JULI

The Kindness of Strangers

The Kindness of Strangers

Julie Newman

Urbane
PUBLICATIONS

urbanepublications.com

First published in Great Britain in 2018
by Urbane Publications Ltd
Suite 3, Brown Europe House, 33/34 Gleaming Wood Drive,
Chatham, Kent ME5 8RZ
Copyright © Julie Newman, 2018

A CIP catalogue record for this book is available
from the British Library.

ISBN 978-1-911583-76-9
MOBI 978-1-911583-77-6

Design and Typeset by Michelle Morgan

Cover by Michelle Morgan

Printed and bound by 4edge Limited, UK

URBANE

urbanepublications.com

For Doris.

My beautiful Nan,
who was always kind.

Part One

The Strangers

Helen

A SLIVER OF SUNLIGHT forces its way through the tiny gap between the blind and the window frame; it's enough to tell me that night has given way to day.

I stretch and realise I'm precariously close to the edge of the bed. I roll over and move towards the centre of the bed reaching out with my arm, searching for him, for his touch and his warmth. The coldness stills me. I allow my eyes to focus properly, and the outline of his pillow greets me. It is smooth and free of indentation suggesting no head has lain upon it. I sit up and stare at the space where he should be, wondering where he is and worrying that he is okay. Then it descends, the gloom and the anguish, for now I remember…

One

I DON'T KNOW WHERE TO START. I've never felt so daunted by a task, ever. Which is quite ridiculous as it is a relatively simple task, not one that requires any particular skill; and yet it challenges me. I've brokered million-pound deals, chaired more meetings than I care to remember and managed teams of people. Yet I can't seem to do this one simple thing.

As I stand in the doorway of his dressing room I am immobilised; I feel like I'm standing on the high board at a swimming pool, not only afraid to jump but unsure if I can swim when I hit the water. And I feel like a trespasser. This was his space, as my dressing room was mine; is mine, for I'm still here. Not that we weren't allowed into one another's rooms, of course we were, but rarely was there a need. Yes, I know, his and her dressing rooms sounds rather grand and over-indulgent, but to be honest it suited our lifestyle. It was a necessary convenience. A convenience that allowed us to have our own space and time, either to get ready for whatever the day held or to unwind at the end of the day. There were many occasions when one of us had a function to attend or a late night at the office. I recall reading somewhere that it's quite common for couples to argue before going out as they often get in each other's way while getting ready - and let's be honest, men can leave bathrooms in a complete state of disarray. Therefore these

The Kindness Of Strangers

additional rooms probably prevented many cross words or heated exchanges. Robert's mother couldn't understand why we didn't just use one of the guest rooms if either of us were late home. She thought the dressing rooms an unnecessary extravagance; but then she thought that of most things we had or did, unless it involved her of course. She was happy enough to accompany us on luxury holidays, and she didn't refuse when we paid for her new kitchen. What she didn't understand was that despite having these rooms we still liked to spend the night together; we rarely spent a night apart. There was the odd overseas business trip, but whenever possible we would accompany each other on those trips. In fact, I can count on one hand the nights we've spent apart. Well I could, before ...

We bought this house over twenty-five years ago. It was a house we would often drive past and admire, both saying we'd like to have something similar one day; although at the time that notion was just fanciful daydreaming. Over time the house began to look a little shabby and uncared for, eventually becoming rundown and derelict. Such a shame we thought; we hoped someone would come along with time and money to restore it to its former glory. Never daring to think it might be us who would take on that mantle.

It was 1992 and we were in a taxi on our way home, following a very boozy evening. We'd been out celebrating Robert's bonus - which was unexpected and an extraordinary amount - when we passed this house. There was a sign outside saying it was for sale at auction. Robert got the taxi driver to stop and we both got out of the car.

"What do you reckon?" Robert asked. I looked at him and shrugged, thinking he was asking me how much I thought it was worth. "It might need work, but with my bonus, well I think we could do it."

"Do what?" I asked a little densely, for I was feeling the effects of my alcohol intake in the cold night air.

"Buy it."

"Really?"

"Yes, really. We've always loved this house and as you keep telling me, we have outgrown the flat."

"That's true, but I'm not s–"

"Meter's running pal and I do have another job to get to," interrupted the taxi driver.

We got back into the car and headed home, but I could tell Robert wanted this. It wasn't just an alcohol fuelled fantasy, this was a long-held dream that now seemed attainable. For him, it felt like the stars had aligned and it was the right thing to do. He was convinced it was what his bonus was meant for. So we bought it. It was two years before we moved in though, two long years. It needed a lot of attention: wiring, plumbing, structural reinforcement. And none of these things were cheap. We seemed to be writing endless cheques, and to me the house didn't look any different from the day we first picked up the keys for it.

"That's because all these improvements are unseen," said Robert, "but they're essential. I know you just want to get on with the business of decorating and furnishing and you will, soon. Then you'll see the difference." He was right, as he so often was.

The house is magnificent, it oozes charm and character. It has a large entrance hall with a wonderful sweeping staircase in the centre. The original stairs were removed as they were rotten; I wanted the staircase to be a strong feature, make a statement, which it now does. Up the stairs and to the right are two guest bedrooms and a bathroom, and to the left is our bedroom and the dressing rooms. When we first moved in we didn't have his and her dressing rooms. There were three bedrooms, one fair sized one and two smaller ones; we knocked down walls and created a master bedroom with an en-suite bathroom and just one dressing room, a dressing room that in time would become the nursery. Well, that was the plan, but as time went on we realised that it probably wasn't the best use of the space. I think it was me who first suggested each of us having our own dressing rooms with bathrooms. I love a bath, laying in the water, relaxing, allowing the cares of the day to float free from you. And back then was no different, I liked nothing more than an uninterrupted soak. Increasingly I'd been using the bathroom across the landing. Self-indulgent, uninterrupted me time; time for solitude, during which to reflect and contemplate without Robert's analytical input. He liked to talk, find a solution or reason for every problem or situation, but sometimes there is no reason. Sometimes things just are. So we had our own dressing rooms and very soon we forgot that the room was ever meant for anything else.

❧

I step across the threshold and into the room, still keeping hold of the door jamb, steadying myself. This feels wrong. I would never come in here without him being here, but I have to do this, it's time. Tentatively I take another step. I decide to start with the wardrobe. I slide open the door; it's very ordered, shirts together, trousers together, etc. and all arranged by colour. Many of his clothes are still draped in the plastic covers that the dry-cleaners put on. I begin with the shirts and they are as good as new; all sharply ironed and neatly hanging in regimented rows. It seems a shame to remove them from the hangers, so I don't. I lay them on the bed as I sort through them. It seems he liked blue, almost all of his shirts are blue: blue stripes, blue checks, plain blue.

I hadn't noticed this before. If anyone had ever asked me what colour he likes to wear I would have said … actually what would I have said? I don't know, I don't know what he liked anymore. Why don't I know? Did I ever know? Clearly it was blue as that is the over-whelming colour of his wardrobe, but I don't think that's right. I don't think blue was his favourite colour at all. As I struggle to recall this one thing which I feel I should know, my eyes moisten. I didn't think it would be this hard. I coped just fine with the legalities and financial issues that had to be dealt with, but this is different. It could be because these are his personal things, maybe that's the difference; clothes he wore, books he read, music he played, the things he touched and that touched him. I have to do this. If I can just sort out his clothes today; that would be something. I dab my eyes with a tissue and continue removing things from his wardrobe. When it's empty I look at the mountain of clothes on the bed. Nothing has made the throwaway pile, it's all too good, but as I have no-one to give them to I'll take it all to the charity shop – tomorrow, I'll do that tomorrow.

Two

IT TAKES QUITE SOME TIME to load up the car with Robert's clothes; who knew he had so many? And he had the cheek to say that I bought too many clothes. 'Is that new? Another new coat? More shoes?' Not that he was complaining; after all I was earning more than he was in the latter years of my working life. But there was always an edge to his voice, suggesting many of my purchases were frivolous and unnecessary. One of the over-loaded carrier bags splits and clothes spill onto the driveway. As I begin to scoop them up I spot his holiday shirt; one of many holiday shirts but this was definitely a favourite. It's adorned with palm trees and brightly coloured exotic birds - it's rather loud. So unlike the conservative style that he generally adopted. I remember him buying it many years ago at Freeport straw market in the Bahamas. He bartered for some time with the stall holder, getting it quite cheaply in the end, although she did persuade him to buy other items which I'm sure she inflated the cost of to make up her loss on the shirt. Still, he did feel rather pleased with himself and his purchase. I think I'll keep this one. I tuck it under my arm as I squeeze the last bag into the boot. I nip back indoors to make sure I have everything I intend to take. Nothing left in the hallway, I go upstairs to check the bedroom and his wardrobe. As I slide the door, the emptiness emits a hollow groan; inside it is bare and cold like a discarded tomb. I stare into the void. It is a stark reminder of my loss and I can't bear it. I can't leave it like this. I run downstairs, go to the car and begin sorting through the bags. Before long the wardrobe is once again home to some of Robert's clothes, just a few, enough to revive it. I know I'm being pathetic, trying to enliven an inanimate object, but removing everything seems so wrong and besides I can't completely let go, I don't want to, not yet. I am no more able to leave his wardrobe empty than I'm able to sleep on his side of the bed.

❧

There are a couple of charity shops on the retail park just the other side of town, and that's where I decide to go. I don't really want to carry these bags from the car park to the shops in town - there's every possibility I may bump into somebody I know. Although on the one hand it may be nice to see someone and have a chat, it's been a while you see. There were lots of phone calls and visitors at first, but since the funeral they've slowed. I understand why, they all have their own lives to concentrate on; families, children, grand-children in some cases and work, but mostly I think they don't know what to say. They offer their condolences and ask how I'm coping. Then they offer up a memory of Robert, often a humorous tale I know to be full of embellishment and we laugh a little, although the laughter is stilted and unnatural. Then as the conversation lulls they fill the void with senseless platitudes. So perhaps it's best to avoid people altogether; after all I only have tales of a dead husband or deranged cat to offer.

Thankfully I'm able to park in front of the shops. There are two and they are next door to each other, so I have a choice to make. Cancer Research or NSPCC? The answer is obvious really. Before

I begin unloading the car I go into the shop to find out who I give the things to; secretly I'm hoping someone will give me a hand so I can do this as quickly as possible. There is a bit of a queue, so I decide to look around until it's lessened a little. As I'm browsing the shelves and rails I hear snippets of a conversation between one of the assistants and a customer, the words chemo and pancreas hang in the air. I think they're talking about me, so I exit the shop.

Of course they weren't talking about me, but those words … they are the words that changed my life. Halting my plans - our plans. Having no control was the worst thing, cancer was in charge and it was in a hurry. Barely had I processed the diagnosis when it was done. My heart was torn apart and pain now occupies the space where Robert once was.

I take my bags into the NSPCC shop, the lady behind the counter is so cheerful. She's very smiley and happy and incredibly grateful, you'd think the things I'm donating were for her personally. She asks me how my day is, talks about the weather and what else I have planned. It's wonderful to have a conversation that isn't strained and awkward because someone is fearful of upsetting me. She talks to me about gift aid, I sign the relevant forms and find myself telling her that I took early retirement.

"That's nice," she says. "Is your husband also retired?" And there it is, just like that the conversation hits an impasse, but it's me who doesn't know what to say. The smiley lady realises her error almost immediately.

"Oh my goodness, I'm so sorry." She grips my hand as she speaks. "It's very common for me to put my foot in it like that. My mouth just runs amok sometimes."

"It's fine," I say, removing my hand from hers as I try to maintain my composure.

"No, it's actually not. I've been in your shoes, a while back now, but even so, I should know better. It's what brought me here you know."

"Really, how so?" I ask. My curiosity piqued and grateful that the conversation has switched to being about her instead of me.

"Yes, I was bringing Gerald's - Gerald was my husband - I was bringing his things here and there was a sign in the window asking for volunteers and well, here I am. In fact we're still looking for volunteers, if you have time on your hands?"

"I ... erm, I still have lots to sort through and I ..."

"Don't mind me, just a suggestion, it's not for everyone. Helped me though, I have to say."

"Thank you, I'd best get on now."

"Well it was lovely talking to you, take care."

On the way home I pick up some cat food and a ready meal. I despise ready meals, but I hate cooking just for me; it yields no pleasure anymore, it is now a thankless task borne out of necessity. I used to love cooking, but the fun of it was sitting down and sharing your culinary creation with someone. Eating alone is depressing, there is no joy in it as it's a constant reminder that I am, in fact, alone. And these ready meals are awful, they are loaded with salt and have the texture of soggy cardboard; but quite frankly everything tastes the same anyway. I'm unable to finish my lasagne - if that's what it was, it looked and smelt no different to what I put in the cat's bowl – so I scrape my plate and clear up before deciding to put some music on and read a book.

I wake with a start, I'm cold and a little disoriented. Not for the first time I've fallen asleep on the sofa. I pick up the discarded paperback and try to flatten the pages that have been creased by its fall. It's a little after three and although I know I should go up to bed I don't want to. Instead I settle on having a cup of tea; how very British of me.

Robert always said I drank far too much tea; he was a coffee drinker, or wine, beer and the occasional whiskey. I don't mind wine, but a nice gin and tonic is my favourite, although I wasn't so keen on that when I first had it. It was on my first date with Robert that I had my first gin and tonic ...

Our paths had crossed several times at various work functions. I was a money broker and Robert a banker. It took him a little while to ask me out and then it was a while after that before we actually went out. Our first date was at Rules, a restaurant near Covent Garden, apparently the oldest restaurant in London and still going strong to this day. It was recently used in a James Bond film. I think Robert chose Rules as it was mentioned in novels by Graham Greene and Evelyn Waugh, two of his favourite authors; he thought that would impress me. The décor was rather opulent and so the ambience it created was not particularly romantic. The fixtures and fittings were highly polished and gilded, and the walls were thick with art, a little cluttered for my taste. It had plush red velvet seating and dark wood panelling that some may call dated - I prefer traditional. It was an enchanting place, definitely somewhere to observe social graces, which is why when asked if I'd like an aperitif I opted for a gin and tonic despite being a non-drinker at that time. To ask for a lemonade seemed a little juvenile and rather unsophisticated, although that's what I would have preferred. Nevertheless we had a wonderful evening and six months later he moved in with me.

Those early days were at times ... well, let's just say a little fraught, largely on account of his mother. Robert was an only child and his father had passed away many years before, so for a long time it was just the two of them. This led to an inevitable closeness that occasionally left me on the side-lines. I pointed this out to him and he did try hard to remedy it. It wasn't helped by his mother telephoning endlessly with all manner of imaginary problems, all with the intention of getting Robert to rush over to her, which he so very often did. I learnt many years later that she considered me someone who probably had loose morals since I lived alone. Eventually, after embarking on a charm offensive, I won her over. The main problem was that she was lonely. She told me once that she thought she had lost him to me forever and she grieved for him, until she realised that there was room for both of us in his life. Now she really has lost him, we both have. I'll pop and see her in the morning.

The Kindness Of Strangers

Three

JOAN LIVES ACROSS TOWN, in a bungalow on a newish estate that's not far from the retail park, so I decide to drop off some more things at the charity shop on the way. These aren't all Roberts's this time, I've had a bit of a sort out too. I have clothes I haven't worn for years and I'm unlikely to wear them again, not now. There is a stack of books too; Dick Francis and James Patterson aren't my thing and neither are the DIY and gardening books. I don't think they were Robert's thing either, he wasn't particularly practical and all the books in the world wouldn't change that. He would say, 'why waste time doing it yourself when you can pay a chap down the road to do it for you'.

The smiley lady is behind the counter again.

"Hello, more goodies for us?"

"Yes, and probably still more to come," I reply.

"That's good to hear. We always need good quality donations." I'm slightly affronted by this remark, does she not remember why I have these 'goodies'? I'm feeling a little low this morning so I'm probably over-sensitive. "Well, look at this," she says picking up one of Roberts gardening books. "May treat myself to this one. I'll put it aside and get Sheila to price it for me."

"Have it," I say.

"I can't just take it, somebody else has to price it and I buy it just the same as anyone."

"I don't mind."

"It's not up to you to mind, it's not yours to give, not anymore. You've donated it, so now it belongs to the charity, therefore I have to pay. That's the rules."

"Sorry."

"Don't apologise, I hardly think it'll break the bank."

I offer her a feeble smile. "What are you up to today?" she asks.

"Off to see my mother-in-law. I'd forgotten this must be difficult for her too. With Robert gone ..." as I say his name I feel a lump in my throat. "Well there's only me to look out for her now," I continue.

"What's she like? Your mother-in-law? Mine was a harridan."

"A harridan, what an old-fashioned word."

"It is, isn't it? It's the politest word I can think of to describe her."

"In that case, I think I'm quite lucky with mine. It took me a little while to convince her that I wasn't the enemy, but all-in-all she's not so bad."

As I leave the shop I feel a little lighter and not just because of the donations. The conversation I've had with ... goodness, I don't know her name, for now she'll have to remain the smiley lady, but I will find out her name. The conversation I've had with the smiley lady was entirely normal, free-flowing and not driven by sympathy. Yes it was short, but it had the power to make me feel normal, for a few minutes anyway. It's hard to explain but I feel my grief shrouds me in a fog that I can see out of but nobody else can see through; certainly not those that know me anyway. They see my grief and don't know how to address it, they don't realise that I'm here, beneath the fog, I'm still Helen. I'm still here and despite my sadness I would like people to see me. Smiley lady gets it; she sees me and in doing so lifts my spirits ever so slightly.

As I reverse onto the driveway at the front of Joan's house I notice the curtains twitching in my rear view mirror. I smile to myself for I know she'll take her time answering the door and pretend that she didn't realise I was here. When she finally answers the door, I'm surprised at how dishevelled she looks.

"Helen, how nice to see you. I didn't realise you were here. How are you?"

"I'm fine thank you," I say as she ushers me along the hallway towards the lounge.

"Good, good. I'll put the kettle on." I offer to do it, but she remonstrates with me and tells me to go and sit down. I do as I'm told. Spread across the floor are countless envelopes and books. I bend towards the floor in order to take a closer look. They're not books, they're albums - photo albums - lots of them. The envelopes contain photographs too, mostly of Robert. I don't think I've seen them before. When Joan comes in with a tray of tea I ask her where they've come from.

"They were in a box in the garage, right on the top shelf, I think Robert must have put them up there when I moved here. I knew I had them somewhere. Thankfully a nice young man helped me get them down as I couldn't reach them."

"I don't think I've ever seen these," I say. "Hang on, what 'nice young man'?"

"Oh, he was one of those green people."

"What?" I ask with trepidation.

"A green, for the local elections ..." I breathe a sigh of relief, she wasn't going ... well, you know. "He was after my vote and asked if I could spare a few minutes. I said I could if he would help me retrieve a box from the top shelf in the garage. I'd already got myself covered in dust trying to reach it, so he got it down for me and then we had a discussion about politics."

I smiled to myself at the thought of this; he wouldn't have known what had hit him. Joan has a razor-sharp mind and enjoys a good debate, and despite her advancing years she would've been a formidable opponent, of that I'm sure.

"So what was the outcome?"

"Sorry?"

"Are you a convert? Did he get your vote?"

"Don't be daft, too much tofu and yoga with them for my liking."

We drink our tea and spend a couple of hours sorting through the photographs. We laugh and cry and laugh some more and cry some more. When I leave she hugs me tightly, something she's never done before, and I realise I've rather neglected her. I apologise - for which I am admonished - and I tell her to call if she needs anything and not to rely on strangers, especially politicians.

"Helen, strangers are only friends not yet met."

I stick my arm out of the window and wave as I drive away.

Four

AGAIN LAST NIGHT, or early this morning depending how you look at it, I woke to find myself fully-clothed on the sofa, book on the floor. I did make myself go up to bed this time and I did sleep some more, but this morning I feel exhausted, which is ridiculous as I have slept. I sleep a lot at the wrong times and I'm sure an expert would say it's not good for me, but it's the only time that I'm free of … free of what? I'm tempted to say Robert, but that's not what I mean. His memory? No, it's not that either, well it kind of is. It kind of is because it's the wrong memory, I can't seem to process my brain to deliver me a nice memory, particularly when I'm on my own. Every time I try my recall is overwhelmed by images of him at the end, or from the funeral, or just by nothingness. A blackness that is my sorrow.

Grief is just a word to so many people; a word used to describe the feelings or the process that death brings about. But when grief descends upon you it is no longer just a word; it's a thing, a real thing, so real I see it. I see it watching me, I see it following me, I see it taunting me. It is an actual thing, albeit a thing of indeterminable state or colour. It has no gender, it has no name, it simply is. And it doesn't want me to forget, as if I could. But I do very occasionally have a moment where my focus drifts from it. Maybe Harvey - the cat - does something amusing which causes me to smile, or God help me, even laugh, and grief is there chastising me for displaying some form of joy. Grief is the worst housemate you could find, for it is everywhere without respite. Sometimes it's right beside me, other times it is draped across my shoulders, its immense weight immobilising me. When I wake, just for a millisecond it is gone, then I see it, skulking in the shadows waiting to ambush me. People tell me time heals but I cannot imagine time ever diminishing its potency. So I sleep, for sleep is my shield.

The phone rang several times today and the answer machine is full; it may well have been close to full before today. It's ringing again now. I look at the caller display and although I recognise the number I can't think who it belongs to. So I don't answer. The ringing stops; I suppose I should listen to the messages. I know, that will be the task I assign myself today. I get a notepad and pencil from the dresser drawer and press play:

'Helen, it's Marilyn. I'm so sorry I was unable to make the funeral, I was overseas. You know how it is here, when duty calls. Anyway, I hope you got the card and flowers and I wondered if you were up to meeting for lunch or coffee yet? Well, tea for you of course. Call me. Bye.'

Marilyn was my assistant when I was working, I trained her and now she has my job. It took a while for me to convince the powers that be that she was the ideal replacement. They were looking to headhunt from a rival firm but in the end my argument citing continuity won out. I make a note to call her back later. The next two messages are marketing calls followed by a message from Joan. I replay her message and check the date, it was recorded the day before I went to see her. That's fortunate, I'd hate to think the message has been on here for a few days and I haven't responded. The following three messages are from Anthony.

'Helen, Anthony here, have some things I need to run by you and I require your signature on a couple of papers too. Give me a call and we can fix something up. If you don't want to come into the office I can swing by the house one evening. Ciao.'

'Helen, Anthony here, I called a couple of days ago re some things I need to talk over with you. Maybe you didn't get the message, but it is important that I see you. I'm happy to come to you if you prefer. Call me.'

'Helen darling, it's Anthony. Starting to get a little worried now, unless you are actually trying to avoid me, ha-ha. I'll drop by later. Ciao.'

Oh God, that's all I need. Anthony Villiers, our solicitor. A great legal brain but a man who can't keep his hands to himself. He's been a good friend over the years, but he is a man of dubious morals. I realise I'll need to call him back ASAP so I make a note before listening to the final two messages. One is a marketing call offering life insurance, oh the irony. The last one is Anthony again, saying he's leaving the office early and he will … the recording ends before he has finished as the machine is full.

Damn it.

I decide to phone him straight away. I get through to his secretary who informs me that he has already left.

Damn it.

I seek out my mobile phone as it has his mobile number stored on it. I find it but the battery has run out. I rummage through drawers eventually locating a charger. I plug it in and once it has enough battery life, I scroll through my contacts. When I reach Anthony's number I press the call button, it goes straight to voicemail. I try again, same thing.

Damn it.

What was that noise? Was it a car? A knock on the door confirms my fear. I let him in.

"Helen, darling. You've had me so worried."

"Sorry Anthony, I've been up to my eyes, you know."

"Yes, yes, I'm sure. Well I'm here to help if you need me to."

"Thank you, but I'm getting on top of things now. Tea?"

"Something stronger would go down a treat."

"Bit early isn't it? Even for you?"

"It's almost five, darling, so I'm sure it's fine."

"Five?" I look at the clock standing in the hallway for confirmation. "It is five, goodness. Well in that case, what can I get you?"

"A malt will suffice." I pour Anthony a whisky and go into the kitchen to make a cup of tea for myself, he follows me.

"So, what have you been doing with yourself?" he asks me.

I tell him I've been sorting through Robert's things and I've been to see Joan. "You know, this and that. Keeping busy."

He nods as he sips his whisky. We go through to the lounge. He waits for me to sit down. Foolishly I sit on the sofa and he sits down next to me, a little too close. From his briefcase he extracts a couple of forms that require my signature.

"Just formalities for shares etc. to be transferred into your name." I sign the forms and he drops them back into the open briefcase, then sits back, downing the whisky as he does. "That's a fine malt," he mutters. "Robert always had good taste and not just in whisky." He leans forward and puts the now empty glass onto the coffee table. He turns to me, putting a hand on my knee. "How are you Helen? I mean really, how are you?"

"I'm good." He raises his eyebrows at me. "No, really, I am doing okay."

"I'm glad, but if ever you're not okay, you can call me. Day or night, I don't mind. I imagine the nights must be the worst. Hour upon hour of darkness and nothingness and nobody to share it with. You must be lonely."

He's hit a nerve.

"I ... erm, I'm ..." I am trying to answer but the words are stuck on my tongue and I can't release them. I close my eyes briefly, in an effort to hold back the tears. I blink and hope he won't notice but then the tears begin to travel silently down my cheeks. Anthony puts an arm around me and pulls me to him. He strokes my face with his other hand, wiping my tears as he does so. Then he gently kisses my forehead, then the tip of my nose and then my lips. I kiss him back, the taste of him is ... a taste I remember and his smell is redolent. I inhale the suave, leathery scent which coupled with the smoky aroma of the whisky is intoxicating. His hand is back on my leg, but this time higher than my knee, much higher, too high. I pull away and look at him.

"What are you doing?" I shout. I'm not sure who I'm shouting at, Anthony or myself?

"I'm sorry, I thought ... you seemed to want ... I'm sorry."

"I thought you were Robert, just for a second, you smell like him, your aftershave ... and you taste like him, the whisky ... you'd better go." I stand up, he takes my arm.

"You have needs Helen and you're still a fine-looking woman. I'm happy to ..."

"Happy to what?"

"I mean, look, you know I've always thought a great deal of you. I ..."

"Anthony, just go."

As I close the front door I crumble and slump to the floor. The tears flow again, guilty tears. I'm ashamed and disgusted. I haven't kissed anyone other than Robert in over thirty years. What was I thinking?

"I'm sorry, darling." I whisper.

Five

EACH NEW SUNRISE does not just herald a new day, it is a new beginning offering new possibilities and the opportunity to be better than before. That's what I always used to believe. It was the mantra of my boss when I first started working in the city. But now, well now it sounds like a pretentious soundbite that has no validity in the real world, certainly not in my world. Every day is the same for me. There is a brief moment when I first wake when I've forgotten he's gone, then boom, it hits me and the darkness descends once more. Today is no different. Perhaps if I still worked my focus would be on what I have to do rather than what I can no longer do. Maybe that's the answer, to go back to work; but where? Marilyn has replaced me and I couldn't go back at a lower level than before. There are other firms, but would they be interested in a 56 year-old woman who's been out of the game for almost eighteen months? I know I wouldn't employ me and I know how good I am. Even if I considered a junior position I'd be competing with a new crop of graduates and interns. And besides, there is still more to do here; papers, accounts, and all the interests we pursued together. I must cancel our golf club subscription for a start; I won't be going there alone and I never liked playing much anyway.

The study is incredibly stuffy. I've opened the window but that hasn't made a great deal of difference. I think I'm going to take some of these files and sit in the garden and sort through them. I make a pot of tea and go outside. It's surprising how many things we signed up for over the years and more surprising is the fact that I'd forgotten we had them. Our joint account has already been dealt with, as have a couple of accounts that Robert had. But what I'm looking at now is an old account of mine that I haven't paid attention to for a long time. I transfer money into it each month to cover the direct debits, but I don't use half the things I'm paying for. This is the downside of not receiving paper statements anymore, I'm rather remiss at checking my accounts online. This is the account that the golf membership comes out of; I write down the account and membership numbers so I can cancel it. There are also a couple of magazine subscriptions, a consumer group subscription and insurances for appliances which I don't even know if I still have. I write down the relevant information so I can cancel them all. When I'm done I pour another cup of tea - well half a cup as the pot is almost empty - sit back in my chair and look around the garden. Somebody comes to cut the lawn every couple of weeks, everything else in the garden Robert and I do, or did. Well Robert mainly. I suppose I'll have to get on with it myself now, not that it takes much, it is quite a low maintenance garden. We had a designer revamp it many years ago, and her brief was simple; it had to be full of colour and easy to maintain. It certainly is that, although parts of it are looking a little neglected. The roses catch my eye, they need dead-heading. I go back into the kitchen for a pair of scissors. As I take them out of the drawer I picture Robert standing in the garden waving a pair of secateurs at me and saying, 'the right tool for the job, Helen'. I smile to myself; a nice memory.

It takes me a little while to locate the shed key. For some reason it's in a small pot at the rear of one of the dresser drawers, instead of hanging with the garage and summer-house keys in the kitchen. I unlock the shed hoping the secateurs will be easier to find. I never go in the shed, it was Robert's domain. He liked to sit in there and read; he complained the summer house was too hot, something that never bothered me. I'm pretty sure he used to have a bottle of whisky hidden away in there too. The door creaks a little as it opens and warm air is emitted from within. It smells stale and fusty. It's clearly in need of ventilating. I pull the door wide, putting a large terracotta pot in front of it to keep it open. I peek in before actually venturing inside; Robert's old chair sits proudly in the centre, there is a work bench to the right on which sits several pots of various sizes, a couple of gardening books - maybe he did read them after all - and the secateurs. I pick them up and look around the rest of the shed; there is a lot of stuff in here, another thing to sort through in time. As I turn to go back out something catches my eye. It's the old picnic blanket we used many years ago, I thought it had long since been thrown out. We enjoyed going for picnics, although to be honest they weren't really picnics. We would head out somewhere for the day, weather permitting of course, and find a nice spot and put the blanket down. We would lay and read for a while; I always took a flask of tea, something for Robert to drink and a few snacks. On the way back we would look for a nice country pub and have a meal before heading home. I pull at the blanket which is draped over something, as it comes off it reveals an old, battered filing cabinet. It's made of metal, grey in colour and mottled with rust spots. I pull open the top drawer; inside are two glasses and an almost empty bottle of whisky, an unopened bottle of whisky, a box of matches and a half-smoked cigar, and various bits and pieces that include garden ties and string and plant labels. I try the next one but that won't open. There is a lock at the top of this drawer, and I look around for a key. I can't see one, but I'm puzzled as to why the drawer is locked and I want to get it open. The roses will have to wait.

After spending almost an hour in the shed looking for a key -to no avail - I've come back inside. Where might the key be? I go through the dresser drawers again and the kitchen drawers and I search the utility room. It's a mystery. There might not even be anything in the drawer, but I won't be satisfied until I know. I go back out to the shed, pulling the drawer a few more times, but it won't budge. I look around to see if there is anything I can use to force it open. Bashing it with a hammer doesn't work, neither does poking around the lock with a penknife. I'm frustrated now, but I won't be beaten. Maybe, I could ask the gardener when he comes to do the lawn if he could get it open, that's not for over a week though. Anthony would do it, but after the other day, I don't think I want to ask him. I'll have to go and buy something so I can do it myself. The lock can't be that strong, I'm sure if I had the right tool I could prise it open.

❧

The DIY superstore car park is full. That's because half of it is taken up with a car wash service and the other half is people who park here and hop on a bus into town so they don't have to pay the exorbitant parking charges. I pull out again and go across the road to the car park by the charity shops. Thankfully they are never full. As I get out of the car I spot smiley lady, she sees me and comes over.

"Hello, what brings you this way, more things for us?"

"Not today I'm afraid."

"I've done my bit for today and I was going to treat myself to coffee and cake. Fancy joining me?"

"I really need to get on …"

"Oh okay, another time maybe." Smiley lady waves as she walks away. As I turn to go I pause and think, why not.

"Excuse me, excuse me," I call. I wish I knew her name. I catch up with her. "Sorry, I've had second thoughts and I'd love to join you if that's okay."

"Of course it is," replies smiley lady, smiling all the more. "I often pop in here when I've finished at the shop," she says as we sit down at a table by the window. "The cakes are delicious, I know I shouldn't, but I can't resist."

"I'm Helen, by the way," I inform her.

"Audrey."

"Well it's very nice to meet you properly, and thank you for asking me to join you."

"You're very welcome. It's nice to have some company. I don't see many people outside of the shop." We place our order and there is a moment of silence before she speaks again. "How have you been? I remember those early days, it was hard."

"I'm fine, mostly. Well not that fine. It's been quite a few weeks now but …" I sigh before speaking again. "When does it get easier?"

"I don't know that it ever does."

"Oh, I er … because you said the early days were hard I assumed that meant it gets easier in time."

"Not easier, just different."

"How?"

"Well, in the beginning the grief is new and raw and for me it was overwhelmingly scary." I nod as she speaks. "Sometimes it was just too much to bear and I couldn't function. Other times I would try and ignore it, but it wasn't going anywhere so I surrendered to it, just went wherever it took me. It seemed endless, then little by little the dark moments became less. Now I do have down days and moments when I miss Gerald terribly but I'm able to get on with whatever I need to do. Working at the shop helps."

"I was only thinking this morning that maybe going back to work would help me, but I still have so much to sort through. I've found that quite hard to do, I have to steel myself to go through Robert's things. It feels so wrong, not that there were any secrets between us but it ... well, I feel like I'm prying."

"Is there no-one who can help you?"

"No, it's just me, no children or family, other than Robert's mother."

"Well if you need a hand with anything, I'm happy to help. I know it's a difficult thing to do. The boys helped me, I wouldn't have wanted to do it by myself."

"You have sons?"

"Two, I don't see a great deal of them though. Simon lives in Edinburgh and Philip is in New Zealand."

"Oh, you must miss them."

"I do. Philip comes over once a year, normally for a couple of weeks. Simon I see more frequently but for less time. He pays me fleeting visits, generally on the way to somewhere else." Just for a second her smile fades.

"Have you ever been to New Zealand?" I ask.

"Twice, it's very beautiful."

"Yes, I've heard that. I visited Australia when I was younger, but never made it to New Zealand. Robert and I did talk about going, I think he has a cousin out there, but we never got ... " I pause as suddenly my head is awash with plans no longer possible.

"Are you alright, Helen?"

"Yes, sorry. I erm ..."

"I know. I often recall things that Gerald and I talked about doing but never found the time to do. I have done some of them by myself, not the same I know but I know he would've wanted me to. Maybe in time you'll be able to do that."

"Maybe," I say with a nod, yet knowing full well I won't. Nothing has the same appeal anymore, the plans we made were for us both to undertake together. It isn't fair, we worked so hard, foregoing holidays in order to take early retirement believing we'd have time for travelling and savouring the delights that the world has to offer.

"I'd best be going," says Audrey. "I've got to pick up some shopping for a neighbour on my way home."

"Yes, I need to get back too. Thank you for this, it's been lovely."

"How about same time next week?"

"Yes, why not?"

The drive home is slow and I'm relieved when I finally pull onto the drive. As I do I remember why I went out in the first place, to get a tool to open the filing cabinet drawer. I look at the time. I won't make it back before the shops close - my curiosity will just have to wait another day now.

Six

I'M GOING TO GET that drawer open today, I can't begin to do anything else until I find out what is in there, if anything. It will probably be a big fat nothing but I still need to know. I go out to the shed and try to open it; if I can avoid going to the shops again I'd prefer that. I bang and shake and kick, the drawer does nothing. Again I try and pick the lock; well it seems so easy in the films. It looks like I'll have to go out. I need a cup of tea first. My second cup of tea is interrupted by a knock at the door. I don't get many visitors and my first thought is Anthony, he's called a few times since … Each message is very apologetic; in the last one he was pleading with me to forgive him. It's not just him I have to forgive, I still feel rather guilty myself so I can't talk to him, not yet. But I will have to at some point, no matter how much I'd like not to. I know I can't avoid him forever.

Reluctantly I open the door, but it's not Anthony. It's a young man, smartly dressed but in need of a haircut and a shave.

"Good morning," he says. "How are you today, Madam?" Oh God, I thought the door-to-door salesman had been replaced by telemarketers and spam emails. I smile politely, preparing to cut him off before he begins his spiel. "I'm Dominic Stewart and I represent The Green Party," he continues waving a laminated ID card in front of me. "I wonder if you could spare a few moments of your time."

"I'm sorry, I'm a little busy right now." I close the door on his crest-fallen face. I wonder if he was the same person who called on Joan; 'the green man'. Yes, the green man. I open the door again. "Excuse me, hello," I call after him. He stops and turns around. "I'm sorry I didn't mean to be so rude, it's just I am a little busy but, well, if you give me a hand with something I'll be happy to listen to you."

"What exactly do you need a hand with?" he asks suspiciously.

"I'll show you." He follows me into the garden, I show him the cabinet and explain that I've lost the key. "I've tried everything." He picks up the hammer. "Yes, I tried that, I've bashed and bashed."

"I can see that," he replies, referencing the fresh dents on the front of the drawer. "You're sure it's okay to force it open?"

I nod enthusiastically, hopeful that I'll finally get the bloody thing open. "Here goes then." He turns the hammer around hooking the clawed end into the top of the drawer. I hadn't thought of doing that. It takes a few goes and a small gap appears. He looks around the shed, spots a large screwdriver which he pushes into the gap and hey presto, it's open.

"Thank you so much." We walk back up to the house and I listen to what he has to say. "Well, you've convinced me," I tell him. "You've got my vote." He leaves a happy man and I scoot off back to the shed.

The whisky burns the back of my throat, I cough and the stinging sensation burns some more, but I don't care; I need its warmth and I need its strength, but above all I need to be numb, I want oblivion. I'm not really a drinker, not whisky, not usually, but then this is not a usual day. Today, this day, everything I know, everything I believe, everything I love has changed.

I refill my glass.

What is worse, a secret or a lie? I always thought a lie was worse, but now, this, the secret, is worse. But then, the lie is the secret … well lies actually, so many lies. Probably many secrets, the two go hand in hand; secrets and lies. You can't have one without the other.

I refill my glass.

The irony is that Robert is the one I need, it's him I've always turned to when shit happens. But this is his shit and if he wasn't already dead I would kill him right now.

I refill my glass.

I need to read these letters again, but the words are jumping around a lot. I pick up the photographs, they're all a bit blurred. And all these statements and invoices and …

I refill my glass.

I squint, hoping that will enable me to focus better. A sheaf of papers falls to the floor. I bend down and pick them up. They are in the wrong order now. I try and sort them but the words are still jumping.

I refill my glass.

I drop my glass.

I … oblivion …

❧

Nausea, dehydration and a headache that can only be likened to having a small animal trapped in your head gnawing on the very bones of your cranium in the hope of securing freedom.

I must be ill.

I try and raise up from my horizontal position; again I'm not in bed. My eyelids are finding it difficult to raise themselves. One in particular is like a broken roller-blind that gravity is determined to keep shut. I concentrate hard, forcing them open, but daylight offends them.

I must be very ill.

I try and manoeuvre myself so I'm more comfortable. My back and legs ache and my stomach is objecting to the movements I'm making.

I must be dying.

Tentatively I sit and I focus. There are papers strewn around me. A glass lies on the floor; an unattractive stain emanating from it has formed on the carpet. From the coffee table an almost empty whisky bottle stares at me.

So, not dying.

Everything I do hurts. It's going to be a long day. I take a shower hoping that may help, it doesn't; although the water feels nice the effort it's taking to stand upright in the shower is negating any pleasure or relief I am feeling. I'm thirsty and hungry, tea and toast is all I fancy and I suspect it may be all I'm able to keep down. Tea and toast is good and thankfully it doesn't revisit me. I'm exhausted now, a nap is required. Three hours later I wake, not feeling any better off for my sleep. I make more tea and toast. I've avoided going into the lounge as I don't want to be confronted by the mess, not just the physical mess on the lounge floor but the mess that it represents. The mess that is now my life. I could just leave the door closed and never enter that room again. An image from *Great Expectations* dances in front of me, you know the one, the room in which everything is left exactly as it is; ignoring all it represents in the hope that decay will void its meaning. Yes, I could do that and just continue as before but I'm no Miss Havisham, and besides it's already too late. Already the contents of those pieces of paper have started seeping into my brain. They say knowledge is power but what kind of power? At this moment knowledge is destruction. Destruction of a life and a memory and a reputation. I have to face this, I know. I need to because maybe then I might understand – bloody unlikely – but I have to try because if I don't the life I have lived over the past thirty years will be rendered meaningless.

With a deep breath I stand tall, open the door and go into the lounge. I pick up the papers that have fallen to the floor - this takes a monumental effort because every time I bend down my head reacts angrily - and gather the rest from the coffee table. I need to put them into some sort of order before I begin going through them properly. I sort them into piles: photographs, letters, statements and invoices. I then decide to order each pile chronologically. I start with the statements and invoices, trying carefully to only look at the dates and not the content. I do the same with the letters, which are all hand-written, although they take a little longer as only the top copy in each letter is dated and some of the pages have separated from each other. Thankfully each page is numbered. Again I try to only look at the dates and numbers although the juvenile scrawl is hard to ignore. The pages are peppered with spelling mistakes and grammatical errors that are screaming out to be corrected. I resist the temptation and continue with my task. Finally, I begin to sort through the photographs. Each one has a date and short description on the back, although to be honest they are easy to put into chronological order without looking at the dates. When I'm done I sit and look at the three piles that are sitting neatly in front of me. I notice that the address on the letters and statements is that of Robert's office. I suppose that makes sense; although I would never open his mail I may well have enquired about it. I decide to start with the letters as it's clear that they came first. I begin with the earliest date, which is almost seventeen years ago:

Dear Bobby

Im sorry to write you at work but I decided not to do it. I know this will make you mad but I cant do it so im keeping it. The money I will use for things I need. You wont here from me anymore so don't worry about your nice life being messed up. This will probly be a good thing for me as the council will need to give me a flat and you know I hate my bedsit. I will miss the hotels and I will miss you. You might even miss me a bit. Don't think shell do what I do for you. Love from Lizzie xxx

'Bobby'. Nobody calls him Bobby, although I do recall him once telling me that his mum did when he was a little boy, but he made her stop as he said it sounded babyish. Babyish - that's what this letter is. Has she never heard of apostrophes? '*Probly*' not. And what does she mean, '*don't think shell do what I do for you*'. I assume that 'shell' is supposed to read she'll … I move on to the next letter which is dated a few weeks after the first.

Dear Bobby

I know I said you would not here from me again but I wanted you to see this. It's the first pic of my baby girl yes a girl. We have made a girl. These scans are amazing. I had to drink loads and fought I might pee everywhere the way she was pressing on my belly but worth it to see my darlin daughter and yours. I said the dad cant come cos of work so that was ok and she gave me two fotos so you can have this one. Love from Lizzie   xxx

The '*foto*' is stuck on the back of the letter.

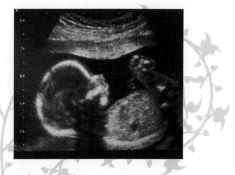

The next letter details Lizzie's desire and need for a new home. It's full of rantings and moans about the state of her accommodation. She clearly expects Robert or 'Bobby' to do something about it. It seems the council are not prepared to rehouse her straight away, she needs to go on a waiting list, but she can't do that until her baby is born. She doesn't want to wait, and the council and social security have suggested she speak to the father, after all '*it's his responsibility too*'. A sentiment I would ordinarily agree with, if the father wasn't my husband. In the letter she continues ranting and venting before finally saying, '*I suppose if I put your name on her birth certificate when she comes you'll have to do something*'. I'm sure this suggestion worked for there is quite a gap in the personal correspondence after this. I surmise that he must have seen her during this period. I begin to look through the photographs. The first few are baby photos. On the back is written the date and the child's age: 6 weeks old, 3 months old, 6 months old. I continue looking. There are half a dozen or so toddler pictures, then, oh my goodness, a school photo, and she looks just like Robert. Only the other day, at Joan's, I was looking at his school pictures. This is too much. I put the photos down. If the thought of alcohol wasn't so abhorrent at the moment I'd have a drink. I compose myself and start going through the letters once more:

Dear Bobby

My car broke down again. I took it to be fixed and the bill is here.
They said it aint gonna last much longer so I need a new one. And I
dont have money for that so you have to by it. Its for our girl so dont
make a fuss. Winter will be here soon and we need a car that works
and a new coat would be good.
Love from Lizzie xxx

I cross reference this with one of the invoices which is from a
garage I know, then I read the next letter.

Dear Bobby

I need some more money. I know you send us money but it dont
cover everything and I cant work as much anymore on account of
your daugter I could do more if you had her sometime. And dont
start about proper jobs cos turning tricks is all I know and its what
im good at. You said that plenty of times. Or maybe you could see
me again and you could see your daugter too. Pay me instead of
someone else or is your missus doing that stuff now. It wood be nice
if you came to see your daugter now and again. She does ask about
her Daddy or I can bring her to see you at your work or your house.
I reckon I can find it. Yeah I can do that!!!!!
Love from Lizzie xxx

That last letter sounded like a threat. I wonder what he did about it.
She had better not have been here, in my home, with my husband
and their daughter. Their daughter. As this point properly registers
with me, I break down. I am utterly destroyed. I take hold of a
cushion, hugging it tightly, rocking on the sofa as uncontrollable
sobs unleash unyielding tears. How could he? What was it I didn't
do? I believed we were happy and everything was perfect; clearly

not, something was missing, for him anyway. Maybe the child was what he wanted, but the letters make me think otherwise. He had a daughter who he paid no mind to. Yes he sent money, an obligation he fulfilled though it seems begrudgingly. I wish I knew what he had to say, but now I never will.

Unless … I ask Lizzie …

Seven

THIS MORNING I FEEL ENERGISED, despite being up until the early hours cross-checking all the documents I have regarding 'Lizzie'. My grief has been usurped by anger, an anger that is fuelling every part of me. I will find her, Lizzie, and I will ... what? What will I do? I haven't thought this through completely but I know I need to find her, I want to know why. At the very least that's what I want to know. And what she did that I apparently didn't, and what she knows of me.

I've noted down all the addresses on the various invoices and bills that she had sent Robert. They include the garage that repaired her car, a plumber, a number of shops and a manicurist who features several times; I think the manicurist is the most promising. Some of the addresses I recognise, others I've found on Google maps, what a great app that is. I plan out a route and put the relevant papers into a file. I also put in a couple of the photographs, one of the girl in her primary school uniform and the last one in which she is thirteen and clearly unhappy about having her picture taken. Then again she may just be a sullen looking child, although the earlier photos show a happy little girl with a cheery smile. Perhaps it has something to do with being a teenager, or maybe she learnt what a piece of work her mother is. This thought engenders angry feelings again so I take a deep breath and calm myself; people will not give me the information I require if I go in with my fury on display.

Firstly, I shall visit the shops Lizzie frequented. I want to try and get a feel for what kind of person she is. I know what she does or did, I know what 'turning tricks' means, but maybe there's more to her. I somehow doubt it. At the moment I don't have a very flattering image of her at all, not that I want to like her. I just want to understand why Robert liked her I suppose, or is it that he just liked what she did?

The shops are just what I thought they would be, down-market and second rate. I'm not even going to venture into them. So far the stereotypical image I've conjured up seems to be the right one. I continue along the High Street looking for Priory Lane, that's where the school uniform shop is. I'm thinking that someone in the shop may recognise the uniform in the photograph I have. If I know what school she went to I may get an idea of where they live, the area at least. I find Priory Lane and walk up and down it several times, but there's no school uniform shop. I look again at the address I have; 42 Priory Lane. I find number 42. It's called Cash Converters, a modern day pawnbrokers I think. I'm about to go in when I hear my name.

"Helen, hi. I thought that was you. How are you?"

"Hello, Audrey, I'm good."

"If you're on a shopping trip you won't find much round here I'm afraid."

"I'm actually looking for the shop that sells school uniforms. I thought it was here." I nod towards the cash converters store.

"Goodness, it hasn't been here for, let me see, I'd say at least five years or so. I think most school clothes can be bought at the supermarkets these days, at a fraction of the price that they once were too. Do you need anything in particular? We get a lot of school stuff at the shop. Children grow so quickly these days and not everything gets worn out."

"No, it's fine. I don't actually want to buy anything I just wanted to know what school this uniform is from." Before I can stop myself I'm showing Audrey the photo.

"Pretty girl. Family or friend?"

"Sorry?"

"I'm being nosey, just wondering if she's a relative or a friend."

"Oh, erm. Neither, she ... erm, long story," I say.

"St. Hilda's."

"Excuse me?"

"The school, you wanted to know the school, it's St. Hilda's."

We say our goodbyes and agree to meet as planned in a couple of days. I can feel Audrey's eyes on me as I round the corner. I know she's probably wondering about the photo and what I'm up to, but I'm not ready to talk about it, and don't know that I ever will be. Manicurist next I think. It's back at the other end of the High Street, but the walk will do me good. It takes a while to find it as the entrance isn't actually on the High Street. It's above a letting agency, you get to it by going along an alley between the agency and another shop and up a flight of metal stairs on the outside of the building. I open the door, and I'm greeted by a girl sitting at the counter thumbing her way through a glossy magazine.

"Go through," she says without looking up.

I do as she says, and I'm greeted by someone else who actually does look up at me.

"You're not Maureen."

"No, I'm not."

"Where is she?"

"Who?"

"Maureen."

"I don't know."

"You don't know. Jesus. Is she not coming? I have better things to do than sit around waiting for her. She could've phoned."

"Yes, she could."

"So, what's her excuse this time?"

"I don't follow."

"Maureen, why isn't she coming?"

"I don't know."

"You don't know. So what she send you for?"

"She didn't send me, I don't know anyone called Maureen."

"Look lady, I haven't got time for games." She stares at me for a bit before barking at me. "So what do you want?"

"I'm looking for someone, a manicurist."

"Oh right. Okay, sorry. Didn't realise. Take a seat."

"Thank you." I sit down at the desk and the girl sits down opposite me. She takes hold of my hands.

"So what would you like today? Acrylic, gel, nail art, manicure?" She looks at me and I realise I'm likely to elicit an unpleasant response if I don't partake in one of these services. I opt for a French manicure. She looks a little disappointed that I don't want some exotic nail art or at the very least a bright shade of nail polish. "Most people who come here are after me blinging up their fingers, you know."

As she begins work on my hands I start chatting, general questions like how long she has worked here etc. I need to get her talking a bit before I ask about Lizzie. It turns out that The Nail Bar - that's what it's called, original I know – is owned by her mum. The girl at the front is her sister. Her mum's not there today, she only comes in a couple of times a week. She tells me about her boyfriend, a tattoo artist, and shows me examples of his work that are dotted across her person. Eventually I pluck up the courage to ask about other clients, regulars. I tell her about someone I used to know, called Lizzie, who used to come here.

"I know a couple of Lizzies."

"Do you know where they're from?"

"No."

"You don't keep addresses or phone numbers?"

"You're asking a lot of questions and if this Lizzie is your friend you must know her address."

"I think she moved," I say hesitatingly.

"You don't know Maureen, so I reckon you don't know Lizzie."

Something about her response suggests she knows exactly who Lizzie is, what she is and where she is. She has also told me, in a roundabout way, that Maureen knows Lizzie. She finishes my nails in relative silence. When I ask her how much and reach for my purse she tells me to pay Gemma, her sister. I thank her and go to the front of the shop.

"That'll be twenty pounds," says Gemma. "No cards," she adds as I reach for my plastic. Thankfully I have a twenty-pound note. I hand it to her and as she turns to put it in the till I glance at the appointment book that's next to her magazine. When she turns around I make idle chat regarding the article she was reading. Gemma likes to talk and as she does I'm able to read and memorise a phone number that's written alongside the name Maureen in the diary. Once outside I take a pen from my bag and write the number down before my aging memory cells discard it.

When I get back to the car I sit there for a few minutes pondering my next move. I had intended to visit the garage next and then the plumber. I decide to call them instead, I'm going to call Maureen too. The garage isn't able to help me, it has changed hands a couple of times since Lizzie used it. It was always a long shot. I try the plumber next but it goes to his voicemail. I listen to his cheery greeting before opting not to leave a message, I'll try again later. Maureen next. I type in the number carefully, pausing before I press the last digit. As it rings I feel a nervous fluttering in my belly. The voice is not what I expected, it's soft and polite with a hint of an accent that I'm unable to place. I apologise for calling and say I'm trying to get hold of Lizzie but I've lost her phone number. She enquires as to how I have her number and I say Gemma from the nail bar gave it to me, (not a complete untruth). At the mention of the nail bar she goes quiet, perhaps she has recalled she had an appointment there this morning.

"She didn't have Lizzie's number but said you would be able to give it to me," I continue.

"Well I don't know if I can just give it to you." I half expected her to say this. "I'd need to check first."

"Yes, of course."

"So who are you?"

"I'm …" What shall I say? Do I give a false name? Would she recognise the name Helen? Did Robert ever tell her my name? Probably not, but I don't know. "Tell her I'm calling about Ro … Bobby. I'll call you back this afternoon."

"No need, I'll give her your number."

Before I can say no Maureen has gone. I haven't given her my number, but then I realise I didn't withhold it so it will automatically come up on her phone. Bloody technology. Last thing I want is for Lizzie to contact me, I want to be in control, I want to decide when I speak to her. I stay where I am for about fifteen minutes or so, but my phone doesn't ring so I decide to head back home. There's nothing I can do now, other than wait.

It's almost six when my phone finally rings, and the display shows a number that I don't recognise. This must be her. I sit up straight, business-like, close my eyes and inhale then open them as I exhale. Then I answer the phone.

"Hello."

"Hello luv, Carl Marsh here, plumber. How can I help?"

It isn't her. I slump back in the chair, deflated.

❧

Robert came to me last night. I felt his arms around me, his breath on the back of my neck as we lay together. I asked about her, and he whispered gently that I was having a dream, just a very bad dream. There could never be anyone else, never had been and never would be. He pulled me closer, holding me tight, tighter, too tight. I couldn't move, breathe even. I asked him to loosen his arms; he didn't. He wrapped himself around me, completely engulfing me until I felt he was crushing me. I began flailing around, writhing and thrashing, anything to try and loosen his hold on me. I was drowning in his arms, but a scream punctured the air, loud and shrill like a siren issuing a warning. Robert's arms relaxed then faded as he vanished into the shadows. I put my hands to my ears to muffle the incessant scream, my scream, a scream fuelled by grief and anger.

❧

Three missed calls are logged on my phone, all from withheld numbers. They have to be from her. All I can do is wait and hope that she tries again. An hour later she calls. I think she's surprised a woman has answered, as she asks for Bobby. I wince as she says his name, even though he was never Bobby to me. I say he isn't here and tell her that I need to speak with her.

"Is this about the money? It's well late you know and I need it."

"Perhaps we can meet and discuss it."

"Are you from the bank?"

"No, I'm not from the bank."

"Look, I don't understand. Do you know why I haven't had my money, it normally goes in the bank regular like and now it's stopped. It were his idea to do it like this and I need it, so if it's not in the bank I'll have to go and get it from him, from his house. Tell him that."

"Bob …" I pause, I am not calling him that. "Robert won't be there."

"What? Why not?"

"Because he's dead."

"Are you kidding me?"

"No."

"That's terrible news."

"Yes, it is. I'm sure it's a shock. That is why we ne …"

"So how do I get my money?"

"What?"

"I still need my money."

"Listen, there is no more money …"

"Who is this?"

"I'm Helen, Robert's wife."

"Oh shit."

"Quite. I think you and I need to meet."

"No way. That paper said I was never to see you or the money would stop."

"It will stop, it has stopped. My husband is dead and you're not getting any more money. Do you understand?"

"I'm gonna speak to that solicitor."

"What solicitor?"

"The one that made me sign."

"What solicitor?" I repeat, although I'm pretty sure I know what she is going to say.

"That posh one, Vil ... Villers, something like that."

Eight

ANTHONY IS STARING AT ME, motionless and very attentive; he knows better than to interrupt me. The shocked expression doesn't fool me. He really is a loathsome, odious man. When I finish my tirade of questions interspersed with obscenities and insults I sit down.

"How did you find out?"

"Does that matter?"

"I suppose not."

"Just tell me what you know, Anthony, the truth, all of it. Don't dress it up with any of your horse-shit."

Jesus, what a mess. I've only got myself to blame, I know. It just started out as relief, I suppose. Helen was unreachable, on all levels: emotionally, spiritually, sexually. Despite all we have been through and despite all I have learnt. I needed something, someone. But I loved Helen, still do, always will. I needed to be touched. I could never contemplate an affair so this seemed the best answer. No strings, no attachment. A temporary fix until Helen was herself again. She'd been through so much, we both had. The treatment exhausted us and then the miscarriages. It was too much, I know, but she wouldn't

The Kindness Of Strangers

speak about it. She threw herself into her work; that was her support. She became more successful than me, as you know, well certainly in monetary terms. Don't get me wrong I was proud of her, am proud of her. I just didn't feel part of her life at that time. I was marginalised and isolated. She didn't realise I was hurting too, but worse was that I had to watch her and I knew she was suffering. I knew and I wasn't allowed to help her and in turn she didn't want to help me. So Lizzie was my outlet, my escape, my therapy even. I could indulge my fantasies and get some relief from the everyday grind that was just so hard to deal with at that time. After a few weeks I suggested meeting in a hotel, I didn't like where she lived, rather damp and not particularly clean. A couple of times I tried to stop but it had become habitual like a drug. Lizzie had also begun to rely on my money, she liked having 'regulars' she said. Then one day the veil seemed to lift on Helen's sadness and we started talking again and you know ... well things were better between us. I suppose we were beginning to heal. I stopped seeing Lizzie, but then she called me up at work insisting that I meet her, begging me almost, so I did. We met at the hotel and she told me she needed money, said it was in my interest to give her some, otherwise she might forget to be discreet; I paid her of course thinking that would be it. It wasn't, every now and again I'd hear from her and she would want more. Helen and I had started getting back on track but things were different, the sex was different, it was good but it wasn't ticking all the boxes and so I thought if I'm paying Lizzie anyway, I may as well get more than her silence. What a stupid fool I was, big bloody mistake. What does she go and do then? Falls pregnant, that's what. She didn't want a baby and neither did I, well not with her. So I gave her more money, money that was needed to, you know, for a termination. I should have taken her myself, made sure she went through with it. I didn't hear from her for a while, then I get this letter basically saying she had changed her mind. She was keeping the baby, a girl, our daughter. I thought about telling Helen but I daren't risk it. I was pretty certain that would be the end of our marriage if I did. I met Lizzie and told her I had no intention of being part of her life and I was not going to play house with her. I gave her some money, quite a lot of money and told her not to contact me again. Of course the respite from her was short-lived. She would send photos and updates along with bills and requests for more money. She even got me to buy her a car for Christ's sake. Now I need your help old chap. I need to put this on some legal footing. A contract in which I agree to give her a sum of money, a regular payment and she must agree to stay away from me and more importantly Helen. I assume that's possible. You won't need to handle any of the money, I'll open a new account just for this and arrange a monthly transfer.

☯

"And that's about the size of it," said Anthony.

"Did you not think to tell me?"

"I couldn't. Not only was he my friend but he was my client and as such I had to keep his confidence. I did suggest that he should tell you, I didn't think that there should be secrets between you. He disagreed with me vehemently saying *'everyone has secrets'*."

"After he died, Anthony, you could have told me then, surely."

"No, I couldn't and to be honest I thought it was long since over. He never mentioned it again after I arranged the contract and they both signed it. That was a long time ago."

"You met her?"

"Of course. She came here to sign the contract."

"Have you heard from her recently?"

"No."

"I think you might."

Anthony's face is very animated as I relay recent events to him. He in turn reiterates that he had no knowledge of the financial arrangement. He will go through Robert's files and look at the accounts he had but he is sure all the ones he was aware of have now been closed and all monies transferred to me.

"There has to be another account somewhere," I say.

"Maybe Robert closed it when he knew he was ... when he became ill."

"Possibly, but I'm not convinced. It was all so quick, as you know. Do I need to worry that she may come after me for money?"

"Who? Oh, Ms Dawson."

"Is that her name?"

"Yes. Elizabeth Dawson. She may do, but it's more likely that the child may make a claim. She'll be what, sixteen now?"

I'd forgotten that a child was at the centre of this mess. Oh, Robert how could you have kept this from me?

Nine

AUDREY IS WAITING for me in her regular spot. As she sees me she starts waving one arm excitedly, beckoning me over. She uses her other arm to move her shopping that she has placed on the seat she has saved for me. I apologise for being late, blaming the parking facilities when in reality I'm late because I have been going through more of Robert's things. I've been looking for evidence of the account he used to pay Lizzie and anything else he may have kept from me.

"Yes, the parking here is awful, it gets busy so early, commuters I think. They park here and get the free bus into town and go to the station. Anyway, how have you been?"

"Fine," I reply.

"Are you sure? You look rather tired Helen."

"Oh I'm just a little busy. There's still so much to sort out."

"Did you sort out the thing at St. Hilda's?"

I'm not sure what she's talking about, but then I recall bumping into her and showing her the photograph. I nod my head and then do something I would never normally do, I begin telling her the whole sordid story. It's so unlike me to reveal myself like this, especially something that is not only upsetting but also deeply embarrassing; but there is something about Audrey that makes her so easy to talk to.

The Kindness Of Strangers

"Good grief," she utters once I've finished. "That's awful, that's erm, well it's awful."

I smile at Audrey's uncharacteristic loss of vocabulary. She is genuinely stunned, I don't think she hears many tales like this. She is rather strait-laced and lives a very suburban and uncomplicated life. The only scandals she ever encounters are in episodes of the soap operas she loves to watch. Once the shock has settled she asks me what I plan to do about it.

"There's nothing to do. I did think I wanted to meet her, to try and understand why, but I don't know that I will achieve anything by doing that and I don't want to stir her up. I'd rather she crawled back under her rock. Hopefully she or her offspring won't try to make a claim on Robert's estate, but if they do I'll just have to cross that bridge when it comes."

"Are you not a little curious though, about the girl, Robert's daughter? I think I would be."

It's easy for Audrey, she has her children, her boys, she doesn't understand the pain my childlessness has caused me. To be fair I haven't told her of the years I spent longing for a child. The unrelenting, soul destroying treatment I endured, all to no avail. She no doubt thinks I was a career woman by choice. She has no idea of the anguish and helplessness I suffered. An anguish deepened by the fact that women all around me were having babies at the drop of a hat. Many of whom did not deserve to be mothers, just like … her. I discarded so many of my friends simply because they had something I wanted. I found it impossible to share their joy. Alongside them I felt incomplete and inadequate and jealous. The jealousy was soul-destroying, but the feelings of inadequacy were far worse, that's why work became so important. I had to prove myself; if I couldn't equal them by having a child then I would surpass them in other areas. And I did surpass them and many of their husbands too, and I let them know it. I looked down on them all, even ridiculing them for giving up everything for the convention that is motherhood. But they never knew that I wanted nothing more than to be part of that convention too. My vanity and conceit knew no bounds; in fact it bordered on the narcissistic. But those traits weren't me, well not the real me.

They were generated by my anger and envy; an all-consuming anger generated by my vulnerability; a vulnerability generated by my failure.

A failure that haunts me still.

So no, I don't want to meet her, because she should have been mine.

Martin

I WAKE WITH A START. My face is cold. Actually, not cold, wet. The tent must have a leak, or maybe something hasn't been tied off properly. How many times do I have to remind the lads to check that everything is secure? You can survive many things, but the weather will beat you every time if you're not prepared. I sit up and look around; there's nobody here, well, nobody that I know. People are walking past me, fast. They seem to be in a hurry and so they should be, do they not realise they have no business here? Why are some of them staring at me? I shout at one woman whose eyes linger on me too long. Bloody civilians. And it's not just my face that's wet, I'm feeling wet all over; curse those lads. When will they learn and where the bloody hell are they? I look down at myself; what appears to be a flattened cardboard box is laying across my damp sleeping bag, and there are empty lager cans strewn about me. I look around again, nothing is familiar, panic rises within me. Where am I? Am I dreaming? It's a strange dream that's for sure. But this dream feels real, very real. That's because it's not a dream, it's my life. My life which more resembles a nightmare, a nightmare that I am living, for now I remember …

One

I DISPOSE OF THE CANS and soggy cardboard in a nearby skip, roll up my sleeping bag and put it into my back-pack. The rain has eased off but I'm still wet and cold and now I need to pee. I know I look dreadful and I need to remedy that before I see Joanne. I look around hoping there is a public toilet somewhere close, but I can't see one. The desire to pee is becoming more urgent now, back of the skip will have to do. I'm so engrossed in the relief that peeing is affording me I don't see the people approaching, but soon enough I hear them. I hear their disapproval. Mutterings of disgraceful and loud tutting accompanied by faster footsteps as they pass by me as quickly as possible. As I do up my trousers and pick up my bag, a group of schoolgirls walk past, and I can't help staring at them. I am thinking of Amy. My thoughts are interrupted by a loud bang; it's a car back-firing in the next street but I don't know this and throw myself to the ground. When I realise that danger isn't imminent I slowly get up. It's the girls' turn to stare at me, stare and laugh before walking away giggling at the freak who is afraid of a car.

I head off down the street and at the junction I spot a supermarket. I'm sure they will have toilets that I can use to tidy myself up a bit, so that's the direction I go in. Thankfully there isn't a security guard on the door, if there was it's unlikely he would let me in. A couple of shoppers have spotted me and they are giving me strange looks; I'm used to that. There is nobody else in the toilets, so I put down my bag and remove my jacket and top. I fill the sink and have a wash. I wet my hair and with my fingers attempt to add a little style to my unruly mop. Small pieces of grit fall into the sink, a reminder that last night's bed was in fact the pavement. When I'm satisfied I've done all I can to make myself look a little better I dry my clothes by holding them underneath the hand-dryer. When I put them back on they are warm, and it reminds me of when I was a boy; Mum would put my clothes on the radiator the night before so they were warm when I put them on the following morning. Dad would complain that she'd make me soft; he was old-school, believed hardships made a man. I fill up my empty water bottle and go out into the shop. I'm hungry now, so reach into my pockets to see how much money I don't have. Forty-three pence is all I can find. Eyes are on me again so I exit the shop. As I walk across the car-park I spot a woman putting her baby into her car. The shopping trolley is standing behind the car, unattended - her full shopping trolley. I do a quick scan of the surrounding area and of the laden trolley. A bacon quiche and a packet of chocolate biscuits catch my eye. I'm in stealth mode now and very quickly and quietly I liberate said items from the trolley.

Without breaking into a run I up my pace; I need to put some distance between myself and the supermarket before I can eat my booty. An unoccupied bus shelter is the perfect place, especially as it has just started raining again. This shelter is one of those new types, rotating advertisements on one end and an electronic timetable at the other. There aren't any seats, well not what I'd call a seat, just a thin metal bench; no not a bench, more like a rail that you lean your backside against without actually sitting on it as it's far too narrow. I like the old-fashioned bus shelters. When Joanne and I first started going out we would spend hours sitting in the bus stop in our village. It was a wooden affair with a bench inside, a proper bench. We'd sit in there and snuggle together and … you know. It was our own personal shelter, hardly anyone else ever used it on account of the infrequency of the bus service. Happy days. I lean my behind on the rail and eat the quiche. It's not bad, would be nicer hot, but better than nothing. I'll save the biscuits for later. Now I need to get directions to Heron Way; apparently it's on a large development commonly known as the Bird Estate so hopefully it shouldn't be too hard to find. I can see a small parade of shops up ahead, maybe someone there will know the way.

The guy in the newsagents knows the estate and more specifically he knows Heron Way. Sadly I have to go back the way I've come. It seems my sleeping quarters were closer to Heron Way than I am now. Oh well, at least my mission isn't time sensitive. I start retracing my footsteps, striding out quickly in an effort to make myself a little warmer. As I walk along I wonder what made Joanne choose here to live, as she's a country girl at heart. Although it seems pleasant enough; it's a relatively new town that apparently started life as one of those 'garden village developments', but has grown somewhat since its inception. The roads are wide, offering dedicated bus and cycle lanes, and at the centre is a pedestrianised shopping centre. I have to go through here and then past the retail park to reach the Bird Estate. The shops are quite busy and I study each face as I walk past the shoppers, just in case she is here. Joanne likes to shop; correction, she loves to shop. It has always been her favourite pastime. When we first met we used to go shopping almost every Saturday. It was an escape from the quiet village we lived in but I never really enjoyed it. Hated it, still do, but back then my desire to be with her outweighed my dislike of shopping, so I went along happily carrying her bags for her.

As I exit the shopping precinct the pavements are replaced by roads, extremely busy roads, though thankfully a subway system runs beneath them. How I wish I'd known about the subway last night; it would have offered a drier spot to rest my head. I come out of the subway by yet more shops; these are much larger though, superstores. This must be the retail park that the guy in the shop was talking about when he gave me directions. I must be close now. Trouble is I can't remember which way to go. C'mon think man, which way did he say? My mind has gone blank and I know my anxiety levels are rising. I crouch down holding my head, and take several deep breaths. I hear two voices, one is berating me for forgetting simple instructions, while the other is telling me to remain calm. Calm wins, this time. I stand up and look around. I still cannot remember the way so I will have to ask someone for help. I imagine someone in one of these shops will know where I need to go. DIY shops, electrical shops, sports outlets, charity shops and a pet store. I decide to ask in one of the charity shops; I reckon they will be more willing to help me. A lady who reminds me a little of my mother is behind the counter; her face is split by a wonderful smile and she is happy to give me directions. Apparently she lives on the Bird Estate and she tells me it's quite a walk, suggesting I get the bus. I explain that I need the exercise and when she asks who I'm going to see I pretend not to hear, thank her for her help and leave the shop.

Heron Way is ahead of me, I can see the sign. I hope Joanne is home; I would've called if I had a number for her. Until recently I didn't even have an address. Not her fault, I think the move was rather sudden and to be fair she probably didn't know how to contact me. I'll surprise her. She likes surprises - at least she always used to. I would try and give her the wrong day for my return from overseas, or at the very least the wrong time, and then land on the doorstep earlier than expected. She would leap into my arms screaming, smothering me with kisses, tears flowing; happy tears of course. A lot has happened since then, I know, and many things have changed, but bottom line is we're meant to be together, always, and I miss my kids so much. They're growing up fast and I need to get to know them, properly. I've spent too much time away from my family already, too much time away from my beautiful Joanne.

Two

THE HOUSES ON THE BIRD ESTATE are not too dissimilar to our house in Cottesmore. Well, newer versions but they still have the same design and uniformity that most barrack homes have. Heron Way is just ahead of me, I can see the sign. I want number twelve; ah, I see it now, looks nice enough. I stop at the end of the road, I'm a little nervous and I need to compose myself. This is a big moment after all, our reunion. I wish I had a mirror, just to make sure I look okay. It has been a while and I really want to look my best, I don't want to disappoint her. Previous homecomings I always looked smarter than this, but then I was still in uniform. How she loved me in my uniform, the kids did too. Jack would always salute me and want to put my cap on, Amy was just pleased to see her Daddy. I suppose they'll both be at school now. That's okay though. It'll give Joanne and I time to catch up. I know my homecoming is different this time so there are probably a lot of readjustments required. Yes, it will take time and patience but when two people belong together like we do it will work out in the end. Despite all that has happened I know that I can't be without her any longer. What is that saying? We are two halves of ... no, two sides of the same ... or is it two halves? Whatever it is, that is us. Right, here goes! I cross the road and walk purposefully towards number twelve. When I reach the front door I run my fingers through my hair, stand tall and prepare to dazzle her with my best smile. I press the bell … and wait … and wait … and wait. I press it again … still I wait. I bend down and look through the letterbox, I can't see anything. I walk around the side of the house and look over the fence into the garden, I look through windows, nothing. I go back to the front door, pressing the bell and knocking on the door simultaneously. Surely she can hear me, unless she's not in. She has to be in. Please be in.

"Joanne. Joanne." I call her name several times while still banging on the door and ringing the bell. "Joanne." This isn't how it was meant to be. She should be here. "Jo." I bang harder. Nothing. My chest hurts. Where is she? I can't breathe. I need her to be here. I hold my head, I know I must calm down, she can't see me like this. C'mon Martin, breathe slowly, calm down mate. The voice in my head is reaching me, I breathe deeply and slowly. I feel a little dizzy so I crouch down for a minute. The panic is receding and I'm breathing properly now. Slowly I stand up, I can't believe she isn't here. I've planned this moment, rehearsed it endlessly and now I'll have to … have to what? Do I go and come back? Do I wait? Perhaps I can get into the house, wait for her inside. I walk around the house, no windows open, no obvious entry point. Maybe there's a key somewhere. My mum always used to leave a key under a pot in the garden, despite Dad and me telling her it was foolish. I look around, but there aren't any pots or anything else under which to hide a key. I decide to wait, but not here. I'll wait further up the road where I can still see the house but I won't be so visible. I still want to be a surprise. I need to recreate that moment, that moment when returning from a tour or exercise earlier than expected; Joanne's joy at seeing me was uncontainable. That's what I want.

I recall my return from Iraq, when the unit came back a couple of days earlier than expected; I knocked on the door and she burst into tears as soon as she opened it. Grateful tears she said, because every time there was a knock on the door she was convinced she would open it to find a senior officer standing there waiting to convey bad news. And happy tears because her man was back home. She hung onto me and made me promise never to leave her again, said I belonged to her and the kids and my place was at their side. She was adamant she never wanted to be apart again; I think it had been harder on her this time, our separation. So I promised her we wouldn't be parted again. A foolhardy promise that I was in no position to make as it was impossible to keep. Despite being a husband and father I belonged to the army first and it would be up to them to decide if and when we were separated again, but I didn't say that. How could I? I wasn't going to let anything sour that moment; that wonderful moment when nothing else mattered but the two of us. So if false promises were required, then I would make them. We barely made it up the stairs before we were making love. It had been well over six months since I'd last held her in my arms so it was magical. Then later we walked to the school together to collect Jack and Amy, my arm hooked across her shoulders and her arms knotted around my midriff. A few of us returned at the same time so there were several family reunions at the school gates. The children were all taken to the school hall at the end of the day and a number of them spotted their dads through the window. They were desperate to get out of school, so much so that when the home time bell rang the children came charging out through the doors and coursed across the playground like a herd of migrating wildebeest, all anxious to be the first to reach their waiting parents. We settled back into a lovely routine very quickly, the kids were great and hadn't suffered too much during my absence. It was the best time, a perfect time, we were all so happy. But then … then I was sent to Helmand. Game-changer …

I almost miss her from my vantage point at the end of the street. I hadn't taken into account another access point. I watch as she gets out of her car and walks to the front door. She opens it and then returns to the car, opening the boot to remove several large shopping bags. I keep watching as she ferries the bulging bags into the house. I can see she is trying to carry too much at a time, hooking bags around her wrists. I want to help her, I should help her, but that would alter my plan. I have to stick with my plan, I can't have our reunion encumbered by shopping bags. I stay in my spot, munching on a chocolate biscuit while observing her. She looks so beautiful - just like the girl I used to cuddle at the bus-stop - untouched by time. As she closes the boot of her car and goes indoors my stomach tightens, just a little. I decide to give her time to put the shopping away. I've been waiting for this moment for a long time now and I don't want any distractions. I'll give her fifteen minutes, maybe ten, ten should be plenty. After eight minutes I begin walking towards the house. Before I knock on the door I run my fingers through my hair again. I knock and wait, and hear light footsteps as she approaches the door, it squeaks as it opens. I'll oil that later. The door is fully open now and there she is, my Joanne, my beautiful Joanne. I deliver my best smile as planned. The shock is visible, I knew she would be surprised. In fact she is so overwhelmed she can't speak.

Three

SHE STANDS WITH HER BACK TOWARDS ME as she fills the two mugs with boiling water. The curve of her back is visible through her dress. Her hair is up, held in place by a large hair-clip. A few strands have slipped free of the clip and are sticking to the back of her neck. She has quite a long neck, which she has always hated and tried to hide by keeping her hair long, so I'm surprised her hair is up. She has beautiful hair, which is still the same gloriously rich chestnut hue. She turns and puts the mugs on the table and sits down opposite me. The steam from the coffee spirals up in front of us. I pick up the mug, slipping both hands around it. Its warmth courses through my hands and up my arms; it's only then that I realise how cold I am. I lift it to my lips and the steam heats my face.

"It'll be hot," she says.

I smile and sip it anyway; it is hot but I don't mind. I can't remember the last time I had a hot drink.

"Martin. What do you want?"

"At the moment this coffee will do."

"Don't try to be funny. You shouldn't be here."

Why is she saying that? Of course I should be here. This is where I belong. I take another sip of my coffee. It's so good to have a hot drink at last, and I'm so involved with my coffee I don't realise

Joanne has started speaking again. Not until she raises her voice.

"Are you even listening to me?"

"Sorry."

"You can't just turn up here. If you want to see the children you have to go through the proper channels."

"I wanted to see *you* and the kids." I emphasise '*you*'. For some reason she thinks I only want to see Amy and Jack. This isn't going right and my head is beginning to hurt.

"I know, but things are different now. I won't ever stop you seeing the children, but it needs to be properly arranged. I need to make sure they are okay with seeing you, it's been hard on them."

"Why wouldn't they be okay with seeing me?"

"Martin. Seeing you like you were ... well, it was scary, particularly for Amy. She was frightened of you. And Jack ..." she shakes her head slowly. "Jack was angry, he is still angry."

"And you?"

"Me, I'm fine ... now. It took a while. I understand what you went through and I know how hard it has been, but I had to think of the children. I still do. Their safety ..."

"Their safety? For Christ's sake, I would never hurt them or you, ever."

"But you did."

"What? No, I never ... I wouldn't ..."

"You did Martin. You hurt us all."

I'm staring at her, but not seeing her. I'm remembering ... something, it's not good. Shouting, screaming, slapping ... a bottle in my hand ... I throw it ... breaking glass, more shouting, I lunge forward and there is Jack squaring up to me, his face almost touching mine, his contorted face ... how dare he. I'll make him look at me with some respect. More shouting, screaming, slapping and ... Amy in the corner sobbing, my baby girl. I try and reach her but someone pulls me back, I spin around and put my assailant on the floor. Then there's more shouting, different voices and the sound of wood splintering as the door is forced open. Many hands are on me and they are dragging me away. I look back over my shoulder. Joanne is lying very still on the floor and Amy is still sobbing in the corner. Jack is standing over his mum, blood on his face, looking at me with such contempt …

"I'm sorry."

"I know, but things …"

"I'm truly sorry and I'm better now, it will be alright this time. I promise."

"Martin, stop it."

"I know what I did was awful but we can put it behind us."

"Stop talking as though we have a future."

"Of course we have a future."

"We don't. Well certainly not the type of future you have in mind. We are divorced. This is my house, my home, mine and the kids, and I'm sorry but there is no place here for you."

"Divorced?"

"Yes."

"How can I be divorced yet know nothing of it?"

"You know."

She's right of course. I think I do know, but I want to turn back the clock, I want it to be before again … but it can't be. But we could start anew, I know we can. I love her so much, her and the kids. We're a family, my family. My head hurts and my chest too, just a little, but I'm surprisingly calm considering all my plans have come to nothing. But one thing I've learnt is if your mission fails, you regroup and adopt a new strategy. That's what I'll do, I will formulate a new plan.

"So now what?" I ask.

"As I said before you have to go through the proper channels and I need to talk to the kids."

"Please Jo, let us sort this ourselves. I could come with you to pick them up from school."

"Amy is almost fifteen and would be mortified if I dared to pick her up from school, and Jack is at college … I hope. Look, leave me your address and phone number and I'll get in touch once I've spoken to them and see how they feel about seeing you."

"I can pop round again in a couple of days, after you've spoken to them, and we can sort something then."

"No. You are not to come here again. Not unless I specifically invite you."

"Give me your phone number then and I can call before I come."

"You're not getting this are you? I don't want you to just turn up or keep phoning …"

"I won't."

"Yes, you will. Give me your number, Martin, and your address and I will get in touch with you, I promise."

I say nothing. What can I say? I feel her eyes on me.

"Where are you living?"

I say nothing.

"Martin, help me out here."

"I'm between homes."

"Okay. Where are you staying at the moment?"

"Here and there."

"Here and there? What does that mean?"

"I move around, that's all."

"Jesus, you're homeless."

"Between homes."

"Are you working?"

"Between jobs."

"Perfect. Mobile phone?"

"Not at present."

"So how am I supposed to contact you?"

"That's why it's easier if I come here or call you," I say with a smile.

"Don't bloody grin at me. You are not to come here and I am not giving you my phone number. Do you still have the same social worker?"

"Yes, but ..."

"No buts. You get him to call me when you're back on your feet, and that means when you have a home and a job. Then I will talk to the kids and only then. Am I making myself clear?"

"Crystal."

"Good. Now I think you should go."

"Any chance of another coffee first?"

"No chance."

Four

CATCH 22. I NEED A JOB. To get a job I need an address. To get an address I need money. To get money I need a job. Catch 22.

Humble pie time. I'm going to have to see Alistair. Alistair is my social worker. Last time we spoke I told him where to go. He was trying to get me settled into some halfway house that was full of fruitcakes and losers. I was having none of it, but things are different now. I have to do this right, I know that now. Especially if I want to see my kids, and I have to see my kids. Who knows, maybe in time Jo will look at me like she used to. Divorce doesn't have to be the final chapter of our story. It's not unheard of for a divorced couple to realise they've made an error and to remarry. Look at Taylor and Burton; yes, I know they went on to divorce again so maybe not the best example. Yep, I'll call Alistair, maybe he can come and get me. I'm done walking. I need to find a phone box. I'm sure I passed one on the way here, one of the old-fashioned red ones. That's why it stood out, so I'm sure it shouldn't take too long to locate it. Thankfully it doesn't. On this grey day it stands out like a lighthouse to a sailor. I pull the door open and placing my bag on a small shelf, I rummage around inside it looking for Alistair's card. I know it's in here somewhere. Ah, got it. I go to pick up the phone, but it's not here. There's no bloody phone in the phone box. I bend down and look below the shelf holding my bag; more shelves, lined with books. Books! I straighten up, and a small handmade poster catches my eye; Stanton Book Exchange. A book exchange, really. As I pick up my bag I notice a book by Andy McNab, and I pick it up and flick through it. He did it right that's for sure. I don't want to read it though so put it back where I found it. As I exit the phone box that isn't a phone box the heavens open again; typical, bloody typical. I do my coat up and wish it had a hood. I stand the collar up and pull it into my neck and walk quicker. I've decided to head back to the supermarket, I'm sure they will have a pay-phone and it'll probably be easier for Alistair to find, once I persuade him to come and pick me up. And at least it will be dry.

There is a payphone but it has a minimum charge, sixty pence. I don't have sixty pence, I have forty-three pence. This isn't good, I mustn't get upset but I can't help it. I can't stop it. I'm feeling sick, my head is starting to hurt, my chest too. So far nothing has worked out as it was supposed to. I can't breathe. I start hitting myself with the handset of the phone. People are looking at me, I just want to scream at them - stop staring at me and give me seventeen pence. Seventeen pence and I can get my life back on track. A man is approaching me.

"Is everything alright, sir?

"I need seventeen pence, I only have forty-three but I need sixty." I open the palm of my hand and show him the coins I have.

"You can purchase a phone card from the till next to customer services."

"I don't want a phone card. I want seventeen pence."

"Or you can use a credit or debit card to make your phone call."

I look at him with growing incredulity.

"Do I look like someone who has a credit card?"

"Or debit card, sir."

He is clearly not listening to me. I know my anxiety levels are rising, I try to control my breathing but this is too much. It's all going wrong, all for the sake of seventeen pence. I open my mouth to speak but words do not come forth. Instead I emit a loud scream. When I'm done an uneasy quiet descends across the store.

"Sir, I think it would be best if you leave now."

I ignore him.

"Sir, I need you to vacate the premises or I will have no alternative but to call the police."

I need to sit down if I'm to regain control of myself. I need to sit quietly and I need to think. There are no chairs so I sit on the floor, cross-legged, waiting for the inevitable. After a couple of minutes I hear a siren. I know it's for me. I start shouting as they approach me, so one of them crouches down and tries to placate me. I know it would suit them to just move me along - less paperwork I reckon - and ordinarily that would suit me too, but that won't help me. I need to see Alistair and I figure the best chance I have of making that happen is if I get arrested - as it's highly unlikely anyone is going to give me seventeen pence - so I persist with the shouting. I also start banging my head and crying … a little. The tears are easy, I'm only ever one step away from despair anyway. I mustn't overdo it though, I want to be arrested not sectioned.

Ten minutes later I'm in the back of a police car. A warm and dry police car. At the station I'm processed, and I politely ask if they will phone my social worker. They agree to this but explain I will have to wait in a cell in the meantime. They apologise for this, but I understand its policy. I can see that they realise I do not pose a threat to them. After about ten minutes or so someone comes along to tell me that Alistair will come for me, he may be about an hour though. I say that's fine, I'm not going anywhere. This elicits a small laugh from the custody sergeant who offers me a tea or coffee. I opt for coffee but when it comes I'm not exactly sure what it is. It's warm though so I drink it.

Well over an hour has passed when Alistair finally arrives, and although I'm not happy at having to wait I decide not to reproach him over his tardiness. One look at his face tells me he is pissed at me. He signs the relevant forms detailing my release into his charge. I sign a form to acknowledge the return of my belongings and I follow him out to his car, in silence. Once in the car I thank him for coming. He ignores my thanks and proceeds to tell me he has made arrangements for me to stay at the night shelter. He will take me there now and return in the morning when we can talk about future arrangements. I begin to talk about Joanne and the kids and getting a job and somewhere to live and …. He lets me talk without interruption. Once at the shelter he checks me in and says he will be back in the morning.

Five

EGGS, BACON, SAUSAGE, fried bread, mushrooms and beans. Full English, something I haven't had in a long time. It even has grilled tomatoes and black pudding hidden somewhere beneath the other ingredients. Alistair has brought me to a café round the corner from the shelter. He's delicately eating a croissant while I'm gorging on this feast. When he finishes eating he begins detailing the things that I need to do in order to bring some semblance of normality and routine back to my life.

"First thing, you need to see a doctor and …"

I begin vigorously shaking my head - I can't speak as I have a mouthful of mushrooms.

"No arguments, Martin. Seeing the doctor and having a psych assessment was a condition of your release yesterday and it would be good to have your medication reviewed anyway. Then we need to find a place for you to stay as the night hostel is for emergency placements only. You can stay for a week, maybe ten days, but that's it. Once we have a placement then you can begin looking for work."

I'm happy that I won't be staying at the night shelter for too long but apprehensive about the alternative. I'm sure it will be the hostel he tried to put me in before. I don't say anything though, we'll cross that one when the time comes. I finish my breakfast; Alistair is talking about benefits now, reminding me of the help available to me as an ex-serviceman. I listen carefully, though he knows I don't want anything from the army. The army cost me my family in the first place, but … if I want my family back I may need to swallow my pride.

The doctor changes my medication and recommends counselling along with cognitive behavioural therapy. This is what he suggested before but I declined. This time however, I agree to it. In my head I'm focussing on Joanne and the children which is making me more amenable. My first session is booked for the following week. The next stop is the benefits office, now called Jobcentre Plus. They explain to me that in order to receive job seekers allowance I need to prove I've been looking for work, and no, they are unable to backdate it. I am due other payments though, so at least I have some money to look forward to. I fill in the relevant forms and sign up for the jobseekers club; yay I'm really looking forward to that - not. Alistair has to return to his office, and he informs me that I'm not allowed in the night shelter before half-past-five. He suggests I use my time wisely and says he will be in touch once he has found a hostel placement for me.

I've spent three nights at the shelter and to be honest, I've had enough. It's not the shelter itself, it is actually quite comfortable and everyone pretty much keeps to themselves. No, it's the days that are the problem, wandering around aimlessly just killing time, which drags when there is nothing much to do. I've tried to utilise the time. I have visited the job centre several times, but I can't actually apply for anything until I know where I'm going to be living. I also tried to reopen my bank account but I need an address for that too, despite having banked there for years. A letter from the warden of a homeless shelter will suffice but not the temporary one I'm staying at now, so I'm rather dependant on Alistair at the moment.

Day four. Hallelujah. Alistair has called, he has a place for me to stay. And it's not the one I didn't like before, it seems they didn't like me much either. Apparently I have a strident manner that upset some people, so Alistair has warned me to tone it down at the place he has found. My new home is still a hostel, a new one, not far from the supermarket where I was arrested. It was a former residential home that has been converted and upgraded. It has three floors. The ground floor has a large communal room with television, table football and a pool table. There is an office and a meeting room for residents to meet with their case worker, whether that be social worker, probation officer or whomever. The two upper floors have six bedrooms each, a kitchen, a bathroom and additional toilet and shower room. It's been nicely renovated and I think it will do. I'm quite pleased by its proximity to Joanne and the children, although I don't reveal this to Alistair.

Now the real work begins; I have to find a job. Alistair suggests I invest in some clothes, particularly a suit for job interviews. He loves making 'suggestions'. I know he is only doing his job but at times he is a little overbearing and borders on the sanctimonious. Mind you, he's right, new clothes would be a good idea, or perhaps I could collect my old clothes. I'm sure Joanne must have something of mine as I have no idea where everything went. Maybe not yet though; Alistair has said he will apprise Joanne of my situation and let her know that I am keen to see the children, so I should probably wait until I hear from her. If I can get myself a job before then I'm sure that would go some way towards helping my case. So, shopping it is; not my favourite activity but needs must and I need something suitable to wear for an interview. Another of Alistair's 'suggestions' is that I purchase a mobile phone. Apparently I can pick up a reasonably cheap pay-as-you-go one from a supermarket; but probably not the supermarket in which I was arrested. Everything is so expensive; well, certainly too expensive for me. I need suit, shirt, shoes, a tie and a mobile phone. Okay, I have some money now but it's really not going to stretch that far, not at these prices. I decide to get the phone first, that way I can call Alistair. He may be able to help with regard to the clothes that I need. I get a very cheap phone; it looks cheap, cheap and nasty, but I don't care. It fits in my pocket and comes with ten pounds worth of credit pre-loaded so it'll do for me.

I call Alistair asking what he 'suggests' I do about the clothes. I'm not happy with his answer; I've never worn second-hand clothes in my life. Who does he think I am? I tell him this in no uncertain terms, to which he responds by telling me that many people buy second-hand and that often the items are of a good quality. He has even worn second-hand, although he prefers to call what he buys vintage. I don't think he realises that his last comment isn't actually aiding his argument, no matter what adjective he uses to dress it up, pardon the pun. Despite my reluctance it appears I have no choice if I want some 'new' (new to me at least) clothes. So second-hand shop it is then. I think I'll go to that charity shop I went into before, the one that I asked for directions to Joanne's house.

I hate to admit it but Alistair was right, most of the clothes here are pretty good. In fact everything is. The shop is clean and well laid out, just like a regular shop. It doesn't have that musty, mildewy smell that I associate with this type of shop, and the clothes aren't the moth-eaten, old-fashioned rags that I was expecting. Some things don't even look as though they have been worn. I find a pair of jeans, a suit and a couple of shirts that are my size, as well as a pair of shoes. I take them up to the counter and a very smiley lady asks me if I would like to try them on - it seems they even have a changing room. I say I would and she takes me to the back of the store and ushers me behind a curtain. They fit perfectly. As I'm admiring myself in the mirror I realise I haven't got a tie. I pick up a dark blue one with diagonal stripes across it on my way to the till.

"Is that everything for you?"

"Yes, thank you."

"Did you find the Bird Estate alright?" she asks, as she neatly folds the clothes for me.

"Sorry?"

"You were in here a few days ago asking for directions to the Bird Estate. I wondered if you found it okay."

"I did, yes. You have rather a good memory."

"For faces, yes I do. Terrible with names though. I live on the estate."

"Yes, I recall you saying actually."

"I wonder if you were visiting somebody I know?"

This is clearly a question and she is eagerly awaiting my answer. I don't want to be rude but I have no intention of telling her about Joanne and the children. Thankfully a phone ringing interrupts our conversation. It takes a few seconds before I realise it is my phone that is ringing. I answer it; it's Alistair. Who else would it be? He is the only one with my number at the moment. I ask him to hang on for a minute as I take my change from the lady and pick up my purchases. She waves as I leave.

"Hi Alistair, sorry about that, I was just paying for some clothes."

"I hope you bought something smart, I've had a call from a friend at the job centre and he says a new job has just been listed that he thinks would be right up your street. If you go over and see him he'll set up an interview for you."

I have to hand it to him, Alistair does seem to get things done. In a week I've gone from being a man living on the streets with no prospects to a potential employee.

Six

SECURITY WORK WAS NOT REALLY the employment sector
I was hoping for, but it appears my military background makes
me quite desirable and besides, there is not much else out there
for a guy like me. Still the pay's not bad and I'll be based locally
once I've completed a period of training. The hostel is working
out too. I keep myself to myself mostly, but there are a couple
of good guys there who are a similar age to me and seem to be
on my wavelength. All in all, things seem to be heading in the
right direction. I've been pressurising Alistair to get in touch with
Joanne, to let her know that I'm making progress. I hope he does,
then she might agree to let me see Jack and Amy. I miss my family.

Off to see the M.O today; sorry, I mean doctor. I've had a
few sessions with him now and they have been quite positive. I
recognise things that upset me or make me angry, but I've still
been reluctant to go into detail about my experience in Helmand.
He has asked me to write it down with a view to reading it to him.
He says that writing might be easier. It's not, as I've never been one
for writing. Never been one for talking much either, not proper
talking, you know, feelings and that. Apparently it's the next
step though and I want to get better. I have to; Alistair says that
Joanne needs some assurances that I'm stable. She doesn't want
me upsetting or frightening Amy, who does want to see me. Jack's

not so keen, he still has some reservations about seeing me at the moment. Fair enough. Maybe if everything goes well with Amy she can persuade her brother for me, but first I have to complete my therapy ...

... it was the loudest noise I'd ever heard and for what seemed like an age, although probably just a few seconds, it was all I was aware of. A thunderous, ear-splitting boom, a powerful, vehement explosion that had surely laid waste to everything. And I mean everything, because in that moment, that second, I thought the end of the world had arrived. Then an eerie silence descended; a great quiet that despite the hush and stillness was deafening. I looked around; there was a lot of dust and smoke which added to the eeriness. Then through the smoke I saw movement; people, well silhouettes of people, and they were moving towards me. Everything seemed to be happening slowly; little by little the silhouettes approached me and as they got closer the silence was broken and there was noise, lots of noise, frantic voices filled with panic. An urgency spread over me and I knew I had to get up. I tried to get to my feet but before I could balance I was hauled up by my tunic and pulled along, the toes of my combat boots dragging on the ground. I was unceremoniously dumped behind a huge boulder. I looked into the faces of those who had manhandled me. They were faces I knew and I was so relieved. We were alive and safe, for the moment at least, but then I realised someone was missing ... Pete.

As the cloud of dust settled I risked a look from behind the rock; our vehicle was upended, but I still couldn't see Pete. I tried to edge out a little so I could see beyond the truck but a short burst of machine gun fire caused me to throw myself back behind our stone shield. A gun was thrust into my hands and we returned fire. We couldn't stay behind the rock; the insurgents knew exactly where we were now. They had the upper hand and before long they would come for us. We couldn't allow ourselves to be pinned here, we had to make a move before they did, and we still had to find Pete. Mack had radioed for help, and although the chopper wouldn't take long, we would still be on our own for a while longer. The next few minutes were vital if we were to have any chance of getting out of here alive. Towards the left of us was a pocket of trees and the terrain fell away slightly. It would offer us far more protection than our present position and a better vantage point too. I offered to go and told the lads to cover me. One, two, three ... I ran as fast as I could, concentrating solely on reaching the safety of the trees, hoping that none of the bullets that were whizzing through the dusty air would find me. Once behind the trees I scanned the surrounding area. Across from me I could see movement; two insurgents, and they were pointing at something. I tried to follow their sight line and I found what they were looking at. Crouching down behind a small thicket was Pete, they were going for him. I had to make him move, but I needed more firepower. I signalled to the lads behind the rock to come over to where I was, one at a time. Pete had now spotted us, but he didn't seem aware of the rebels who were watching him. There was still no sign of the chopper, and I knew that the enemy would also have radio communications and back-up on the way. We had to get Pete over here with us. We took up positions that would enable us to effectively cover him, then I signalled for him to move, fast. He didn't. He kept shaking his head and pointing at the ground. I again signalled for him to move. Still he didn't, but the insurgents did; we exchanged fire again and as I expected there were more of them now. We needed the bloody chopper and Pete had to move now. I shouted at him to run. He was aware of the imminent danger but still seemed rooted to the spot. I shouted again and again and again until finally he moved.

The explosion was worse than the first one, probably because instantly I knew what it was and what it meant ... again a silence fell, a silence halted by Mack yelling into his radio, 'Contact IED, one times casualty, T1.' I ran to Pete, and he was in a bad way. In the distance I could hear the familiar sound of the rotating blades of an approaching helicopter - at last. Thankfully the explosion had dispelled the advancing rebels. It was a small mercy but one we needed right now if we were to save Pete. The chopper landed and I heard Mack call for a medic. Pete's legs were a mess and we had to stem the blood flow. Mack applied pressure as the medic tied tourniquets around the severed arteries. I held Pete's head talking to him, assuring him he would be fine. I was lying to my best friend. As I held him he looked at me and said, 'I knew there was another one, I knew.' I didn't respond. I couldn't. I had been the one who had made him come out into the open from the relative safety of his hiding place. Instead of trying to take out the rebels I had taken out Pete and now as I looked at him, there were no words, no comfort could I offer. We put him on a stretcher and carried him to the helicopter and despite the fact that he had been administered morphine he still managed to say, 'It's fine mate, you did what you had to.' ...

I can't look at the doctor. I think he is waiting for me to say something else, but I can't. Relating my Helmand experience has exhausted me. My head hurts and my face is clammy and damp. I've laid bare my shame and at this moment I really can't see how doing so will be of any benefit.

"That was very brave."

I snort at his assessment. Brave, what a strange word to use in relation to me; I'm a coward. I know it. He knows it. Everyone knows it.

"You don't agree?"

I say nothing.

"It would help if you offer some response."

"I thought you were being rhetorical."

"No."

"I'm not brave."

"Bravery takes many forms and acknowledging past trauma takes immense courage."

"Facing life without your legs takes courage."

"That is very true. How is Peter doing?"

I stare at the doctor. What a stupid bloody question! And his name is Pete, he hated Peter.

He watches me, waiting for an answer. "Have you seen him recently?"

My breathing is becoming rapid and I'm fidgeting nervously. I'm getting angry, I know. I hold the arms of the chair to stop myself from banging my head. The doctor senses my discomfort and he tells me to breathe slowly. I do as he says, concentrating hard. When I'm obviously a little calmer he repeats his last question. I think he knows the answer, but he wants to hear it from me. All I can manage is a shake of my head.

"When did you last see him?"

"When we put him in the helicopter."

"You've not seen him since that day?"

"Alright, I did once, but he didn't see me. I went to the rehabilitation centre and I saw him sitting on ... lying on his bed, on top of the bed so I could see his ... well, they were gone, just stumps ..." I'm aware that I'm whispering now. "That was the day I ... apparently ... I was upset I think and I needed a drink and I ... I don't quite remember ..."

"You do remember."

"I don't."

"That was the day you assaulted your wife and son."

"I don't want to talk about that, or Pete or the army, especially not the fucking army."

"You blame the army."

"Yes … no."

"What is it? Yes or no?"

"This is too hard."

"It is hard, yes, but you're halfway there."

"Only halfway?"

"Acknowledging what happened is the first step. Accepting the consequences for what happened is the next step. I know you're not keen to take advantage of some of the resources available to veterans, but I think you would benefit from attending the group therapy sessions that the army offers. It would help you to recognise that Post Traumatic Stress Disorder is an actual thing and it is that which is fuelling your guilt and your anxiety."

"I don't know, Doctor."

"You will be surprised to find there are many ex-servicemen and women who feel like you do. Think about it."

Seven

GUARDING AN OUT OF TOWN SHOPPING CENTRE. Not what I was hoping for, but it's a job. I'll be outside a lot of the time, which I don't mind; patrolling the shops and surrounding areas. Also on the plus side, it's very near to Joanne and the kids so it's possible I may even see them there. The downside is I have to wear a uniform; I swore I would never put on a uniform again. I suppose as uniforms go it's not too bad, as from a distance it looks like a regular suit; it's only up close that you can see the company insignia and my name badge. Anyhow, if I focus on my end-game, namely being reunited with my family, I can cope. The Doc thinks I'm making progress too, although I haven't taken his advice about the group therapy. But I have been having regular sessions with him. However, his latest suggestion is a step too far. He wants me to visit Pete. I can't. How can I look him in the eye when I know his ... situation ... is my fault?

Pete Marsh and I did our basic training together and passed out at the same time. He was my buddy, my collaborator, colluder and confidante. He was best man at my wedding, Godfather to Jack and loyal ally to Joanne and me. We were not just 'Brothers in Arms', we were brothers, and we swore we would always have each other's back. I let him down. The doctor says I have 'survivor's guilt' as a result of Post-Traumatic Stress Disorder. It's just jargon, a fancy name, but the truth of the matter is I let Pete down. Not only did I fail to protect him, it was me who actively encouraged him to step on that IED. I shouted and screamed at him until he moved, ignoring what he was trying to tell me and making him ignore his own assessment of the situation, for he knew there were other devices. Of course there would be. In my rash assessment of the situation I neglected to consider other potential dangers. No amount of talking will make me think differently, but the Doc can help me control the anger and anxiety that these feelings generate, for I never again want to be responsible for hurting my family.

Alistair has been in touch; Joanne has agreed to let me see Amy. We have to meet somewhere neutral as Joanne does not want me to go to the house. Fair enough I suppose. There is a coffee shop where I work, so I suggest there. I arrive early and secure a place that gives me a good view of the door, and have a coffee while I wait. I see Joanne first. Amy is following her and when she steps out from behind her … oh my, I'm quite overwhelmed, she looks so much like her mum these days. I'm a little nervous about today but as Amy approaches my nerves evaporate, for it is clear from the expression on her face that she is genuinely pleased to see me. Why does that surprise me? I'm her dad after all. She gives me a hug and sits down opposite me.

"Are you joining us?" I ask Joanne.

"No, I'll leave you to it. I've some shopping to do. I'll come back in half-an-hour."

"An hour," says Amy. "We agreed an hour."

Clearly there has been some discussion as to the length of time Amy is to spend with me.

"Forty-five minutes."

"No, an hour."

I feel the need to interject before this develops into an argument.

"Forty-five minutes is fine, your mum can join us for a coffee after she has done her shopping." Neither of them speak straight away, they are both staring at each other - a stand-off.

"Fine. I'll be back in forty-five minutes or so."

"So, what do you want, cake, ice-cream?"

"No just a drink, I can't have cake or anything."

I begin to worry that my daughter has body image issues until she asks for a hot chocolate topped with whipped cream, marshmallows and chocolate flakes. I smile to myself as I order it.

"So, we have a lot of catching up to do. Fill me in on what's going on."

"You know, this and that."

"I don't know, Amy. It's been a while since I've seen you." She's not forthcoming so I press on. "Tell me about school."

"School sucks."

"I used to think that."

"Yeah, they treat us like kids."

"No, that's terrible. Being treated like a kid at your age." She ignores my sarcasm.

"I'd rather be at college like Jack."

"How is your brother?"

"Fine. I think. We don't see him much."

"No? Why's that?"

"He's got a girlfriend. Mum doesn't like her and Jack doesn't like Ray."

"Who's Ray?"

"Stop asking so many questions. Tell me what you are doing. Mum says you got a job and a new place to live." She takes a huge slurp of her hot chocolate while she waits for me to answer. I bring her up to date on what I'm doing although really all I want to know is ... who the hell is Ray? When I've finished telling her about me,

I'll ask again, but maybe not so directly.

"Why doesn't Jack like Ray?"

"Jack doesn't like anyone, except himself. And he doesn't want to see you, before you ask."

"I know," I say sadly.

Sensing my sadness, Amy reaches across the table and takes my hand. "I've missed you, Dad."

"I've missed you too sweetheart and I'm so sorry for what happened."

"It's fine, Dad. I don't really remember a lot of what happened. Jack would try and tell me sometimes, but I didn't want to know about it. Will I be able to come and stay with you?"

"Not while I'm at the hostel. We're not allowed visitors but hopefully I won't be there for long."

The door opens, it's Joanne. I'm dismayed to see her so soon, but when I look at the clock above the counter I see that she actually left us for almost an hour, it just went so quick.

"All good?" she asks.

"Yes, great. Do you want a drink?"

"No thanks. We need to be getting home."

I follow the pair of them out of the shop. Amy is busy texting so while she's distracted I ask the question.

"Who's Ray?"

Joanne's face colours instantly and her lips purse together as the contours of her face tighten.

"He's a friend, Martin."

"A friend?"

"Yes, a friend and it's none of your business. Amy, say goodbye to your dad, we need to get going."

Amy turns and gives me a hug.

"Do this again next week?" I ask.

"Sure, bye."

I watch them as they walk towards the car. I'm thinking about 'Ray'; a bit of a setback perhaps, a fly in the ointment, a bump in the road. Well, I've encountered bumps in the road before. Bumps just need to be flattened, that's all. I wait until they have driven away and then head back to the hostel. My thoughts are dominated by Ray: Who is he? How long has he been on the scene? Does he visit the house? And does he have to wait for an invitation like me? Or does he live there? The possible scenarios and endless questions run through my head. I try and recall if there were any obvious signs of a man living at the house; I wasn't there for long enough though and we only sat in the kitchen. I need to stop thinking about this. I'm on the early shift tomorrow so I need a good night's sleep.

The Retail Park is deserted when I arrive. It's barely light and a gentle breeze is blowing a discarded carrier bag across the car park. Its flight is delicate and graceful, giving it an almost ethereal presence. There are a couple of cars parked, and one belongs to the guard I am to relieve. I hope he's awake. I've been told he can often be found sleeping in the back office. I sign in and go to look for him. He is awake, although that is clearly a state he hasn't been inhabiting for long. His eyes are a little bloodshot with drooping lids, his hair is sticking up, and one side of his face is quite red where he has obviously been laying on it. He gives me a handover of sorts, 'nothing to report mate, quiet night', signs out and leaves, farting on the way. Cheers for that. I lock up the office and go outside to do my first patrol of the morning. Everything seems to be in order. A few cars are parking in the car park. I should really go and ask what business they have here as it's far too early for shoppers and still a little early for staff to be arriving, but I can't be bothered with that. I'm aware that most of them will be commuters; they park here and walk to the station. It's a ten to fifteen minute walk depending on your pace, but it will save them about six quid a day, so you can hardly blame them. Anyhow, I'm not challenging them, I'm not a bloody parking attendant.

Most of my day is spent looking at CCTV images or patrolling the site. Nothing much happens, which is good. Primarily we are meant to be a deterrent, but occasionally you'll be called upon to sort out some joker intent on causing a problem. As I'm looking at the monitors I notice a group of lads running from one of the shops. It's one of those discount chains, you know the sort, pile it high and sell it cheap. I watch the group being pursued by a couple of assistants from the shop. They are going to run straight past the office in a few seconds, if I time it right I'll be able to stop them. They don't see me and I'm able to get hold of a couple of them. My presence has slowed the entire group and the shop assistants grab another. The others look at me and run; no loyalty amongst thieves then. The two I've nabbed are telling me to let go of them, shouting something about their rights. I tell them their rights disappeared the minute they ran out of the shop with armfuls of cheap booze without any intention of paying for it. The shop assistants are struggling with the one lad they have hold of; he manages to free himself from one of them and as he battles with the other I catch a glimpse of his face. I know it instantly. He's bigger than I remember and clearly much stronger as he has now shaken off the other assistant. Before he has time to take off I lunge for him, grabbing him by the shoulder. In doing so I lose the two that I had hold of.

"Oh mate, you've lost the other two," bemoans one of the shop workers.

"This one will do. I'll take it from here," I say.

"We need to take him back to the shop, the manager will want to call the police. Company policy, we always prosecute."

"I said, I'll sort it now. He's in my custody, you boys get back to work." Thankfully they choose not to argue with me and trudge back towards the store a little despondently. I go back to the office along with my reluctant companion. In the office I tell him to sit down. We stare at each other, and his contempt for me is obvious. Who knew today's joker would turn out to be my errant son?

"Well this isn't how I hoped to see you."

"No shit."

I ignore his comment and ask him what he thinks he's playing at.

"Look who's playing dad! Well, guess what … it's too late. Just make the call and I can get out of here."

"Call?"

"The police."

"No, no police."

"Great. I'll be going then," he says as he stands.

"Sit down. We are going to make a call, but not to the police. We're going to call your mother. Well you are actually."

"I'm not."

"Yes, you are. Call her now." I hand him the telephone. He doesn't take it, instead he gets his mobile phone from his jacket pocket. I watch as he explains to Joanne that he needs her to come and get him. He says he is with me and then hands me the phone.

"She wants to talk to you."

"Martin. What is going on? I can't just drop everything."

"Jack is in a spot of bother and unless you'd rather pick him up from the police station I suggest you do drop everything and get over here." I hand the phone back to Jack. He takes it from me and begins playing around with it. "Perhaps you can put your phone away and you and I can have a chat while we wait for your mum."

"I have nothing to say to you."

Eight

DAY OFF TODAY, but still a busy day. I have a counselling session and a meeting with Alistair and I intend to go and see Joanne. This business with Jack needs sorting. It seems he has been in trouble on a few occasions now and it needs to stop. I can't have him becoming some kind of delinquent. He's a good lad, a clever lad, and I can't sit back and do nothing why he does foolish things that could jeopardise his future. Jo made it clear when she picked him up that I have to accept some of the responsibility for Jack's behaviour and I do, which is all the more reason to be involved. I want to make amends, I want to be a good father. He got lucky this time - if another guard had been on duty he would have handed Jack over to the police, no questions asked.

The counselling session goes well; I know I'm making progress. The medication helps of course, but I am also able to control my anxiety. I recognise the signs now; the breathing exercises help and I've started running. The doctor thought physical exercise would benefit me, and he was right. I feel energised after running and it's a great way to clear my head and, dare I say it, I think I'm looking better for it. A bit trimmer, a bit more toned, another bonus. In fact, Alistair made a comment regarding how I look. He was quite flattering, which is a little disconcerting, hopefully I'm not his type! The meeting goes well. He is pleased with my progress and he gives me details of a housing association that might be able to offer me a flat. We arrange to meet again in a couple of weeks. A brisk walk gets me to Joanne's in no time, though disappointingly there is no-one home. I consider waiting for a while but decide against it. It's Saturday tomorrow and although I'm working, I'm on the late shift so I'll have time to come back in the morning. If I come early I think there'll be more chance they will all be at home.

❧

Joanne's car is in the drive this time so I'm sure she is here. I ring the bell and wait ... nothing, so I try again, holding my finger on the button for a little longer this time. I think I hear something, and bang on the door for good measure. I can hear someone sliding a bolt and unlocking the door; good girl, security is good. The door opens and Joanne is standing before me in her dressing gown.

"Martin. What are you doing here?"

"I thought we should talk about Jack."

"It's eight o'clock on a Saturday morning."

"Yes. I wanted to catch you before you went shopping."

"I'm not going shopping."

"You always go shopping on a Saturday."

"No. I don't. I lay in on a Saturday because it's my day off and as I said to you before I will deal with Jack. You need to go, Martin." She starts closing the door but I put my palm up and hold it open.

"You're up now, let me in and we can talk about it. He is my son too. Is he here?"

"Yes he is, but no I'm ... look it's early I'm not doing this now."

"Hi Dad," says Amy as she comes down the stairs.

Joanne tells Amy to go in the kitchen and put the kettle on. She then reiterates to me that she would like me to go.

"Hey love. Everything alright down there?" asks a tall figure as he walks down the stairs.

"Shit," whispers Joanne as a man walks up behind her placing a protective hand on her shoulder. "Ray, this is Martin."

"Oh right. Hi bud," he says, extending his hand.

Bud, I'm not his bud. I shake his hand though. This is not the time to be unfriendly.

"I came to see Jo to talk about Jack."

"Yes, sure. Shame about that business at the shops, good of you to do what you did. We really appreciate it."

Is this guy for real? He is thanking me for helping 'my son'.

"Martin was just leaving. I've told him everything is alright."

"Yeah bud, we've got it all covered. Kids you know, they do stupid things sometimes. Anyway, really good to meet you finally."

The door closes but I'm unable to move. I look at the closed door with disbelief. Does this guy not realise who I am? I'm tempted to bang on the door and haul his arse out into the street and give him what for. Maybe a few months ago that's exactly what I would have done, but not today. Despite my irritation I'm aware that I have to play this one carefully. There will be plenty of time for flattening the bump in the road, but at the moment Amy and Jack are my priority, particularly Jack.

So for now, Ray can wait. But I will deal with him, for this family is mine.

Charley

HIS TEXT WAKES ME, and sleepily I reach for my phone. It's a cold morning and the chilly air is too much so I quickly retreat back to the warmth of my bed, pulling the cover tightly around me like a cocoon. I open my phone; the harsh glare of its light causes me to blink. The message is brief, '*Sorry XxxX*'. Sorry? Sorry for what? I'm confused, but I'm too tired to care and I don't feel brilliant this morning. I turn over, trying hard not to create any gaps between myself and the quilt as I'm not yet ready to leave the toasty confines of my bed. Beneath the covers I read through the latest Facebook posts. It's unbelievable what some people have to say, they seem to let their life play out on social media. Well not me, I don't want anyone knowing about my life; although it would be helpful if someone could explain to me why he is sorry. I snuggle down a little, I really don't feel great. My stomach is trying to tell me something, maybe I'm hungry. Oh no, it's definitely not hunger; I reach the bathroom just in time. The spewing and retching exhausts me and when I'm done I don't have the energy to move. I sit on the bathroom floor with my head in my hands, and a faint ringing interrupts my thoughts. It's my phone that I hear and I know it's him. I know it's him and I know why he is sorry, for now I remember ...

One

AS THE BLUE LINE SLOWLY APPEARS, so the room becomes smaller. The walls are marching towards me, closing in, and the air feels thinner. I'm breathing too fast. I sit on the edge of the bath tub, holding onto the cold porcelain to steady myself, for suddenly I don't feel sure of anything, least of all my ability to remain on my feet. A maelstrom of emotions courses through me like a sickness. Fear and dread wrap themselves around me so tightly that I can't see beyond their bounds. Not that there is anything to see, not at this moment, not with a baby. The promise of a future is fading, replaced by an unending … an unending what? That's exactly it though, an unending ….

I don't want to be a mother. I have plans you see; well maybe not plans, not definite concrete plans, more like dreams. I do have dreams and my dreams do not include a baby. I'm not sure that they include anyone. Everyone has something they long for and for many that may be a baby, but not me. I do long for something, but a baby would push it further out of reach. Yes, I know, it's a very selfish sentiment but I can't help how I feel. And it's not just that - it's scary. There I've said it, I'm scared. Me; street-wise, self-sufficient Charley is scared. Actually, I'm terrified. I can look after myself and I do it well, I've had to; but a baby? Jeez, I can't, I just can't. And he won't help; he'll want to, of course, but he's no more than a baby himself. Although slightly older than me in years, emotionally he's still a little boy and that temper of his. Take last night, he flew into a ridiculous rage just because I didn't want to go to the Feathers. And as for her; I can't look for help there.

I don't want to be a mother. I'd be rubbish at it; I don't have a role model to follow. Don't get me wrong, she's never hit me or anything like that. It's just, well … she has always made it quite clear that I'm a nuisance who is in the way.

"I have to work now, so you go in your room and keep quiet. Here are some pencils and paper."

A glass of milk, a couple of biscuits and the door locked behind me. I would stand there looking at the door, silent tears sliding down my cheeks; not because I was afraid, but because I really wanted to watch television. I knew not to make a sound though, otherwise I wouldn't get to watch television after she let me out either. In the beginning I would just sit on the floor waiting for the door to open, but eventually I picked up a pencil and began to draw and then I wanted to draw all the time. I was so absorbed by the colourful creations that I put on paper that I didn't even notice the noise from Mum's room stopping and the sound of the front door closing, signalling that she had finished working. As I got older she would send me out when she had to work - all weathers – and by this time I had progressed to a sketch book, which I took with me wherever I went. Thank goodness for those pencils and paper; they revealed my talent and became my best friends.

I don't want to be a mother. I want to be an artist. I don't want people looking at my child saying, 'what a gorgeous baby'. I want them to look at my paintings and say, 'what a fabulous use of colour'. Yes, selfish, that's me. His mum says that about me and she is right. I could blame my mum, say I get it from her, she's selfish alright. Selfish or not, bringing an unwanted child into this world is wrong and I won't do it. I would become her.

If I were to have a child, I would want to give it a life, not just life. I would want them to do and have what I didn't. Jeez, what a bloody cliché.

❧

We weren't poor. I was never hungry or cold or anything like that, but I didn't do the things that most of the other kids in my class did. There were no dancing lessons or gym club. I never went swimming other than with the school. I can't even tell you now if Mum can swim or not. We didn't have holidays or days out, except on my birthday when we would always go shopping and then to McDonalds. I had friends at school but those friendships did not transcend school. I was never invited round for tea or to birthday parties. Actually that's not strictly true, I went to Eloise's party and I had the best time, but then when everyone was being picked up no one came for me. Eloise's mum had to drop me home. I don't think she was very pleased about that and Mum certainly wasn't. She said she was running late and couldn't understand why they didn't just wait for her. I don't think Eloise's mum was very impressed with my home or Mum's attitude. I was never invited to a party again.

Mum wouldn't make an effort; that was the problem. She kept away from the other mums. Standing at the end of the road instead of by the gates at home time. Some thought she was aloof, others thought her irresponsible – especially after the party incident – but Mum didn't care. She called them the witches. I cared though. I wanted to come out of school and stand with my friends while our mums chatted. I wanted to walk home with them all, across the park instead of cutting through the alleyway. Most of all I wanted them all to be friends with us. I wanted Mum to like them and them to like Mum because then I would be included. None of them would allow their son and daughter to be friends with someone if they didn't know and approve of their parents. Mum's ambivalence towards them and refusal to conform led them to make their own conclusions about her.

As I got older friendships were a little easier as they weren't so dependent on your parents' input. Although I was still not openly invited into people's homes. I often learnt of sleepovers after the event, when someone accidentally let slip that one had occurred. That said, I didn't invite anyone to my home either. She didn't like it as she worked at home. Even I had to go out when she was working. Still I was happy enough, I had my sketch book and if the weather was good I could often be found sitting in the park drawing. If the weather was bad I would decamp to the library. The library was my safe haven, peaceful and warm. The light was good too; I would often use my oil pastels while there. And then it got flooded! Burst water pipe or some such thing. It was closed for several weeks; thankfully the weather was good. Except that one time …

I really had no choice but to go home. The rain was torrential and when the thunder started, well I wasn't sheltering beneath a tree during a storm. I'd take my chances and go home - I could sneak into my room and she'd never even know I was home. As I opened the front door I could hear the tinny sound of the radio in the kitchen. Gently I closed the door behind me. I wanted a drink so went into the kitchen. I could've done with a hot drink but knew the kettle would alert her to my presence so settled on some juice. It was as I closed the fridge door I saw him, coming from the bathroom and going into Mum's room. He hadn't seen me, not until I dropped the juice carton at the sight of him in all his naked glory, then he looked straight at me. His expression a strange blend of horror, contempt and embarrassment. The next thing I knew there were raised voices and a flurry of activity. The man appeared again, running past me to the door, tucking in his shirt and pulling on a jacket as he exited. Then she came out, her little robe draped around her, and boy did she let me have it. That was the day I discovered what she did for a living.

Two

ALL I WANT TO DO is lock the door and shut out the world.

Hibernate.

Or hide.

Or sleep.

Or ...

I can't and I won't. And I don't have time to wallow, as much as I'd like to. I know what I need to do and self-pity is a luxury time won't afford me.

I don't want to go to the Doctor. I've looked online and there are a few places I can go. I think the best one is the Brook Centre. I don't need an appointment for a start and as it is a little way out of town there is less chance of bumping into someone that I know. I'm going to go today.

I have to get two buses. It takes over an hour on account of missing the connecting bus and having to wait almost twenty minutes for the next one. When I reach the centre I linger outside a while, I'm not normally one for nerves, but this is ... well this is different. Finally I go in. The receptionist gives me a reassuring smile and places a sheet of paper on the counter. It's a list of services available, and she tells me to point at what I want to discuss. She then gets me to fill in a form and gives me a ticket with a number on. I have to wait about half-an-hour, although it feels much longer than this. A lady with exactly the same smile as the receptionist calls my number - I wonder if they are related. We talk for quite a while, and she says I'll need to take a pregnancy test. I explain I've done one already, but she says another one is required just to make sure.

"I'm not sure I can pee."

She gives me a glass of water and tells me not to worry, there's no rush. She ushers me back toward the waiting room.

"When you're ready tell Emma, she'll do the test for you," she says pointing at a lady sitting at a desk at the end of the corridor. Emma waves; she too has the smile. I'm sure they can't all be related. Maybe it's a pre-requisite for a job like this – must be able to offer reassuring smile to nervous teenagers – either that or it's part of their training.

The test is positive, as I knew it would be. Emma explains the options to me. I tell her that I know what I want to do. She nods and continues to smile as she tells me that she will need to refer me to a Doctor.

"I can't have letters or anything sent to my home."

"No problem. I can phone and make the appointment for you while you are here."

An appointment is made for the following week. Emma gives me some literature and directions to the clinic that I need to go to.

"It's not far from here. The doctor will talk to you about a termination and if you are certain that's what you want it will be arranged."

It is what I want.

"How long will I have to wait? To have it done?"

"Not long. It will probably be the week after you see the doctor."

As I head back to the bus stop I feel lighter already. In two weeks' time my nightmare will be over.

My journey home is punctuated by endless texts and phone calls that I do not answer. I have to mute my phone as I can tell the constant ringing is irritating some of the other passengers on the bus. It's always him. I know he's sorry. I'm just not sure I want to do it anymore. We always had such a lot of fun together, but lately he is so angry. He won't tell me why and I know there is something going on. As I get off the bus I feel my phone vibrate in my pocket. I look at it, a message on the screen tells me I have several voicemails. I stop in the park on the way home, sit on a bench and listen to the messages. They are all versions of the same thing: he's sorry, he loves me, it won't happen again. I delete the messages, then send him a text telling him I'll meet him later, before heading for home.

As I walk up my road I pass a smartly dressed, middle-aged man. He is a bit on the paunchy side with thinning hair. He has a furtive look about him, not surprisingly. I know where he has been.

She is in the shower when I go in, I'm grateful for that. I'm really not in the mood for conversation at the moment. Once in my bedroom I take the leaflets that the Brook Centre gave me from my bag and I put them in my art folder, amongst some of my work. She never looks in there; my pictures don't interest her in the slightest. This morning has left me exhausted so I decide to have a nap. I slip beneath the duvet, but my head has barely touched the pillow when she comes in.

"You lazy mare."

"Ever heard of knocking?"

"It's alright for some," she continues. "I wouldn't mind going to bed in the middle of the afternoon."

"I thought that's where you had been," I mumble. Annoyingly she has supersonic hearing so heard my mumble.

"Don't speak to me like that. I do what I do for us. I don't have a choice, my back's to the wall."

Backs to the wall – is that a new position? I don't say this out loud.

"I'm going out now so you can cook dinner tonight, I'll be back about six."

"Fine, shut the door on your way out."

Three

WE MEET AT THE TAVERN. Thankfully he didn't even suggest The Feathers, although I'm sure that's where he would rather be. He starts off by apologising, again. I watch him as he speaks. He is incredibly good looking and he is so funny, normally, but his humour has been lacking of late. He has finished talking and is looking at me, he wants me to say something. He wants me to say it's fine, I'll let you off, don't do it again. I don't know that I can. I know he doesn't mean it but the anger is too much. He needs to talk to me. If we are to stay together I need to understand what is going on with him. So, that is what I say. I can tell by the look on his face it's not what he expected to hear. He really did believe I was going to say 'it's okay'.

"I think that's a bit unfair. I'm not always angry."

"Mostly you are."

"Look, there's a lot going on, maybe that's why I lost it. But you don't help, sometimes you deliberately set out to wind me up."

"That's not true."

"It is. Take last night, you knew I wanted to go to The Feathers."

"And you could've gone. I was happy to go home."

"You're always happy to go home these days."

"Look, blame me all you want, point is, you seriously lost it."

"Alright, I overreacted a bit, but you know how to push my buttons."

The Kindness Of Strangers

"We aren't getting anywhere here. Maybe it's time to call it a day."

"Don't be stupid."

"I'm not being stupid, I just don't think …"

"C'mon, what don't you think? Tell me. You seem to have all the answers, c'mon."

"See what I mean, you're getting angry now."

"I'm not, it's just … you wouldn't understand."

"Understand what? Tell me what is wrong. I might be able to help."

"You know what, you're right. We are wasting our time." He stands up abruptly, tipping his chair over as he does. "See you around, Charley."

And he's gone.

Four

I HAVE MY APPOINTMENT with the doctor today. I'm a bit nervous, which is probably why I was sick again this morning, or maybe not.

I have to get the same buses as before, but today the connections are faultless so I get there much quicker than last time. Typical, I left really early as I didn't want to be late and now I'm probably going to have to sit around for ages.

The clinic is literally just around the corner from the Brook Centre. I decide to go in, it's too cold to hang around outside and you never know I might get seen earlier. I inform the receptionist that I'm here and she directs me to the waiting room. The seats are in rows. I pick a chair in the last row, behind a middle-aged couple. I wonder why they are here, it can't possibly be for the same reason as me. There is one other person, a lady, probably nearer Mum's age than mine. She is staring intently at a television which is suspended from the ceiling; it is muted and subtitles are moving across the bottom of the screen. It looks a bit out of sync to me as the words don't seem to have any bearing on the picture I'm seeing. I look around the waiting room. To the left of me there is a water dispenser and a small coffee table that is covered with a layer of magazines. I'm going to get a drink and something to read. I leave my bag on my chair, just in case somebody else comes in and like me, decides they want to hide at the back. The magazines are really disappointing, there are several copies of Peoples Friend, Country Interiors and Good Housekeeping and a couple of kid's books. I settle for the water. As I go back to my seat I spot a copy of Hello magazine on one of the chairs. There is nobody nearby so I pick it up. It's really old and the cover feature is about the wedding of some soap-star; I'm pretty sure I read somewhere that she's divorced now.

I read the magazine from cover to cover, and it doesn't take long. There are more pictures than words. The lady who was watching television has been called in and a couple of other people are now sitting in the waiting room. They are all wearing the same expression. A look that hovers somewhere between boredom and expectation. I look at the black-framed wall clock for the umpteenth time, it's still not quite my appointment time yet. I hope they aren't running late. I look at the clock again, only two minutes have passed. The disquiet and unease I feel is not lessened by the slow passing of time. I know I must stop looking at the clock. I gaze around the room, though apart from the clock and television there is nothing else to look at except dirty grey walls that are badly in need of a fresh coat of paint. They could smarten it up a bit, it wouldn't take much, put some pictures up maybe. The dentist I visit has a couple of seascapes hanging in his waiting room, he even has a picture on the ceiling in the treatment room. I used to think that was funny, but it was good to have something to look at it while he was fiddling around inside my mouth.

A nurse is calling someone's name, it takes a few seconds for me to realise that it's actually my name. Nobody calls me Charlene except Mum, and that is normally when she's cross with me, which is often. So it's strange when somebody else calls me it. The nurse takes me through a set of double doors and then tells me to take a seat in the corridor. She then disappears into one of the rooms. So, I've just been moved from a waiting room to a waiting corridor, and there is even less to look at here. Ten minutes later she calls me again.

Oh dear!

I was really hoping for a lady doctor. He introduces himself and offers me his hand; he has a firm, yet friendly handshake. His voice is gentle, with a hint of an accent that I can't place. I don't think it's English though. I think he senses my unease that he is not female, and he assures me that the nurse will stay with us throughout the consultation. She nods at me and tells me her name is Katie. Most of what he tells me I already know from the leaflets, but he goes into a bit more detail about the actual process. I don't really want to hear this, I just want it done. I tell him this, and he nods patiently while I talk. When I've finished talking he examines me and then goes to his computer.

"We can make the appointment for next Tuesday. Can you do that?"

"Yes, I can. Do I come back here?"

"Yes, you do."

I nod. It's sooner than I thought, less than a week away.

❧

To the untrained eye my picture is nothing more than a mismatch of colours and shapes. Most will think it is not representative of anything because it lacks form. Some may delight in the array of shapes and patterns that are swirling and dancing on the page. Others may simply like the colours, very few will see the emotion and fear that fills the page. Even less will know it is an image of my heart and mind; my thoughts and emotions laid bare. The paper is saturated in colour, lustrous and glossy. I've used mainly reds and orange; these colours are an expression of anger and distrust. A dark purple hue evokes sadness and despair. Amid the colours are flashes of white, with parts of the page deliberately left untouched. These few white spaces create shadows and it is the shadows that tell the story. For the shadows house my fear, alongside my dismay, disquiet and distress.

❧

I hear the front door close and then giggling and whispering; she's brought someone home. I listen carefully, it's a female voice, one of her friends. That's a relief as I really don't want to listen to her entertaining a one-night stand or worse, have to go out because it's a paying guest. I look at the time on my phone; it's much later than I thought. I've been totally absorbed in my picture. I look at it again before laying a sheet of glassine paper over it and putting it in a folder under my bed. The folder is quite full. I'm not sure how many pictures are in there or even what pictures. I rarely look at them again, but I like to keep them as they are a record of how I feel. Instead of using words in a diary or notebook, I create pictures, then file them away.

Five

A STRANGE RUMBLING sound filters through to my bedroom, I lay there listening to it for a while before going to investigate. As I open my bedroom door the source of the sound becomes apparent. A prostrated figure is lying on the sofa, deep in sleep, unaware of the resonant rumbling she is emitting. I tiptoe past, stepping over an empty wine bottle and go to the kitchen to make a cup of tea. Another wine bottle is on the worktop, also empty, and alongside it is a cardboard box with the remains of a pizza in it. There are no cups in the cupboard, so I wash one up that is in the sink. It's then I notice the milk carton, it's been left on the side all night. Tentatively I lift the carton towards my nose, the offending smell confirms what I already suspected. I look in the fridge, but there is no fresh milk and now the rumbling in the lounge is joined by a whistling. The whistling is not a melodic accompaniment, it's too much. I need to get out of here.

The café on the corner of Finch Lane is empty except for a solitary man sitting in the corner, reading a newspaper and eating a bacon sandwich. He is wearing a uniform, not police or anything that official, maybe he's a security guard or something similar. I take a seat in the opposite corner. A lady steps through the wooden beaded curtain that hangs across the kitchen door and from behind the counter asks me what I would like. I order a cup

The Kindness Of Strangers

of tea and a round of toast. She brings the tea over to me.

"Toast will be a couple of minutes, love."

I nod and thank her for the tea, which is rather strong. Builder's tea I think they call it. I add extra sugar to make it more palatable. I smell the toast before it arrives and my stomach begins to make noises, I hadn't realised how hungry I was. When it comes, it's unbuttered; a small silver rectangle sits on the side of the plate alongside a small single portion of marmalade. The butter has clearly been in the fridge a while and won't spread easily. As I'm battling with the butter I notice someone looking in the window. It's him. I wave, indicating he could join me if he wants to. For a moment I think he's coming in, but then something stops him and he moves on quickly. The man in the corner puts his paper down, drops some money on the table and runs out of the café. Hearing the door, the lady comes out from the kitchen again and starts to clear the man's table.

"Would you look at that, he's hardly touched his coffee. Must be running late I reckon."

I silently express agreement with her, although I'm not so sure. If I didn't know better I'd say he had seen someone he knew and was keen to catch up with him.

☯

I'm not surprised when he calls, only surprised it wasn't sooner.

"Hey. How're you doing?"

"Good thanks. What made you rush off this morning?"

"When?"

"Outside the café. You could've come in and said hello."

"Yeah, sorry. I just remembered I had to be somewhere. What you up to?"

"Nothing much, walking about."

"Want some company?"

"Sure."

"Where shall I meet you?"

"I'm over at Barnwell at the moment."

"Okay, see you in a bit."

I see him before he sees me - eventually he spots me and comes over. He gives me an awkward hug.

"What you doing over here?" he asks.

"You know I like being outside." He rolls his eyes at me as I continue. "I love it here. No cars or shops. Not too many people, or if there are you don't notice them. Big open spaces full of fresh air and countryside."

"Yeah, whatever."

"When I'm walking here I could be anywhere in the world."

"So where are you at the moment?"

"Sorry?"

"You said, you could be anywhere. So where are you?"

I look around. We are near the lake which is the heart of Barnwell. Barnwell is a country park, it was established when the new town was built. It is the mandatory green space and I love it. I will often come here to sketch or escape or both.

"At the moment I am walking alongside one of the Great Lakes of America."

"Really? This lake is just a puddle in comparison."

"Use your imagination, okay?"

"Okay. Point of reference though, I think the Great Lakes are in Canada."

"America."

"No, I'm pretty sure it's Canada. I'll Google it."

I watch him while he studies his phone.

"Well?" I ask.

"We are both right."

I'm not sure he's telling the truth, I'll check when I get home. We walk around the lake, not saying much. I think he is going to say something and when he does it's not what I expect.

"Fancy getting a sandwich?" he asks.

"Yes, sure."

We get a sandwich and go and sit on one of the benches. When we've finished he puts the rubbish in the bin.

"Shall we head off?"

"Not yet," I say. "I'm enjoying sitting here."

He sits back down next to me, silence joining us once again. This time it is me who speaks. I ask the question I've been wanting to ask all day.

"So, what spooked you this morning?"

"When?"

"On Finch Lane. Outside the café. I was sure you were going to come in."

"I told you I had things to do."

"I don't believe you."

"That's up to you."

"Come on, whatever it is, maybe I can help."

"Leave it, Char. Don't spoil a nice day."

He is right. It is a nice day, but now he's as good as admitted there is something going on I can't leave it.

"Who was the guy?"

"What guy?"

"The one who chased after you, this morning."

"Jesus. You're like a dog with a bone."

"What does that mean?"

"A dog with a bone – never gives up, relentless."

"Yep, that's me. I'm relentless alright."

He laughs at me and I laugh too. I'm still aware he hasn't answered me though.

"So, who is he?"

"He's my dad."

"I thought he was dead."

"I never said that."

"You said he was gone, I assumed you meant ..."

"You shouldn't make assumptions. That was my mistake, I assumed he was gone forever, how wrong could I be ..."

"It's not a good thing then? Him being back?"

"Nope."

"Do you want to tell me why?"

"Nope."

"Like I said before, I could help."

"Do you want to talk about your dad?" he shouts.

"No."

"So don't expect me to talk about mine."

"I don't have anything to say."

"Me neither."

"No, I mean I really don't have anything to say because I don't know anything." He looks at me quizzically as I continue. "I don't know where he is or who he is, if he is dead or alive. I don't even know his name."

"You must know his name."

"No."

"And you've never asked your mum?"

"I did when I was quite young. I said, who is my daddy and she said, you don't have one and don't ever ask me that again. So I didn't."

"Haven't you ever tried to find out some other way?"

"I wouldn't know where to start."

"What about your birth certificate?"

"Just has her name on it."

"Wow. I don't like mine very much but at least I know who he is. Aren't you just a little bit curious?"

"Not anymore. I used to be, but now I figure he may not know about me anyway and if he does he clearly doesn't care."

"I get that. Mine doesn't care."

"I don't think that's true."

"And how would you know?"

"Well he's back isn't he?"

Six

YESTERDAY WAS A STRANGE DAY. A good day, but strange. I had a lovely time at Barnwell and it took my mind of off my situation for a few hours, but it's thrown a light on other issues. Mainly my parentage. He reckons I should ask her again and maybe I will. Problem is, she may not even know, I was too ashamed to tell him that though.

She's cleaned up the kitchen but hasn't been shopping, so still no milk. I grab my purse and head up to the corner shop. When I get back she's in the kitchen.

"No milk," she shouts. "No sodding milk."

I go into the kitchen, throw my keys and purse on the side and wave the carton at her.

"Make us a cuppa then, kettle's boiled."

I make two mugs of tea and take them through to the lounge. I hand one to her.

"Thanks. Two sugars?"

"Yes."

She takes a sip, remarking that it's hot. What does she expect? I've only just made it. She puts it on the floor by her chair then picks up her cigarettes, takes one out and lights it. She inhales deeply which elicits a harsh cough as she exhales

"They'll finish you off," I say to her. She just sneers at me, inhales again and blows smoke rings in my direction. She knows I hate smoking.

After a long silence she asks me if I have any plans. I respond by asking if she wants me out of the way.

"Pardon me for being interested," she says feigning indignation.

"No work today then."

"It's Sunday."

"Oh yeah."

"So what are you up to?"

"Nothing."

"No arty project on the go then." Her sarcastic tone reveals she isn't really interested in what I'm doing.

"Thought I'd stay in today. Thought maybe you and I could have a chat."

"Have a chat?"

"Yes."

"About what?"

"Oh, you know, life, love and the universe."

"You what?"

"Or we could start with something simple like, what's my dad's name?"

Her anger shows on her face long before it reaches her tongue. Normally, at this point I would leave, a barrage of insults helping me along, but not today. Today I sit firm, because today I will make her tell me.

She has stopped shouting now, for the moment at least. She is standing over me, glowering at me, fury etched on her face. This contorted look ages her.

"Just his name. It's not difficult."

"Give it a rest."

"Okay, so you don't know his name. A description maybe?"

"Charlene, stop it."

"Tall, short, slim, fat, dark, fair, come on you must remember something about him."

My tone is unnerving her, I can tell. I don't do confrontation, not normally. But today is different; today I am emboldened, and I want answers. She lights another cigarette, inhaling hard. I watch as the red heat sears through it, grey flakes of ash floating delicately from the tip. She sits down, picks up the remote and turns on the television. I watch her as she flicks through the channels. This is her way of telling me this conversation is over. That's what she thinks. I turn off the television.

"I was watching that," she protests.

"Mum, you are going to answer my questions."

"No, I'm bloody well not."

"Yes, you are. I have a right to know."

"Don't talk to me about rights."

"What is my dad's name?"

"I've told you before, you don't have a dad."

"Am I like him?" She is staring past me now. "Am I like him?" I repeat.

"Do you know what? You bloody well are. You have the same attitude: self-righteous, holier-than-thou, think you're better than everybody else."

"Not better than everybody else, just you. Which isn't hard."

She jumps up from the chair and stands very close to me, spitting her words at me.

"How dare you judge me? I have done the best I could for you."

"The best?" I scoff.

"I could've got rid of you, you know. People said I should, including him."

"Well maybe you should have."

"Yeah. Well if I'd realised how ungrateful you would turn out …"

"Ungrateful? I'm ungrateful? What have I got to be grateful for? Tell me."

"I've fed and clothed you and put a roof over you."

"I know, but that's all you've done."

"All? I've worked bloody hard to do that."

"Let's not get started on your work."

"I don't do what I do by choice."

"There's always a choice. You could choose to do something different. You could choose to tell me about my dad. You could have even chosen not to have me."

"But I wanted you. That's what you don't seem to get. I wanted you."

"It's not just about what you want and it's not just about food, clothes and a roof. Kids need more. Nobody should have a child if they can't give them what they need. Nobody."

Seven

SLEEP IS ELUDING ME TONIGHT. I'm trying hard not to think about tomorrow. But by thinking about not thinking about it I am in fact thinking about it.

I look at the time on my phone, it's just gone half-past-one. I switch on the bedside lamp and reach for my sketch book. I start doodling. I let the pencil do as it pleases, I'm too tired to allow thought into the process. I scribble, sketch and shade until I finally succumb to sleep.

The alarm wakes me. I hit snooze and turn over, and a sharp pain in my side causes me to flinch. I reach down and discover the source of the pain is a pencil. I remove it and sit up. I'm not going to sleep anymore so I turn off the snooze. It's then that I remember what the day has planned for me. My fear manifests as nausea and the nausea seeks some release. I quickly get out of bed, slipping on some paper before running to the bathroom. This morning the heaving and retching produce nothing. I go to the sink and splash my face with some cold water. I lift up my head and look at my reflection in the bathroom mirror. I look dreadful and it's not just my usual morning face. The circles around my eyes are deeper and darker today, a marked contrast to my pale skin, which is much lighter than normal. Bed hair completes the look. I try and smooth down my hair while telling myself that tomorrow I will look better, because tomorrow it will be gone.

I go back to my room. There are sheets of paper strewn across the floor. They're from last night, I remember now. I pick them up, smoothing creases from them as I do. Some of them aren't bad. I sit on the edge of the bed and go through them. They are all variations of the same theme. A female form in various poses: sitting, standing, laying. And she is holding something …she is holding something to her breast …

❧

My appointment was half an hour ago. I'm still sitting at the bus stop opposite the clinic. I'm neither able to cross the road to go in or get on a bus to go home.

Someone is walking towards me. I recognise her, I think she is from the clinic. What is her name?

"Hello, Charlene. Do you remember me? I'm Katie. Are you okay?"

"I erm …"

"Do you want to come inside?" she asks pointing at the clinic.

I shake my head and look down at my feet. I don't want her to see me.

"Look, if you are having second thoughts that is fine. If you come with me we can have a chat, but please be assured you will not be made to do anything you don't want to."

We walk into the clinic together and she takes me straight through to a small room. She offers me a glass of water, which I accept although I'm not really thirsty.

"I can't do it," I say.

"Okay. Is it because you are worried about the actual procedure?

Because I can get the doctor to come and talk to you again or I can run through it with you?"

"No, it's not that. It's just that ... well I've erm ... I've changed my mind."

"Right. That's fine but you need to be sure as ..."

"I'm sure." As I answer I start going through the backpack that I have with me and I take out a sheet of paper. It's folded several times, I unfold it and hand it to her.

"This is very good. Did you do this?"

"Yes. It's me and ... with ..."

"You and a baby."

I just nod. I can't speak anymore. I'm crying as quietly as possible, but my sniffing gives me away.

"Charlene, it's absolutely fine to change your mind. But obviously we need to make sure that you get the care and attention that you need. So, I have to get the doctor to come and talk to you. Is that okay?"

The doctor was nice, considering. I was a bit scared that he would be cross with me, but he wasn't. He asked me quite a few questions though and said he would write to my G.P. As I left he wished me good luck. I think I'm going to need it.

When I get home I phone my surgery for an appointment. My doctor can see me on Friday. I have another phone call to make but chicken out and send a text instead.

'Hey, fancy meeting up on Saturday? We could go to Barnwell again? Xx

He replies instantly.

'Defo. Working in morning though. Can meet at 2?'

We arrange to meet by the visitor's centre. I try and imagine the conversation we might have, but running through possible responses exhausts me. Either way, telling him will be easier than telling her. We haven't spoken since Sunday. I think I'll wait a bit, no need to tell her just yet. But perhaps I need to start talking to her, try and get her in a slightly better mood before dropping my bombshell.

Eight

I'M NOT SURE I like my doctor very much. He told me to consider all my options - again - including adoption. I think I made it clear what I want though, in the end. Thankfully I don't have to see him very much; I have to see the midwife and she is nice. She is quite old, I think. Well probably older than Mum; yes, definitely older than Mum. Her face is heart shaped, it's quite lined, but it's a kind face and she has a soft voice that matches her face perfectly. Her hair is red but flecked with grey. I suspect she had very red hair when she was younger. She keeps calling me pet, which I quite like. Her name is Geraldine. She reminds me of a grandmother, or what I think a grandmother should be like. I don't have one, but if I did I wouldn't be disappointed if she was like Geraldine.

☯

He's late. I'm just about to text when I see him walking towards me.

"Sorry I'm late. Got caught up at work." He hugs me as he apologises. The smell of beer tells me he's lying. I don't say anything.

"It's fine. I've only just got here anyway," I lie.

He laughs and asks if I'm hungry. I'm not actually but I reckon he is. He wouldn't have asked otherwise. I say I am; I want to keep him in a good mood. We each order a panini in the restaurant by the visitor's centre. It is delicious and I eat every last bit, clearly hungry after all.

"Are we staying here?" he asks.

"Yeah. Is that okay?"

"Fine. Or we could go to The Feathers?"

"I'd rather not. I need to talk to you and The Feathers is a bit noisy."

"Fair enough."

He concedes quite easily, which is a relief, probably because he has already been there.

"Actually," he continues, "there's something I want to talk to you about too."

"Oh, alright. You go first."

"No. Ladies first."

I'm not sure it's a good idea for me to go first. What I have to say is quite major and very possibly a conversation stopper and I'd like to hear what he has to say. I reckon it's about his dad and as I've been pushing him to talk … I should let him.

"No, you go. I can wait."

"Right. Well, I've been doing a lot of thinking, about us and about what I want to do and … well … the thing is I like how things are, now. We're friends again and it's good. We're not arguing, so maybe we should erm …"

"Should what?"

"Maybe for now we should just be friends."

"Friends?"

"For now. We could see what happens, but yeah."

I did not see this coming and I don't know what to say. I thought we were getting back on track. I did think, well before, that maybe we shouldn't be together, but now I'd convinced myself we should be and I kind of thought we were. But obviously not.

"Char? You okay? You look a bit …"

"I'm fine, that's fine, it's just …"

"Great, because I have something else to tell you."

Oh God, I knew it. He's met someone else.

"I've joined the army."

"What?"

"I've joined the army."

"You can't."

"I have."

"But why?"

"Because I want to. I've always wanted to."

"I need to get home."

"Don't be like that. I'm not saying we won't get back together, it's just for now. I need to focus on this. The initial training is quite tough and I could do without any distractions."

"Fine," I say, but keep walking.

"This is what I need. I've been getting into some bother lately and I have to do this or who knows where I'll end up."

"Whatever."

"Char, please stop. I still want to spend today with you."

"I want to go."

He catches up with me and grabs my arm.

"Stay, please."

"Let go of me."

"Okay, sorry." He holds his arms up. "Stay. You haven't told me your news yet anyway."

"Who said I had news?"

"You did. You said you had something to tell me."

I can't tell him now, I know that.

"It's nothing really, just an exhibition I'm planning."

"That's brilliant, Char. We both have a future to look forward to now."

Don't we just, I think.

Nine

CIVILITY REIGNS AT HOME, for now. Mum and I have been cordial with each other and on the odd occasion, friendly even. But for the most part our relationship is still overshadowed by distrust and mutual disrespect. Neither of us has brought up the argument and I haven't asked anymore questions of her. I have been busy at college as I still have pieces to complete for my portfolio and she has been busy doing what she does.

The sickness has stopped now, which is a relief. The problem I have now is my size. I generally wear baggy, over-sized tops which have concealed my bump thus far but that won't be the case for much longer. I will tell her. I need to pick my moment though, and it will need to be soon. I haven't seen him since he told me his news. Had a couple of texts, apparently his basic training starts soon, at somewhere called Pirbright, wherever that is. He'll be there for fourteen weeks, so by the time he comes home there will be no hiding it from him either.

My work is being assessed today so I need to take in my folder. I want to go through it before I leave but the bloody zip is stuck. I rub pencil lead along the teeth of the zip; it helps but it is still sticking. I rub some more and pull it hard. The folder opens showering its contents across the lounge floor. I scoop up my work, carefully placing glassine sheets between each piece and put them back into

The Kindness Of Strangers

the folder. The zip won't do up now, this is all I need. I'll have to put a couple of safety pins through it and hope they hold it together. I'm running late now so I need to get a move on. I pick up the folder and my back-pack and head out of the door. In my haste I don't notice some bits of paper that haven't made it back into the folder.

❧

The assessment went well and some of my pieces have been selected to be used in an exhibition at the Civic Centre. I will need to have them properly framed and mounted though. As I round the corner and turn into my road I pass the paunchy man again, still looking guilty; and so he should. I think I'll go to the café for half an hour; she is never in a good place when she has just finished work. I order a hot chocolate with all the trimmings: whipped cream, chocolate sauce, mini fudge cubes and of course marshmallows. Well I hardly need to worry about my waistline, I have no control over that anymore. It goes down a treat and that plus the successful afternoon I've had at college puts me in a great mood. I may even offer to cook dinner for us both this evening.

As soon as I open the front door I know something is wrong. She is sitting in the armchair, cigarette in hand, staring straight ahead. On her lap are some papers. Probably bills, she is never happy when a bill comes. I brace myself. Her regular rant normally includes the line, 'if you got a job instead of fannying about at college, you could pay your share'. But she says nothing. I break the silence by asking what she fancies for dinner.

"I'm not hungry."

"You might be later."

"I don't want dinner."

"Okay."

I don't push it; something has really wound her up today. I think I'll do some pasta, and do enough for two in case she changes her mind. I hang up my coat and go to the bathroom. When I come out she hasn't moved, at all. Not even to flick the ash from her cigarette which is now tilting at a perilous angle and will fall onto the chair or floor imminently. It does, but she seems not to notice or to care.

"Everything alright?" I ask.

She emits a disdainful sniff before speaking.

"You tell me."

"What?" I'm confused, but as I walk towards her, I take a closer look at the papers on her lap. They aren't bills, they are the leaflets from the Brook Centre. Shit, this is not how I wanted her to find out.

"Mum, I ..."

"Don't speak."

"But ..."

"I mean it Charlene. Don't say anything, you have no idea how bloody furious I am at this moment."

I sit down on the settee and wait for her to speak. When she does I'm utterly confused.

"You've obviously done the best thing, so that's fine, but stealing. It's beneath even you."

"You what?"

"I told you not to speak."

"Yes, but I don't know ..."

She is up quick as flash and for a second I think she is going to hit me, so I put my arms in front of my face. She stops and stares at me.

"Put your arms down you stupid bitch. I'm not going to touch you, although you deserve a bloody good hiding. I fell out with

Jenny because of you. I accused her of taking it when she stayed here the other night."

"I haven't taken anything," I shout.

"Don't give me that."

"I have no idea what you are talking about."

"Really. Then how did you pay for it?"

"Pay for what?"

"God almighty, you are testing my patience. The worst thing about this is if you had asked me I would've given it to you."

"Given me what?" My anger will soon equal hers.

"The money."

"What money?"

"The money you stole from me."

"I haven't stolen any money."

"So who paid for it then?"

"Paid for what?"

"The abortion."

"I haven't had an …" The penny has dropped. She thinks I've got rid of it. The leaflets, Emma had written the address of the clinic on them and …

"You haven't had what?"

"I haven't had an abortion and I didn't take your money."

"What are you telling me?"

"I'm pregnant."

This time she does hit me and I don't see it coming. My eyes smart and my cheek stings.

"You stupid, stupid …"

She doesn't finish the sentence, instead she slumps back into the armchair and lights another cigarette. Neither of us speak for what seems like an eternity. Finally she interrupts the quiet that's unsettling us both.

"Are you getting rid of it?"

"I was going to, but I couldn't do it."

"You have to."

"I can't."

"You have to."

"Mum, I'm … I can't."

"You're not listening to me, Charlene. You cannot keep it."

"It's too late," I say and I lift up my top to expose my swollen belly.

She looks at me and shakes her head. Then stands and goes into her bedroom. I can hear talking; she must be on her phone. Odd moment to make a phone call. Five minutes later she comes back, and she is carrying her overnight bag.

"What's that for?" I enquire.

She doesn't answer. Instead she walks to the front door, puts her bag down and puts on her coat. Silently, she walks over to the chair she was sitting on, grabs her cigarettes and keys, putting them in her coat pocket. She looks directly at me as she speaks in a tone that conveys no emotion but is emphatic in its meaning.

"I'm going to stay at Mo's. I will be back tomorrow night. Make sure you are gone before I return."

❧

I've packed what I can into my back-pack; thankfully I left my folder at college. I still have a carrier bag full of art materials that I don't want to lose. She may let me collect them another day but actually I don't ever want to come back here again. The look she gave me as she left was so cold and final. Without doubt it was saying I don't ever want to see you again. Well that's fine by me. I choose a selection of pens and crayons that fit into my bag, the rest

I will have to leave behind.

I put my key on the window sill. I'm tempted to write a note, but what's the point? I look around one last time, waiting to see if I feel anything. I should feel something, shouldn't I? But, nothing, no sadness at all. If I feel anything it's maybe relief tempered with some mild disquietude. And a hint of irritation over the money. I've never taken anything from her or anyone. It probably one of her skanky mates or one of the many guys that come through here. You know, I think I will leave her a message. I go into her bedroom and get her lipstick, the expensive one that she treats herself to and uses sparingly. Thankfully she didn't take it with her. I go into the bathroom and use it to write on the mirror. I press hard to ensure I use a lot of it. I step back and look at my handiwork.

'I did not steal your fuckin' money'

Hmm, something missing. I put some lipstick on my lips and then press them against the bathroom mirror just below my scrawl. That's better. I drop the remainder of the lipstick into the sink and leave.

I have looked online and I have found a hostel I can stay at over the weekend but on Monday I'll have to set about making some proper plans. I think I'll go and see the midwife, I'm sure she will be able to help me.

The receptionist at the surgery says Geraldine will see me but I'll have to sit and wait for a while as I don't have an appointment. That's okay, I don't have college today and I don't have anywhere else to be. I don't have anywhere else to go. I don't tell the receptionist this though. I have to wait about forty minutes, then Geraldine comes into the waiting room.

"Hello, pet. You want to see me?"

I nod and she gestures for me to follow her.

When I've finished talking she takes hold of my hand and sits there shaking her head. I can tell she is a little bit shocked and surprised at what I've told her. In her gentle tone she explains that she will have to get in touch with Social Services. She is disarmingly sympathetic and her kindness releases my tears.

"Oh pet. Don't cry now. A social worker is the person best placed to deal with accommodation and other such issues and I'm here to make sure you and your baby remain healthy. Between us we will sort you out. Okay?"

I manage to voice an okay between my sobs.

She gives them a call and a duty social worker agrees to come out and see me. The receptionist makes me a cup of tea while I wait, and Geraldine finds me a couple of biscuits to have with it. I have to wait for almost an hour for the social worker but I don't mind. It's warm in the surgery waiting room and they have a good selection of magazines. They have books too that you can take away if you leave a donation in the jar on the counter.

The social worker is younger than I expected. She is not very tall, a fact not hidden by the heels she is wearing. I reckon she will barely hit five feet when she removes her shoes. She is smartly dressed in a skirt and jacket and she is wearing tights which are not thick enough to conceal a small tattoo on her left ankle.

"Hi Charlene, is it okay to call you that or do you prefer Charley or something else?"

Not many people ask me that. I like her already.

"Charley, I prefer Charley."

"Great and I'm Rachel. Right, Charley, I'll explain a few things to you. Firstly, as you're pregnant and homeless you are classed as being in a category of priority need so the local authority has an obligation to house you. However, that said, it doesn't mean they are going to give you a house. The accommodation could be a hostel or bed and breakfast or foster care. Although the last one wouldn't apply to you as you are over sixteen. Most likely you will be placed in a council run hostel until you have your baby. Then, assuming there is a space, you will be moved to a mother and baby home until more permanent accommodation is available. With me so far?"

"Yes. Will it be the same one I stayed in at the weekend?"

"No."

"That's good."

"Was there a problem?"

"No. it's just I had to go out during the day."

"Aah, that's because you were at the night shelter. It literally is only open at night. I'm going to make a couple of calls so sit tight and I'll be back in a bit."

She isn't very long and when she comes back she looks quite pleased with herself. She tells me there is a place at the hostel and she can take me there now. I say goodbye to Geraldine who wishes me good luck and reminds me I have an appointment with her at the end of the week. On the way to the hostel Rachel gives me a bit more information. She tells me she is the duty social worker today and she may or may not be assigned to my case. I tell her I hope she is. She fills me in on what benefits I may be able to claim and how I do that. She also asks again if I am absolutely certain that Mum and I will not be reconciled.

"No chance."

"Fair enough. I had to ask and if you do get another social worker you may be asked again. Here we are now."

We pull up outside a large Victorian style house, I'm not sure where we are as I wasn't paying much attention to which way we were going. We go inside and meet the lady in charge, she reminds me of one of my old schoolteachers. After various formalities I am shown to my room; apparently I'm lucky as I have been given a single room.

"Do you have everything you need?" asks Rachel. "I could arrange for someone to visit your mum and collect any of your belongings you may have left behind."

For a second I think of asking for my paints and pens, but then I just shake my head.

"In that case I'll be off. Either myself or another social worker will be in touch tomorrow."

I say goodbye and after she has gone I close the door and sit on the bed. I lay a protective hand across my belly and in a hushed voice I talk to my child. Making promises I hope I can keep; promises I want to keep. I'm under no illusion that I have a hard road ahead but I will make it work for me and for my baby. I will make it work without him and I will make it work despite her.

This is my life and no more will I tolerate being pushed around. I may be alone, but the future is mine.

Part Two

The Kindness ...

The Kindness Of Strangers

One

AS SHE OPENS THE CURTAINS of her living-room, Audrey is surprised to see someone sitting on the wall that borders her front garden. Her initial thought is to tap on the window and shoo them along; most certainly that is what Gerald would have done. However something about the man's demeanour, for it is a man, makes her hesitate. She stands still, watching him through the small holes that are part of the intricate lacy pattern on the net curtain. He looks troubled, she thinks. His shoulders are slightly hunched as his hands cradle his head. He appears weighed down by whatever it is that concerns him. She will have to go out to him. She finds it impossible to ignore someone when they are visibly distressed or in need. Audrey is not the sort of person who walks on by or crosses the street to avoid a situation. She is the one who will stop, ask if you are alright and do what she can to help. Why? Because she is kind, Audrey Stevens is very kind, the epitome of kindness. Everyone knows this; although there are a few who may disagree. They are a handful of people at most, who misinterpret her kindness as interference or just plain old-fashioned nosiness. Some of these people may describe her as an over-bearing busybody, while others suggest she is self-righteous. Both views would be harsh. Thankfully Audrey herself is oblivious to these opinions. She will admit that she likes to know what is going on, but says this is so she is well placed to help people, for she knows that not everybody is able to help themselves. In fact, she is keenly aware that many people do not know what is best for themselves or others, so she is happy to step in and help in this regard. There are occasions when her assistance is firmly rejected, but she will often persevere, for she knows what is right. And today, she believes the right thing to do is to go and see what troubles the man on the wall, but she needs to get dressed first. She has standards and as such she knows it would be inappropriate for her to go outside in her nightclothes. A little bit of colour on her cheeks wouldn't go amiss either. Ten minutes later and more suitably dressed, Audrey opens the front door. The wall is no longer occupied. She is disappointed and chides herself for allowing vanity to get in the way of offering help.

❧

Helen slowly opens her eyes, allowing the morning sunlight to gently filter through. Birdsong drifts into the room through the open fanlight. The delicate warbles bring a smile to her face. A smile that all too soon fades when she remembers; Robert has gone. Although now, it is not his death that grieves her, but his life. A life she knew so little of, his secret life. The revelation that he had a daughter has compounded her grief. But Helen will not let this diminish her. She knows that the grief will fade, along with the anger, and maybe one day she won't look back on her marriage as time wasted. Until then she takes one day at a time, making very few plans as she never really knows how she will feel from one day to the next. Today however is the exception, for she does have plans. She is meeting Audrey for lunch and a spot of shopping. Not that she is much of a shopper; well, not like Audrey. Audrey will wander aimlessly along the High Street, happy to browse, searching out bargains. Helen will happily shop if there is a purpose, if she needs something. Walking from shop to shop looking at things that you don't really need on the off-chance you may see something you like is not really her idea of fun. She does however enjoy Audrey's company. Her capacity for words, bordering on loquaciousness, means she can be very entertaining. Audrey is also her confidante; the only person Helen has told of Robert's indiscretion. She couldn't tell anyone else, certainly nobody who knew Robert. They would just try to understand it from his point of view and make excuses for him. Their clumsy attempts at trying to make her feel better would lead them to somehow exonerate him of blame, exactly as Anthony had done. And if Robert wasn't to blame, who was? That's what she had said to Anthony when he dared to defend him. It wasn't her fault, of that she was sure. Yes there had been difficulties, she will admit that, but she hadn't strayed despite having plenty of opportunities and offers for her to do so. Anyway, there wasn't anyone else to tell, friends were thin on the ground. Helen's superior manner during her working life had not helped endear her to people and many of her old friends had chosen different paths and therefore had very little in common with her anymore. So Audrey is her only friend and Helen is grateful for her, despite her continued assertion that Helen should find Robert's daughter.

Joanne standing in the doorway with Ray, his hand on her shoulder, is all Martin can see. It's as if this image has been seared onto his retinas. He tries hard to shake it off and think of something else, but he cannot. He wonders if he lives there or if he's just an occasional overnight guest. Whatever the living arrangements Martin doesn't like the familiarity Ray has with his family: with Amy, with Jack and most of all with Joanne. This man stands where he should stand, and even worse, lays where he should lay. The thought of someone else touching his Joanne is too much. His head begins to ache and his breathing is erratic. He stops walking and sits on a garden wall, clutching his head. The mercury is rising and he needs to calm down. Anger and anxiety go hand-in-hand for Martin and in his haste to see Joanne this morning he left home without taking his medication. He needs his pills, now. Or maybe a drink. Or both. A drink, definitely a drink. He knows there is a supermarket nearby. He looks at his watch, it's not even nine yet. They are not going to serve him alcohol. He thinks he may have passed a small convenience store on the way, if he can find it he is quite sure they will be less likely to adhere to the licensing laws. Martin heads back the way he came, walking quickly and with urgency now. Before long he is holding a small bottle of vodka. Not that he particularly likes vodka but he has to work later, so the odourless liquid is the best choice. The clear fluid initially burns his throat before releasing a warmth that courses through his body. The warmth elevates his mood just enough to quell his anger. For now.

❧

Charley sips her tea as she stares out of the kitchen window of the hostel. She yawns, shivering slightly as she does. Another disrupted night's sleep thanks to the girl in the adjoining room shouting obscenities through the open window at her boyfriend in the street below. A situation she hopes isn't going to continue for too much longer. As if hearing her thoughts the warden comes in and tells her that Alice, the girl in the adjoining room, will be leaving in a couple of days. Charley expresses her thanks, finishes her tea and goes back to her room. Despite her fatigue she is quite excited today; it's the opening of the exhibition at the Civic Centre. This is a big deal; sometimes it's attended by art experts and gallery owners hoping to discover new talent. Apparently last year someone had a piece chosen for the Summer Exhibition at the Royal Academy and somebody else was offered sponsorship by a gallery. Something like that would be a dream come true for Charley, although she thinks it unlikely. Even if someone likes her work, will they be prepared to fund a homeless, pregnant teenager? She very much doubts it. In reality, she knows her prospects are not great and contemplating an uncertain future takes a little of the glow from her excitement. Despite this however, one thing she is certain of; no matter how desperate things may become she has no intention of following her mother's career path. So for now she will just enjoy seeing her paintings on display.

Two

THE BUS IS A FEW MINUTES LATE, but Audrey doesn't fret over this, she knows Helen won't be waiting for her. Helen is very rarely on time, and although she finds this quite irritating she doesn't let on. Audrey often wonders how Helen managed to have such a successful business career; surely punctuality was paramount. Then again perhaps her tardiness is a new thing, a consequence of losing Robert and everything else that has happened. As she nears the coffee shop that is their meeting place she peers inside. Just as she thought, Helen isn't there. She goes in, orders a coffee and sits at a table in the window. From here she can watch the comings and goings of passers-by and she will spot Helen too. As she waits for her coffee, her stomach emits a low growl which startles her, it is then she realises that she has come out without having any breakfast. Her morning routine was disrupted by the man on the wall. When the waitress brings her coffee over Audrey orders some wholemeal toast. Ten minutes later Helen arrives, offering no apology or reason for being late.

"Morning, Audrey. Are we eating?" asks Helen, spotting the remains of her toast.

"I forgot to have breakfast."

"Oh dear, should I be worried?" Before Audrey can reply Helen has ordered herself a pot of tea and a toasted teacake. "Another coffee?"

"Yes please. I was distracted this morning."

"Distracted … by what?"

Audrey tells Helen about the man on her wall, embellishing the tale somewhat, making the experience sound way more interesting than it actually was.

"Goodness a stranger in your midst. You didn't recognise him at all, not a local man?"

"I don't know who he was, although there was something familiar about him. Maybe he has been in the shop."

"Maybe. Are you finished?" enquires Helen, pointing at Audrey's plate which still has scraps of toast on it.

"Yes, I'm done. The crusts are a little burnt."

"Let's go and spend some of your money then."

❧

Charley cannot hide her delight at seeing her pictures properly mounted and framed and on display. The spot she has been allocated is perfect, allowing just enough natural light to enhance the bold and dramatic colours that are included in her pieces. She wished she looked as good as her work, but she has a very limited wardrobe and the few clothes she does have are beginning to feel a little tight in places. She is going to have to get some new clothes soon and not just for herself. Although how she will do this is a worry; a worry she refuses to acknowledge today, because today is about her art. This may well be the only time her work is ever viewed by the general public and she intends to soak it up and forget about her situation, just for a while. The exhibition opens shortly, the first in will be the press and those who have a professional interest. Then it's open to all.

Charley gets herself a chair and sits alongside her work. She watches carefully as reviewers, fellow artists and other dignitaries slowly move around, studying the very varied collection of artwork. They are all quite taken with a large sculpture that has been positioned at the centre of the room. As a couple of the party move towards her, Charley stands up. The two men smile politely at her and then move on. She sits down, a little disappointed that they didn't make any comment or ask her anything about her work. A few minutes later and some more people come over, they are more interested and do ask questions and make comments to each other. The words 'vibrant' and 'startling' are used to describe her use of colour. Somebody else comments on the movement in her work, saying despite its boldness it maintains fluidity. One lady calls her work organic. Charley is not sure about that, but overall she is pleased with the comments. A photographer takes some pictures of her and her work and informs her that the council are going to buy the large sculpture that everyone is admiring. She feels a touch of envy when she hears this; a commission like that would solve her immediate problems. However, she is very aware that things like that don't happen to girls like her, because girls like her with runaway fathers and whores for mothers end up pregnant and alone, perpetuating the myth that girls like her simply don't deserve anything else.

❧

Helen's feet are beginning to ache. She has been bumped, elbowed and jostled, very often by people on their mobile phones. She has had to dance around a couple having an argument in the middle of the street and avoid the inconsiderate few who think it's okay to smoke while walking along a crowded street. Many of the shops have been too hot and the one time she wanted to buy something she couldn't because the shop in question was unable to process card payments and she didn't quite have enough cash. All in all, she believes her dislike of shopping is quite justified. She tells Audrey it's time for lunch. Audrey is quite happy to stop too; she has just inadvertently breathed in a cloud of second-hand tobacco smoke that was exhaled directly into her face just as she was coming out of a shop with her heavy shopping bags. One of them, a cheap carrier bag which she had to pay for, is threatening to cut off circulation to her index finger. She suggests to Helen they go to The Lemon Tree, she rather fancies one of their homemade quiches or pies, but Helen prefers either The Crown or one of the Italian chains. Audrey knows why this is; The Lemon Tree is unlicensed and clearly Helen would like a drink. She has been drinking more and more of late. Audrey understands this; after all Helen has had a lot to contend with recently, but it is something that needs addressing. They settle on The Crown as Audrey is not a fan of pasta or pizza. She is very British and has tastes to match. Helen orders herself a large glass of red wine, Audrey pointedly orders a soda water and a coffee.

"Busy in town today," says Audrey.

"It is, and it's made all the worse by people's selfishness." Audrey looks at Helen, she feels a rant coming. "If people just observed a few simple rules, navigating the High Street would not be nearly as bad as it is."

"What sort of rules?" asks Audrey, regretting asking the question as soon as she had finished speaking.

"Well, no bloody mobiles for a start," replies Helen rather loudly. "And no arguing, kissing, smooching and definitely no smoking." Audrey whole-heartedly agrees with the last one, although she thinks Helen sounds like a speaking version of one of those posters she recalled seeing at the swimming pool when she used to take the boys swimming. She even thinks she is going to press on with no diving or bombing. "It would help if the pavements had lanes on them too, keep everyone moving in the same direction. Another drink?" Audrey shakes her head, she still has her soda water.

The women finish their food; Audrey got her homemade quiche as it was on the specials board and Helen had a steak baguette. As Helen pushes her empty plate aside and picks up her wine glass Audrey decides that now is the time to speak.

"I'm a little worried about you, Helen."

"Really. Why?"

"Well you are drinking rather a …"

"I've had two glasses of wine."

"Let me finish. I know things have been hard, but drinking isn't the answer." She puts her hand up sensing Helen might interrupt again. "You need some sort of closure and I think you will achieve that if you find Robert's daughter."

"Audrey. I have neither need nor desire to ever find her."

"But what if she comes knocking on your door one day? What if she finds you?"

"I will cross that bridge when and if I come to it, now please leave it."

"I just want what is best for you. You're still so angry."

"And finding his daughter is going to make me less angry, is that what you think?"

"I think it is inevitable that you will meet, surely it's better if you find her rather than the other way around. Do it on your terms. It may help you come to terms with it or at the very least satisfy your curiosity."

"Your curiosity you mean," snaps Helen

"That's unfair. I'm sure you have many unanswered questions, that's all."

"And I'm sure that the daughter he never met will be no wiser than I am."

"Maybe her mother then?"

"I'm going to get another drink. Would you like one?"

"You don't need another."

"You're right, I don't need another. I want another."

Audrey doesn't say anything more, she knows her disapproval has been noted. When Helen comes back from the bar she has a flyer in her hand. She passes it to Audrey. It is advertising an art exhibition on at The Civic Centre.

"Do you fancy popping along to this before we go home? It might be fun."

"Why not," says Audrey, well aware that the previous conversation is now at an end.

❧

Charley is struggling to keep her eyes open; a disrupted night's sleep and the boredom are beginning to take effect. Initially a steady flow of people came through, but after a while it became a trickle. The last hour has seen one person come in. Her early excitement has been replaced by a dull detachment. Her lassitude isn't helped by the fact that she hasn't spoken to anyone for a while, the chair she is sitting on is incredibly uncomfortable, she is hungry and she needs to pee. There is no one around at the moment so she decides now is as good a time as any to leave her post, not that she has much choice in the matter. She has to queue as shoppers are taking advantage of the free toilets on offer at the centre. When she goes back to the main hall Charley notices a couple more people; two women are looking at the sculpture. It is impressive looking, mainly due to its size and prominent position. It dominates the room, drawing people to it instantly. They all walk around it nodding and pointing at it, but Charley suspects that very few of them have any idea what it is or means. The two women walk away from the centre and start looking at the other pieces. One of the women appears to be far more interested in what she is looking at than the other, she is studying the pieces quite intently and is clearly reading all the information cards. The second lady is more pre-occupied with her shopping bags, of which she has many. When they reach her paintings Charley stands up.

"Did you paint these?" asks the lady with the bags.

Charley tells her she did. She explains that she is a student at the college and these pieces were selected from her portfolio.

"They're very good," continues the lady. "Colourful. I prefer traditional art really, like Constable, but I like these."

"Thank you," says Charley politely, fully aware that abstract art isn't for everyone. She knew immediately that this lady wouldn't be a fan, she thinks she is probably here at the behest of her friend who does seem rather more interested.

Helen likes art, particularly modern art, although the walls of her home belie this fact. They are dominated by prints of works by the 'old masters', a few limited edition prints that she and Robert picked up over the years or paintings that Robert himself had done. He was quite talented, although his repertoire was narrow, consisting mainly of landscapes and flowers. As she studies the pictures in front of her, she thinks maybe it's time for a change at home. It wasn't so long ago that the thought of removing Robert's pictures would have been impossible to contemplate, despite the fact they are not to her taste. It would have been a betrayal of his memory but now, well … it seems perfectly right.

"Are these for sale?" Helen enquires.

"Yes, yes, they are." Charley can't believe it, an enquiry.

"They are wonderful, particularly this one. It puts me in mind of work by Sonia Delauney."

"Wow, thank you. I love her stuff and her husband's too, Robert Delauney. Do you like him too?"

"Yes, I do. I think Kadinsky is my favourite though. He was heavily influenced by Matisse and Picasso who I also adore."

"Georgia O'Keeffe is my absolute favourite," replies Charley relishing a conversation that has roused her from an almost languid state.

"Not so keen on her, I like the style of her work but not her love of flowers. She paints too many flowers."

"You don't like flowers?" pipes up Audrey.

"Not so much in paintings," answers Helen. Turning back to Charley she enquires how much the picture is to buy. Charley is dumbstruck, she has given no thought to prices. She didn't think anyone would really want to buy her work. Helen can see the girl hasn't thought this through, which paves the way for her to be a bit opportunistic and buy the painting rather cheaply. Previously Helen may have done this; despite her wealth she likes to achieve a bargain. However, the new Helen has no desire to profit from the young girl's ignorance. Besides, she quite likes her. She finds her enthusiasm delightful and her passion is communicable.

"I assume you can't actually sell anything until the exhibition is over anyway," says Helen.

"I can, you just won't be able to take it away until it's finished," counters Charley, desperate not to lose a potential sale. "The exhibition finishes Wednesday. You could come back then or I can bring it to you."

"I'm not sure what I'm doing Wednesday, but look, I will give you a deposit to hold it for me, then call at the end of the week to arrange delivery or collection."

"Okay," says Charley nodding.

Helen opens her purse, extracts two twenty-pound notes and hands them to Charley, who is rather surprised; she expected a fiver, ten pounds at the most.

"Is that enough?" asks Helen, when Charley fails to say anything.

"What … Oh yes, sorry, yes that's fine."

"Do you have a card?"

"A card?"

"Business card, with your details on."

"No, sorry. This is all a bit new to me," confesses Charley.

"No matter. You can call me." Helen reaches back into her handbag and takes out a small wallet, from it she removes a card which she hands to Charley. "Call me on the mobile number."

"I will, thank you. Thank you so much."

"You're very welcome. Now be sure to put a sold sticker alongside my painting."

When the two women are outside Audrey tells Helen off for not getting a receipt for her money.

"You may never hear from her again and that's forty pounds gone."

"Audrey, she is a young artist who has just sold her first painting. I can assure you I will hear from her."

Three

THE WEEKEND IS OVER, and for this Martin is thankful. It's a new day and he has to look forward. The realisation that others have moved forward with their lives, forged new relationships, and made decisions without him is hard to face, but he has to face it and make a plan. A plan to counter it. He has a day off today, which he needs. He has to regroup, evaluate and assess what is going on but with a clear head. He waltzed through the weekend in a chemically induced daze. Anti-depressants and alcohol, a potent mix that initially made him feel that he could cope with anything, then left him shrouded in a fog of paranoia and anxiety accompanied by a deep lethargy. He is astounded that he made it into work, although he is pretty certain that he has not fulfilled his duties as he should have. He throws back the bedcovers and swings his legs out of bed. His head protests at the sudden movement, his stomach lurches a little and then settles.

Gingerly he stands up and goes into the bathroom. As he steps into the shower he can hear the melodic ringtone of his mobile phone. He decides to ignore it; he assumes it's probably work calling to reprimand him for forgetting to do something.

As he gets out of the shower his phone is still ringing, they're persistent, he thinks. Then he pauses for a second, wondering if in fact he has made some major cock up at work and they are actually calling to fire him. How would he explain that to Alistair? The ringing stops, but still he doesn't move, half-expecting it to start again. When it doesn't he tentatively moves towards it as though it is a wild animal that may pounce at any moment. It beeps as he picks it up, letting him know he has a voicemail. It isn't work. Four missed calls and two voicemails, all from the same person - Joanne. For a moment he wished it was work. Work he could deal with, Jo - well that is a whole different scene. He drops the phone onto the bed and proceeds to get dressed.

❧

As Audrey makes her way to work she mulls over the weekend's events. It has been a good weekend, shopping and lunch with Helen on Saturday and a lovely walk on Sunday morning. She had even finally managed to get hold of the boys, although the conversations were a little stilted and rather brief; Philip bemoaning his Skype connection and Simon claiming he had a bad signal on his mobile. Again there had been no mention of visits by either of them. Audrey was hoping for an invite to New Zealand as she hasn't been for several years now. The manageress at the shop, Sheila, goes to see her daughter in Australia every year. A veil of sadness descends over her, just fleetingly. She shakes it off for there isn't time for her to feel sorry for herself. Helen is her concern at the moment. Her drinking, her inability to face up to things and her odd impulse buy at the art exhibition all lead Audrey to believe Helen is losing it and having some sort of breakdown. She knows she has to help her, although it won't be easy. Helen does tend to disregard Audrey's advice all too readily. But Audrey is tenacious and she is sure her doggedness will allow her to find a solution.

Martin is standing at the end of the conveyor belt packing his shopping when his phone goes. He takes his mobile from his pocket, it's Joanne again. He mutes the phone and puts it back into his pocket and continues with the task at hand. He knows he will have to speak to her and he wants to speak to her; he just doesn't want to hear her.

He knows she will tell him to back off.

He knows she will tell him to stay away from the house.

He knows she will talk about Ray.

He does not want to hear about Ray.

Martin does not want his suspicions confirmed. He settles up with the cashier and heads home. He hasn't even reached the door of the supermarket when he feels vibrations in his pocket. He checks his phone again, she has left another message. At home Martin unpacks his shopping and makes a coffee, then he sits down and readies himself to listen to Joanne's messages.

'Martin it's Jo, can you call me as soon as you get this please?'

'Martin, this is important. We need to talk about Jack. Call me.'

Martin sneers as he hears her mention Jack. He is pretty sure that is just a ruse to make him call her. She didn't want to talk about him earlier. Typical, everything when she wants, nothing new there. He listens to the final message.

'Martin. Where are you? I need to speak to you. You are not going to believe what Jack has done. Please call me, he is getting ready to go to Pirbright and I can't … '

The message ends, it is incomplete but one word fills Martin with dread; Pirbright. He tries to call Jo, this time it's her who doesn't answer. He doesn't bother trying again, instead he picks up his keys and charges out of the door. He leaps down the stairs two at a time and when he hits the street he is already sprinting.

"Where's the fire, mate?" shouts someone as Martin almost knocks them down as he rounds the corner.

When he gets to Jo's house there is no hesitation, he knocks on the door, loudly, calling for her at the same time. She opens the door then walks back into the house, leaving Martin to close the front door.

"You're too late," says a tearful Jo. "You're too fuckin' late."

"What … late for what? Jo, what's happened? Where is Jack?"

"He's gone. He has enlisted and he's gone. If you had answered your bloody phone you may have got here in time to stop him. Don't even know why I'm surprised. It's what he always said he wanted to do. Join the army like his dad. Only I hoped that after what happened … well I hoped he didn't want to be like you anymore."

Martin sits down on the stairs. He feels like all the oxygen has been sucked from the room. Images of Jack as a small boy are running through his head:

Jack wearing his cap.

Jack marching up and down the garden.

Jack saluting him.

Jack with a stick he had brought back from a foray in the woods, brandishing it like a rifle.

Then it's grown up Jack:

Jack wearing his own cap.

Jack marching.

Jack saluting.

Jack the soldier brandishing an actual rifle.

The last image is too much and Martin begins sobbing. He is crushed. Jo sits down beside him on the stairs and they cling to each other. The feel of her in his arms once again is exquisite and despite the sadness of the moment Martin delights in her touch. It isn't long before he is fully aroused and believing that Jo is feeling as he is he begins moving his hands over her. Her sudden rigidity makes him stop.

"What's wrong?"

"What wrong?" she repeats. "You, you're wrong. You need to go."

"No. Don't make me go. I'm sorry. I'm rushing you aren't I?"

"Jesus, Martin. What do you think this is?" Joanne stands up, putting some distance between them.

"Oh come on, Jo. I know you feel it to. We should be together. We need to be together."

"No, no, no. You and I are no longer a couple and will never again be a couple."

"Joanne, I know you. We have shared so much, we belong together."

"What we share are our children and that is all. Do not make that a difficult situation by pursuing me Martin."

"But ..."

"You need to go." She opens the front door. "Now."

Martin lifts himself from the stairs and tearfully moves towards her. She steps back.

"I love you," he whispers as he walks past her.

She says nothing until he is across the threshold and then the words she says crush him once again.

"I love Ray and he will be home soon."

It is a lovely day so Audrey decides to walk home from work. As she turns onto the Bird Estate she notices something ahead. It looks like a pile of sacks or similar. She is quite cross, whatever it is has clearly been dumped on the roadside for someone else to sort out. As she nears the pile, it moves and makes a noise. It is then that Audrey realises that the 'pile' is in fact a man. Her eyesight is not what it once was. The man is distraught.

"Are you alright?" Audrey asks, leaning over to get a better look at him. He says nothing but looks up towards her, it is then she recognises him. It is the security guard from the retail park. "Come on, get yourself up now and you can come with me. I live just around the corner. I'll make you a nice cup of tea." She gently holds his arm and Martin absently stands and walks alongside Audrey. Neither of them speak until they reach Audrey's house. "Here we are then."

"I'm sorry. I can't …" He removes Audrey's hand which is still on his arm and gives her a sad smile before walking away. She watches him go, looking downcast and disconsolate as he drags himself along. She studies the forlorn figure and realises he was the man on her wall. She is angry with herself for letting him go a second time, as she doesn't believe it is a coincidence that their paths have crossed once again. Clearly she is destined to help him.

The Kindness Of Strangers

Four

HELEN LOOKS AT THE BLANK SPACE above the fireplace in the lounge. This is where she will put her new purchase. A rectangular splash of brightness has been revealed, a reminder of what colour the wall once was. The previous picture that occupied this space had protected it from the sunlight that floods this room. She casts her eyes around the rest of the room, and there are several bright spots on the walls. Removing all of Robert's paintings and some of the other pictures that were never to her taste has revealed how badly the room needs redecorating. As she tries to recall when it was last done she takes in the rest of the room. The curtains, carpet, and furniture all look dated now, and worse, all remind her of Robert. His favourite chair, threadbare and tatty, sits by the window. The arms are shiny and discoloured, a dark patch where his head would rest is highlighted as a cloud passes, allowing the sun's rays to filter through the large bay window. She decides there and then to change it all: new décor, new furniture, a new start. And she will use Charley's painting as her inspiration, bold and modern. Definitely modern. Empowered by her decision Helen begins removing some of the ornaments and knick-knacks that adorn the room. She puts them on the table in the dining room, a room she hasn't used since before Robert fell ill; she prefers to eat in the kitchen. Walking through the hallway she glances at the clock and realises she needs to get ready, she is meeting Charley at the college to collect her painting.

When Helen arrives, Charley is just finishing taping brown paper around the picture which she has already covered with a couple of layers of bubble wrap.

"Thank you," says Helen. "That looks nice and secure."

"I hope so," responds Charley.

"Now, we must sort out how much I owe you."

"Yes. I erm …"

Helen realises that Charley is still struggling with putting a price on her work.

"Tell you what. I will make you an offer and you tell me if it's enough."

"Okay."

"One hundred pounds."

"What?" Charley is astonished, she expected her to say fifty.

"No, you're right. One hundred and fifty. That's better I think. Do you agree?"

Charley stares at Helen, mouth slightly open, nodding mutely.

"Excellent," says Helen counting out crisp notes fresh from the cash machine.

"Thank you. Would you like me to write you out a receipt?"

"No, I don't think that is necessary. Although future buyers may need you to be a bit more professional. Maybe get yourself some cards to start with."

"I have some cards." Charley hands Helen one of the cards that she had printed off earlier in the IT suite.

"There is no address. Do you not have a studio you work from?"

"No, I don't have the room at home and anyway I'm still a student so I do most of my work here."

"I see. Well I'm sure that won't always be the case. I see big things in your future."

You're not wrong there, thinks Charley, touching her abdomen.

"I'm having some work done at home and when it's finished your painting will take centre stage, you must come and see it."

"Thank you, I'd like that."

Once Helen has gone Charley begins skipping around the room euphorically waving the money in front of her face like a fan. When she has finished her little celebratory dance she pops the £110 into her purse alongside the £40 she had already received. She can't believe it, at the most she expected another ten pounds. Fifty pounds in total would've been more than she had hoped for so when Helen said one hundred she had been amazed and then for her to up it to one hundred and fifty made her feel like all her birthdays and Christmases had come at once. She thinks she might invest in some new pastels and oils and treat herself to some clothes. She may get something to put away for the baby too.

After trudging around town for a couple of hours Charley heads home. An afternoon that had started out full of hope and excitement has become a harsh learning curve. Her first stop was the department store; she was sure they would have everything you need for a baby. And they did. What she had not accounted for was how much these things cost. It was all so expensive and she hadn't realised quite how much you needed. She did not buy anything, not for the baby or herself, not even any paints. It quickly became obvious that she should hang on to her money. She was quite used to buying things for herself from the charity shops and although she hoped she would not have to do that for her baby, she knew it was probably the only way she would be able to afford what she needed.

Helen takes a few steps back to admire the painting in its new home. She has hooked it onto the hook left from the previous occupant, but it is too high. She always thought Robert hung their pictures too high, although for him they probably looked fine as he was a little taller than her. She will put it lower once the room has been decorated but for now it can stay there so she can study it and use it to help her determine the colour scheme of the room. It really is a fabulous painting, the swirling shapes and vibrant colours appealed to Helen instantly. She loves modern art and the more abstract it is the more she likes it. She likes the indiscernible nature of the genre, the fact that very often there are no recognisable objects to take hold of as you look at it. But, if you take time to really study a piece it often reveals a great deal. Abstract art merits more than a cursory glance to truly appreciate it. Audrey had been surprised that Helen had bought the painting and she wasted no time in letting her know that. Helen smiled to herself as she brought to mind what Audrey had said.

"It's very colourful, Helen, but what is it? It doesn't look like anything."

Helen had tried to explain what she liked about it, it's form and process and what it conjured up for her, but Audrey's reply had been short and sweet.

"Well I don't get it."

"That is the point. It isn't about getting it, it's about feeling it."

Audrey's response had been a disdainful sniff so Helen decided to give up. She also recollected reading a quote by Picasso; 'People who try to explain pictures are usually barking up the wrong tree'. Despite this, one thing Helen is sure of is that she has stumbled upon a talent and she considers her purchase one hundred and fifty pounds well spent.

She pours herself a large glass of Merlot, a congratulatory drink she tells herself. The first drink of the day always imbues her with an assuaging warmth. She delights in this feeling which intensifies with each quaff of her wine. After the third glass and suitably sated, Helen decides it is time for dinner. Microwave meals are still her food of choice and after a rummage in the freezer she opts for a chilli con carne. She sits at the island in the kitchen to eat it, and she has almost finished when she spots one of Roberts drawings poking out from behind a plate on the welsh dresser. Pushing her food aside she goes to the dresser and removes the picture. It is a pen and ink drawing of a willow tree on a small daler board. It is very good, but that doesn't matter, it has to go. Helen has resolved to remove all of his pictures. She is burning with an anger and resentment of all he represented and all that represents him and in a moment of epiphany she made a decision. And that decision is to erase him as best she can, if not from her heart and her memories then at least from her home.

Five

MARTIN HAS SPENT his working week successfully avoiding the lady from the charity shop but today she is to catch up with him. Images on the CCTV show her approaching the office and as Clive is on his rounds Martin cannot duck out the back. Company policy says the office has to be manned at all times, except in cases of emergency, and he doesn't think saving himself from an embarrassing conversation qualifies. As her diminutive frame appears in the doorway he imagines how ridiculous he must have looked to her; a grown man sobbing into the pavement. She taps on the door even though she is well aware that Martin can see her.

"Come in," says Martin in as masculine a voice as he can muster.

"Hello there. I hope I'm not disturbing you, but I just wanted to make sure that you're alright now."

"Yes I am. Thank you."

As an awkward silence falls between them, Martin looks away. He pretends he is looking at the bank of monitors displaying what is happening across the retail park.

"Anything interesting going on out there today?" asked Audrey.

"No, all quiet."

Silence comes again.

"Well I'd better let you get on. Unless there is anything I can help you with?"

"I don't follow," responds Martin, a quizzical look on his face.

"If you need any help or a shoulder. I'm a good listener."

"Oh I see. That's kind of you, Mrs…? Erm … I'm afraid I didn't catch your name."

"Audrey, call me Audrey."

"Audrey, I am grateful for your concern but I was … well just having a bad day. But I'm fine now."

Audrey turns to leave, a little disappointed that Martin doesn't want to share his troubles with her, but she is pleased to see that he is looking and sounding a lot better than when she last saw him.

"There is one thing," says Martin.

"Yes," says Audrey eagerly.

"I would appreciate you not mentioning my er … episode to anyone else."

"Of course. Mum's the word. Take care of yourself."

Martin watches her walk across the car park on the monitors, relieved that the encounter wasn't as awkward as it could have been. What must she think? He imagines she can't have much confidence in him as a security guard. With his hands behind his head he leans back heavily in the chair which creaks ominously under the pressure. He is all too aware that he can't allow himself to buckle like that again. If he does, the next person to find him may well call the police and the consequences of that could be catastrophic; job loss and home loss and Jo would be even further from him than she is now. Regardless of her declaration of love for Ray, Martin is still convinced that he can get her back, but he knows it will be harder than he first thought. He hopes Audrey keeps her word; if the management get any hint of what happened they will get rid of him. He realises he has more to lose than pride, so decides it may be a good idea to be friendly towards her. And maybe having someone like that in his corner wouldn't be a bad thing.

The rest of Martin's shift passes by without incident and after signing out and passing on the keys to the colleague relieving him he walks across the car park towards home. Fortuitously for him he spots Audrey leaving work, she is walking slowly as she is laden with bags so he easily catches up with her.

"Can I help you with those?" he asks indicating her bags.

"If you don't mind. I'm only going to the bus stop just across the road. I did fancy walking home but I've bought rather too much today." She offers him an embarrassed smile as he relieves her of some of her shopping.

"I'm happy to walk with you. Unless you'd rather take the bus?"

"I don't want you to go out of your way."

"It's fine. As I recall you live on the estate and I'm going to see someone over there anyway."

While they are walking along Martin informs her that his family live on the estate. He tells her that he and his wife are estranged. He doesn't mention that they are actually divorced, as he has always refused to recognise the marriage is officially over. After all, how can you be divorced in your absence? And he was absent, in mind and body.

"Had you been to see her the other day?"

He nods sadly as he confirmed this.

"It's always hard when I see her and the children and I think I …"

"No need to explain, I understand the ways of the heart you know." Audrey stopped walking. "This is me," she says pointing at a pretty house set back a little from the road. Martin takes it all in, he hadn't paid any attention last time he was here. A small front garden sits behind a low wall. It is incredibly colourful. The house itself is festooned with hanging baskets that are being gently moved by the light breeze.

"Who's the gardener, you or your husband?"

"I'm a widow actually."

"Sorry. I thought … I saw your wedding ring and …"

"Don't apologise. Easy mistake. Gerald has been gone for quite some time now. It was after he died that I started working at the charity shop, for the company. I'm just a volunteer there, well we all are, except Sheila. Here I go, waffling. You asked about the garden, he was the gardener. I have someone come round to cut the lawn and generally keep it tidy for me, but he's retiring soon so I will have to find someone else to preserve Gerald's hard work."

"I'm not much of a gardener but I'll happily pop by and cut the grass for you."

"I may hold you to that. Would you like a cup of tea?"

"Another time perhaps."

"Well, anytime you're passing you are more than welcome."

Martin waits while Audrey unlocks her front door then he places the bags in the hallway and says goodbye. He continues walking up the road a little longer and then stops. He is almost at Joanne's house although he has no plans to visit despite what he may have told Audrey. For a moment he considers going there on the pretext of seeing if she has heard from Jack, but then he reconsiders; it's unlikely she has heard from him, and if she does he is sure she will let him know and besides he doesn't think a warm welcome would be on offer – not yet anyway.

Charley lays on her bed, the enormity of what is to come is only just beginning to sink in. In truth she has no idea how much having a baby will cost; either financially or emotionally. However, what is obvious is that the task before her is daunting and she has no-one to help her. Despite her good fortune at the art exhibition it is becoming all too clear that the road ahead is not paved with gold and she does not have a fairy god-mother who will wave a magic wand and conjure her up a fairy-tale ending. She is on her own, which doesn't actually feel like a new thing to her. The upbringing she had has forced her to be resilient, self-reliant and self-sufficient. She wished it had been different. She wished she had a mother who was dependable, one she could ask for advice; but she could never do that and still can't. Charley is determined that her child's life is going to be different to hers, so help from her mother, even if it was an option, would not be welcome. You could argue that Lizzie had not done a bad job; after all Charley is a nice young woman with many positive attributes. Charley would argue that this is in spite of her mother not because of her.

Picking up a notebook and pencil from beside the bed Charley begins making a list of things she will need to get. She is good at writing lists, she whiled away a lot of time during her childhood composing them. Lists of toys she wanted, foods she enjoyed, films she wanted to see and places she hoped to go to. Places that now seemed further from her than ever before. The list soon becomes a very long one and still she is sure there are things she has forgotten. She reads through it despondently, knowing she will never be able to afford most of what is on it. She has to prioritise and then shop around for the cheapest options.

❧

Martin is sure the car that just went past him was being driven by Ray. He watches as it turns into the road Joanne lives on and is mortified to then see it turn onto the driveway of her house. He takes a few steps forward to get a clearer view; he is sure it is Ray. He wishes he could get closer but that would put him at risk of being spotted. Whoever it is has got out of the car and is striding towards the front door. Whoever it is has a key. At first a quiet rage flows through him, but it is quickly replaced by indignation and chagrin. He steps back, rubs his head and then turns to walk back the way he came. With each step he contemplates possible ways to deal with Ray, but none of them are feasible solutions; many are illegal and those that aren't would not endear him to Joanne. He needs a plan. A plan that puts him in a good light and paints Ray as a villain. He is sure he can discover something about him, something Joanne doesn't know. Everyone has secrets. In order to do that he needs to know more about Ray. He needs to watch him, find out what he does and find out where he goes. Firstly, he needs to find out his full name; he could then look him up on the internet. He has access to a computer at work and at the hostel. His ideas begin to invigorate him and fill him with hope that he will unearth something unsavoury about Ray. He considers finding somewhere to hide so he can watch him now. But he mustn't get caught. What he needs is a legitimate reason for being on the estate. Like helping a kindly widow look after her garden …

Six

CHARITY SHOPS ARE NOT what they used to be. In an age of upcycling and recycling there are many bargains waiting to be had. They are no longer the home of discarded bric-a-brac, incomplete jigsaw puzzles or well-thumbed paperbacks. Items that were once thought of as old fashioned and dated seconds are often trendy and in demand, largely due to the interest in vintage and retro styles. And the shops in question know how to display their wares. No more do you need to rifle through clothes rails or rummage in large bins in the hope of discovering a hidden gem.

Charley is quite adept at charity shop shopping. As well as clothes she has often found items she can use in her art. But finding things for her baby is proving hard. This is not due to a lack of items, more an ignorance of what is best to buy. She wishes she had found out the sex of her baby at her scan, at least then she could choose between boys' or girls' clothes. As she looks through the array of baby paraphernalia on offer she senses someone watching her. Raising her eyes only she looks towards the counter, where a lady is looking at her intently. *She probably has me down as a possible shop-lifter*, thinks Charley, but then as they catch one another's eye, the lady smiles. Initially Charley does not recognise her and finds the smile disconcerting, but when Audrey steps out from behind the counter and starts walking towards her she remembers.

The Kindness Of Strangers

"Hello there," says Audrey. "Fancy seeing you here. How are you?"

"I'm good, thanks."

"Are you looking for anything in particular?"

"No, not really."

Audrey is aware they are standing among nursery equipment and baby clothes and so can't help but glance down at Charley's stomach. There is a definite bump, but she isn't convinced it's a baby bump until Charley protectively places an arm across her front.

"When are you due?"

"August."

"Goodness, you're about six months then."

"Not quite."

"So no rush for some of these things then," says Audrey pointing at the buggies and highchairs.

"No, I'm just looking."

"Well if you do see anything you like let me know and I'll put it aside for you and your boyfriend or partner to collect."

"Thank you. I have to go now, but thanks."

Charley almost knocks a clothes rail over in her haste to exit the shop.

Audrey watches her go and curses herself for saying what she did. She wasn't making an assumption, she sensed that Charley may be dealing with pregnancy alone and wanted to know. It wasn't very subtle though. She hopes she comes back. Outside the shop Charley walks straight into a tall, uniformed man, and mumbles an apology before hurriedly heading towards the subway.

Audrey is still looking towards the door when Martin comes in. He looks around briefly, then spotting her raises his hand before walking in her direction.

"Hi, I was hoping you were in today," he said.

"Oh. Is everything alright?"

"Yes fine. I was just wondering if you were serious the other day."

"About what?"

"Your garden. And me helping you out."

"Yes, absolutely. Although I can't pay much. The chap who does it at the moment doesn't charge much as he is a retired gentlemen who helps out to top up his pension."

"You don't have to pay me."

"Don't be silly. Of course I'll pay you."

"Whatever. It's up to you. To be honest, you will be doing me a favour. I have far too much time on my hands and it will help keep me fit. I've rather let myself go a little of late," says Martin, patting his abs as if to emphasise the point.

"Well, I will pay you the same as I pay Ron. He is stopping at the end of the month, so after that I will be delighted and very grateful if you could take over."

"Thank you. I'll pop by next week and you can show me what you would like me to do."

"Perfect. And you can have that long overdue cup of tea with me."

Martin leaves the shop with a large grin on his face, a smug self-satisfied grin for the first part of his plan is now in place. And as a bonus, he'll earn a little extra money too.

Audrey goes back to her post behind the counter, but she has barely got there when somebody else catches her eye and starts waving at her. She is quite surprised; it is very rare for her to see anyone she knows in the shop, but today they are like buses - three of them, one after another.

"Hello, Helen. What brings you here?"

"I have some more stuff that I'm getting rid of. It is ridiculous the amount of things I have that serve very little purpose."

"Not everything has to have a use, sometimes it's nice to have trinkets and tokens that remind us of something, somewhere or someone."

"Oh Audrey, you know me well enough now. I really have no time for sentimentality."

Audrey says nothing. She knows Helen's desire to discard so many possessions bought during her marriage to Robert is not due to a lack of sentimentality. Helen is not as hardboiled as that, she is still mightily aggrieved and she is hurting. Audrey wishes there was something she could say to ease the pain but she knows Helen is ready with a counterargument to any suggestion she may make.

"And besides the house needs an overhaul, it is so cluttered. A bit of modernisation is long overdue. Buying that painting has made me realise just how dated everything has become."

"Funny you should say that. You will never guess who was in here a few moments before you."

"No, you're right. I will never guess." Helen did not have the time for one of Audrey's guessing games today. The decorator was due at her house in an hour or so and she still had a few more errands to run before going home.

"Okay, I'll tell you then. It was the girl from the exhibition, the artist. The one you bought the painting from. And guess what?"

"More guessing, how tiresome."

"She is expecting."

"Expecting what?"

"A baby, silly."

"Really? Goodness she is so young. Are you sure? I don't recall her looking pregnant."

"I'm sure. She told me herself, due in August. I may be wrong but I don't think it was planned and I think she is dealing with it alone."

"How very stupid," says Helen.

"That's a bit harsh."

Helen never delights in baby news or pregnancy announcements. Even after all these years it still smarts.

"Not really. I think it's a shame, she has such talent."

"Sometimes accidents happen."

"Not nowadays, there is no excuse for an unplanned pregnancy. Now where do you want my boxes? I have quite a few."

"I'll give you a hand."

There are a lot of boxes and Audrey can't help feeling a little sad that Helen feels the need to rid herself of so many of her possessions. Ornaments, photo frames, pictures; the boxes contain a treasure trove of collectibles. One of the boxes that Audrey picks up is full of some odd bits. She rests it on a concrete bollard and has a little look through. It is filled with pens, pencils, paints and brushes. They all look like new.

"Who was the artist?" she enquires of Helen.

"Robert, he liked to paint and sketch. Most of those are unopened so I thought they might do someone a turn."

"I think I know a 'someone' who would like these. That young girl, the artist. If she's having a baby she may not be able to afford things like this."

"She's welcome to them."

"I'll put them back into your car then."

"No, you take them. Put them aside and if she comes in, give them to her."

"I can't do that. Once they go in there," Audrey nods at the shop, "they become the property of the NSPCC."

"Yes, I seem to remember you telling me something like that before."

"Can't you take them to her?"

"I don't really have time."

"Not right now, another time. Doesn't even have to be today."

"Very well," says Helen taking the box from Audrey and sliding it back into the boot of her car.

The decorator quotes a good price and he can start the following week as his previous job completed earlier than expected. This pleases Helen so she hires him on the spot. Her determination to change everything in the house has an urgency now. For her it is the only way forward. Too many reminders of the past will have her constantly looking backwards. Changing and removing Robert's influence is the only way to eliminate the regret and disappointment.

❧

Audrey wonders if she is a little underdressed for today's lunch date with Helen. It is only at Helen's home but today is the big reveal; the grand unveiling of the newly decorated lounge. She hesitates at the front door, perhaps such a momentous occasion warrants more than a pair of linen trousers and a cotton blouse. The door is opened before she can answer her thoughts or even ring the door-bell. She inspects Helen and is relieved to see that Helen is wearing something not too dissimilar to her. The women exchange air kisses in the hallway.

"Come on then. Let's see the new room," says an expectant Audrey. "Or should we wait for a drum-roll?"

Helen pushes open the lounge door and they are met by a blaze of colour which Audrey finds startling. It is magnified by the sunlight shining through the window, the shafts of light splitting the colours and creating kaleidoscopic patterns on the walls.

"Wow."

"Yes. It does have the wow factor. Do you like it?"

Audrey nods. She does like it and she is surprised that she likes it. Neutral tones adorn her home; splashes of colour are provided by the weekly flowers that she treats herself to. For a moment she wonders if she should make a change but she is sure she could not recreate the same prismatic effect in her home as her rooms are not exposed to as much daylight. And after a while the psychedelic harlequins dancing on the walls would probably be too much. But here, in this house she likes it. Her eyes are drawn to the fireplace and the painting above it. She goes closer to view it properly.

"It fits the room perfectly," says Helen.

"It does," agrees Audrey. "It really does."

Although it is only May, it is a surprisingly warm day, so Helen has set the table on the patio for lunch. She pours two glasses of white wine, placing one in front of Audrey without asking if she wants it or not. She knows she would say no, but also knows she is too polite to refuse it once it has been poured. And she can hardly voice her disapproval of Helen if she too is drinking. They eat a hearty lunch of wild salmon fillets on a pasta salad with a lemon caper dressing. To follow Helen has made a New York cheesecake.

"That was delicious, Helen, thank you."

"You're welcome." Helen has enjoyed preparing lunch for herself and her friend. It is a refreshing change from the pre-prepared ready meals that she has been used to of late.

The two women sit back in their chairs, both facing the sun and determined to soak up the unseasonal rays. For a few moments there is a silence; a serene repose interrupted only by the occasional sound of birdsong or the gentle rustle of leaves as a graceful breeze passes through the trees. It is Audrey who punctures the tranquillity when she compliments the garden.

"I'm afraid it's been neglected of late. I may have to get some help with it. I think I want to make some changes too."

"That's interesting."

"Yes, I rather fancy extending this patio the width of the house."

"Well, I know just the person to help you." Audrey becomes quite animated as she tells Helen about Martin.

"Let me get this straight, you are suggesting I employ a man who, when you first met him was horizontal on the pavement, snivelling and whimpering."

"Helen, I never said that. Anyway, that wasn't the first time I had met him, just the first time I spoke to him. He is one of the security guards at the shop."

"What do you know about him though? Where does he live? Is he married? Does …"

"He is separated from his wife."

"I'm not surprised. Who wants to be married to a cry baby?"

"Helen!" shouts Audrey. "There is no need to be unkind. He is a man who is going through a difficult time. He has a responsible job and he is ex-military. He has started doing my garden, he does it very well and he doesn't cost much. You should give him a chance."

"Maybe."

"Martin would be able to do a patio for you I'm sure, although don't be too hasty with any alterations. You may regret it."

"I will not regret it."

"New curtains and a coat of paint or even a larger patio will not undo what Robert did and getting rid of everything that belonged to him will not eradicate him from your memories. I think you need to deal with this by …"

"Do not tell me how to deal with this. You have no idea how I feel. You did not know Robert and you know nothing about my marriage. You cannot …"

Audrey does not let her finish, she says the things she has been wanting to say for a while. The things she believes a true friend ought to say.

"… counselling may be an idea. But pretending it didn't happen is not good. Throwing out your old life is not good."

"Throwing out my old life, as you put it, is exactly what I have to do. It is the only way I can move forward."

"No, it's not and if you really believed that you wouldn't be bothering with alterations at all. You would be selling up and moving somewhere else. But you're not and that's because you don't want to expunge Robert or your marriage, not really, certainly not completely. What you are doing is occupying your time with needless home improvements in order to avoid facing some unpalatable truths."

Audrey stands up, intending to leave before Helen hits back with a polemic rant. She bends to pick up her bag, then stops. To her shame she notices that Helen is crying, softly and almost silently. She moves towards her; crouching down she puts her hands on Helen's knees and apologises. It was never her wish to make her friend cry.

"You're right though," says Helen removing her tears with the heels of her hands and causing black lines to streak across the top of her cheeks. "I can't leave here, because he is here. He will always be here and I don't want to be without him. But I am so fucking angry with him."

Audrey balks a little at Helens language, but doesn't admonish her for it. She doesn't like hearing the 'f' word but she thinks the use of it in this context is entirely appropriate.

"The anger will pass, in time. But I do think you need to talk this through. I am happy to listen but maybe a professional would be better."

Helen nods her agreement and reaches for her wine glass.

"And you do need to curb the drinking."

Something snaps, not literally, for there is no sound. Not straightaway. But then the fury that has been fermenting within Helen erupts with such ferocity Audrey has to sidestep swiftly to avoid injury. A wine glass wings its way across the lawn, its demise guaranteed as it hits the stone sundial and shatters. The wine glass's trajectory is accompanied by a sustained shriek. A desolate sound full of anguish that ended with the sound of breaking glass. An eerie hush descends. When Audrey is certain that Helen's anger is spent she ventures towards her. She gently takes her arm and steers her indoors. She doesn't say anything to her; she knows to speak may be unwise. After a few moments it is Helen who speaks.

"You don't get it. I know that. You see this wonderful house, designer clothes, money and you …"

"I do get it. I understand grief."

"It's not grief. There is so much in this house that he gave me, so much."

"And you shouldn't discard it all."

"It means nothing because the thing I wanted he gave to someone else."

"What do you mean?"

"The one thing, the only thing I ever wanted from Robert was a child, but he didn't give that to me. He gave that to someone else."

Seven

THE CONFIRMATION that Ray is not an occasional overnight guest but does in fact live with Joanne is not what Martin wanted to discover. Despite his suspicions, he was hoping beyond hope that their relationship was more casual than that. He now knows that the task before him is going to be harder than he first thought, but is still not impossible. He has to step up the surveillance - now that he knows where Ray lives (the vein in Martin's neck throbs as he processes this), it is also time to see where he works and if there is anywhere else that he frequents. Audrey has offered him the use of her car whenever he wants, which will be a big help. She doesn't drive much these days, often choosing to catch the bus or walk. Martin has the next couple of days off and all he has scheduled is a visit to Audrey's. He'll borrow her car and see what else he can uncover about Ray.

꩜

Martin tries to keep at least three cars between him and Ray. He doesn't want to be spotted but neither does he want to lose sight of him, not least because he is driving in an unfamiliar area. Ray has pulled into a filter lane so he can make a right turn. If Martin does this too he will be directly behind him. He opts to stay in the lane he is in and take the next right turn and double back. He's sure he will catch up with him. Martin watches as Ray's car disappears around the corner. He keeps watching until he can no longer see it. A car horn blasts and Martin jumps. A look in the rearview mirror reveals an angry motorist gesticulating at him. His keen observance of Ray has meant he missed the green light. He shrugs and proffers a mimed apology. When the lights change again he accelerates hard, eager to put some distance between himself and the irate driver. The next opportunity for Martin to turn around is a roundabout about half-a-mile up the road, and disappointingly it is governed by yet more traffic lights. He shouts in frustration; a frustration not lessened by every light turning red as he approaches them. When he finally turns onto the road where he last saw Ray unsurprisingly there is no sign of him. The road isn't particularly busy. It appears to be an access road for an industrial estate. Now that he is here Martin decides to cruise around the estate for a while to see if he can spot Ray's car. After several minutes and just before Martin's patience is about to desert him he spots it parked outside one of the units. The sign across the top reads Milner & Sons. Satisfied that he has learnt all he can for now Martin heads back to Audrey's house. He knows she has a computer and internet access as she has told him she often looks at live cams in New Zealand and Scotland. Apparently it makes her feel closer to her sons. When he has finished cutting the lawn he will ask if he can use it; maybe looking up Milner & Sons will give him some information about Ray.

'Milner & Sons - specialists in the manufacture and supply of precision tools. Established in 1987 ...'

Martin scrolls down further and clicks on the button titled meet the team.

Managing Director: Derek Milner, Production Director: Edward Milner, Sales Director: Raymond Milner

Each name is accompanied by a photograph so there is no mistake, Raymond Milner the Sales Director is Ray. Martin is sure the title is an overblown way of saying he is a salesman working for Daddy's company.

Martin clicks off the page when he hears Audrey come into the room.

"Here you are," she says placing a steaming mug of tea alongside him. "Did you find out what you needed to?"

"Yes, thanks."

"Good. Martin, do you recall I spoke to you about my friend Helen, she needs someone to do her garden and a few odd jobs?"

"Yes, I do."

"When you have time I'd like to take you over to meet her. If that's okay?"

"Absolutely. Tomorrow any good? It's my day off."

❧

Helen is a little apprehensive about today. Audrey is bringing over her gardening chap for an informal interview. Helen has interviewed hundreds of people over the years. Well maybe not hundreds but certainly a lot, so it isn't that making her a little nervous. It's that she has not seen anyone, other than Audrey, for two or three weeks. Since her meltdown she has not ventured out at all. Audrey has been very kind, visiting often: cooking, cleaning and comforting her. Helen feels she has regressed as she is feeling considerably worse than she did immediately after Robert's passing. It could be, as Audrey says that grief is a process that often sees you take two steps forward and one back. It could also be, again as Audrey says, that acknowledging the hurt Robert's actions have caused her is a big part of the healing process. Inconceivably she is starting to believe that Audrey may be right. Either way, she feels like shit.

She makes herself look presentable, a touch of concealer helps to hide the dark shadows beneath her eyes and a dash of lipstick adds some colour to her pallid features. She looks in the mirror, satisfied at least that she will not frighten him off as soon as he sets eyes on her. It would be good to get some semblance of order back into the garden and having a handyman around would be useful. She still has the garage and the loft to sort through as well as other things that she is unable to do.

"So, Martin. Would you be able to do three or four hours each week?"

"I don't see why not. Although it won't be the same day every week. I work shifts and it is very rare that I have the same days off. But I always know three weeks in advance what my shift pattern is."

"That's fine. Let's go outside. You can see the garden and my rather messy garage."

Helen opens the garage. Martin and Audrey can see she was not exaggerating when she said it was a mess.

"I really have no idea what is in here and if I need it or if I want it. What I would like you to do is sort through it and perhaps put some shelves up to accommodate what I keep. When winter comes I want to be able to put my car in here. I do not want to have to scrape windows before I can go out. It's a pet hate of mine; Rob … Robert always used to do that for me." Helen stutters a little as she mentions Robert.

"Helen, you still have those paints and things," says Audrey pointing at an overfilled cardboard box sitting in the corner of the garage. "You said you were going to give them to that girl."

"I haven't had time."

Audrey throws Helen a look that clearly disputes that.

"You should invite her to see her painting in all its glory."

"Yes, maybe I will. I did say I would let her see it."

"Well there you go, ask her over and give her the stuff."

"You might want to put it all in a different box," offered Martin. "That one is liable to collapse if you try and pick it up."

After Audrey and Martin leave, Helen pours herself a drink and sits in the lounge. She is admiring Charley's painting. It does look wonderful above the fireplace. As she casts her eyes around the room she notices a space on the wall opposite the door. Another picture might look good there she muses, something to catch your eye as you walk into the room. Helen goes into the kitchen to fetch her handbag. She rummages through it for a few seconds before finding what she is searching for, the card Charley passed her. The card itself is not particularly noteworthy but at least it details what Helen needs, a contact number for Charley.

Charley is surprised but thrilled to hear from Helen. To be able to see one of her paintings hanging in somebody's home is a dream come true for her. That would be enough for Charley, but there is more, a possible commission. She tries not to get too excited; she is very aware how things can change in a heartbeat and at the moment it is nothing more than a possibility. They arrange for Charley to visit a couple of days later.

Helen wakes early the day of Charley's visit and realises she is actually looking forward to it. Possibly because it will be a welcome distraction from the malaise she is currently experiencing, although she thinks it is more than that. She has never commissioned a painting before and the idea is rather intoxicating. It's another glorious day. The sun is issuing beams of light that complement and highlight the splendour of the newly decorated lounge. Indeed the room itself resembles a work of art. Helen hopes Charley will be pleased with the setting in which her work now resides. She glances at her watch, then looks out of the window, squinting a little as the sun is incredibly bright. Then she sees her, walking up the driveway. Shock is what she feels first, then the inevitable sadness tinged with envy. She did know. Audrey had told her, but she had forgotten. Now she can see for herself, as can everyone, for the girl's condition is obvious to all. Helen has expertly avoided close contact with pregnant women for many years. During her working life when some of her colleagues had become pregnant, she had achieved a way of making them feel rather uncomfortable so that it was they who would avoid her. But today is different, she has invited Charley here so she has to be nice to her, and despite the thread of resentment she still wants to see her. She does so love her artwork.

Charley knew Helen's house would be big. However it is more than that; it is grand, impressive and imposing. Yet it has a charm that is not normally present in this style of home. A charm more often exuded by quaint country cottages, not buildings of such grandiosity. It is a home that cannot be pigeon-holed as being of any one style or period. It is well maintained, and the original building has been extended and added to. She likes it though. A mix of old and new; contrasting styles that some so called 'experts' would state were wholly incompatible. She rings the doorbell and waits, and waits. She hesitates before ringing the bell again. This time the door opens, almost instantaneously.

"Sorry, I didn't mean to keep you waiting. I was in the garden," says Helen, who was actually standing behind the door mustering the courage to open it. "Come in. How are you?"

"Thanks. I'm good, considering," says Charley rubbing her swollen belly.

"Yes, quite. Would you like a drink?"

"Something cold would be nice."

Helen fixes them both a drink, a non-alcoholic drink. She figures Charley can't have alcohol in her condition and she is not even sure she is old enough to drink legally anyway; and as much as she would love one it probably is still a little too early. The sun is not yet over the yardarm. She puts the drinks and an assortment of small pastries onto a small tray before carrying it through to the lounge.

"Oh My God, what a fabulous room," says Charley. She is so taken with the room that a few seconds pass before she spots her painting. When she does she stops dead. She can't move or speak. Her eyes become fish-like as they swell with the moisture of unshed tears. Charley bites her lip in the hope of quelling their release. It doesn't work and silently they slide down her cheeks. Helen is moved and a tiny bit embarrassed by this show of emotion. Hastily she hands Charley a tissue.

"Sorry."

"Don't apologise. I'm sure your emotions are all over the place when you're pregnant."

"It's not that," says Charley. "It's erm … this is like a dream I used to have when I was a little girl. A dream in which my picture is chosen from hundreds to hang in a beautiful castle."

"This is hardly a castle."

"I know. The dream changed as I got older. I then began to dream and hope and pray that one day my work might grace someone's home."

"And now it does."

"Now it does," agrees Charley.

"I would like another picture, to go right there." Helen points at the space on the wall. I don't want something as large this time and maybe not quite as abstract, a little more form. Perhaps something reminiscent of Robert Delauney?"

Charley nods enthusiastically. She pulls a sketch pad from her bag and begins to rough out some ideas. Helen watches her with awe for although she has no artistic talent whatsoever, she knows what is good and this young girl in front of her is very good, supremely good even. It doesn't take them long to settle on what the picture will be like and when their discussion is over Helen asks if Charley would like to stay for lunch. Charley readily accepts the offer; she is sure that whatever Helen serves up will be far more appetising than the beans on toast waiting for her at home. Her budget does not lend itself to variety and on the odd occasion when she has bought something different one of the other residents of the hostel has seen fit to eat it. The two women go in to the kitchen, and Charley carefully manoeuvres herself onto one of the tractor stools around the island that sits in the centre of the room.

"Would you prefer a chair?" asks Helen.

"No, I'm fine."

Helen goes to the cupboard, unsure exactly what she will do for lunch. She spots a bag of pasta and decides on that, hopeful that she has enough ingredients in the fridge to conjure up some sort of sauce. While she cooks the two of them chat some more. The conversation flows easily; their love of art has quickly established a connection between them.

"Are your parents art-lovers too?" enquires Helen.

The question flusters Charley for a moment, she has no desire to discuss her parentage.

"Not particularly," she answers. "What about your husband, does he like art?"

There is a slight hiatus before Helen explains that she is a widow. Charley is terribly embarrassed and apologises several times.

"Please stop apologising, you weren't to know."

"Do you have children?"

Helen bristles and her demeanour changes, ever so slightly. Charley is unaware as Helen has her back to her while she stirs the sauce for the pasta.

"No, I was a career woman," says Helen as she tries to regain her composure.

"What did you do?"

Helen is grateful for this question, she is on more comfortable ground. She explains to Charley what her job entailed while serving up their lunch.

"Bon appétit," says Helen sliding the bowl of steaming pasta towards Charley.

As each of them tuck into their food their thoughts are mirroring one another's. They are both thinking how much they are enjoying each other's company. For Charley particularly it is also nice to share a meal with another person. It has been a very long time since she has done that.

"Thank you, that was delicious. Let me wash up for you." Charley lowers herself from the stool and takes her bowl and cutlery across to the sink.

"No leave it. I'll put it in the dishwasher later. I have something I want to show you."

Helen leads Charley outside and opens up the garage, showing her the box of artist materials that belonged to Robert.

"You are welcome to take them if they are of any use to you. My husband was only an amateur but he did buy decent equipment, I think."

"Yes he did, thank you. These are wonderful. Do you want some money for them?"

"No, definitely not. They are no use to me."

"I could do your painting for free, as payment."

"That isn't necessary. I would like you to have them, please."

"I may not be able to take them all today though, that box looks a little heavy to take on the bus."

"I'll give you a lift home. You can take it all then," says Helen, who would prefer to be rid of the box altogether.

❧

Helen remembers Martin's warning all too late for as she picks up the box to put it into the boot of her car the bottom collapses and an array of brushes, crayons and other paraphernalia fall at her feet. A small tin opens, ejecting its contents onto the driveway. One of the items is a small keyring on which there are two small keys. Helen studies them for a moment, she has no idea what the keys could be for. They are quite small; she figures they are probably from an old suitcase or something similar and slips them into the pocket of her jeans.

Charley directs Helen to where she lives. Unsurprisingly Helen is unfamiliar with the side of the town that the hostel is on. When they pull up outside, Charley feels she needs to offer an explanation regarding her living arrangements. She relays a brief account. Helen asks if she thinks she will be reconciled with her mum, and Charley shakes her head.

"This is why I can only work at college. There is barely enough space in my room to stand up let alone set up an easel."

Helen carries the things she has given Charley up to her room for her. When she sees the room she realises Charley wasn't kidding; the room is tiny.

"Do you have anywhere to put this stuff?" she asks.

"There are drawers under the bed that are empty."

On her journey home Helen can't stop thinking about Charley and her situation. She is completely flabbergasted that her mother has thrown her out. She cannot comprehend it at all, rejecting not only her child but her grandchild too. She is also astounded by how little Charley has in the way of possessions. She didn't even appear to have many clothes and there were certainly no visible signs of anything for the baby.

Eight

MARTIN HAS DISCOVERED a great deal about Ray, much of it without having to undertake any legwork. The internet has done that for him. A few clicks have revealed a host of information: birthday, previous addresses, education history and more besides. The most illuminating has been Facebook, where Ray has 364 friends. Martin thinks the term friend in this instance is quite ridiculous. For him a friend is someone with whom some physical interaction is needed from time to time, not someone who clicks a button liking your latest holiday snap or types a few words as a comment on some declaration that they have read. What is interesting about Ray's friends list is who is not on it rather than who is. Joanne is not on it and neither is Jack. Sadly Amy is and Ray is on hers, but then Amy seems to have everyone on her list. She has 641 friends - Martin makes a mental note to talk to her about that. Joanne doesn't do Facebook as far as Martin can tell. After several hours Martin has established who are Ray's closest friends and the places he frequents, along with incidental information such as the football team he supports, the paper he reads and his political leanings. He attempts to appear patriotic, but his views contradict this. His comments are occasionally humorous but at best they are Neanderthal, at worst misogynistic. Martin's opinion of Ray is that he is a self-aggrandising, narcissistic prat who has probably rendered himself unemployable hence the fact that he works for his father. Although he is sure the places that Ray frequents will not be his cup of tea Martin thinks he may have to visit some of them in order to build a bigger picture of this interloper. And with a bit of luck he may uncover something unsavoury about this man that he can present to Jo.

He is up early considering it's his day off, but he is scheduled to work at Helen's today. As he goes down the stairs Martin passes the warden who tells him there is some post for him in the office. He grabs it on his way out, folds it and shoves it into his back pocket. He exits the air-conditioned lobby of the hostel and is met by a wall of humid air. The unseasonably high temperatures show no sign of fading and Martin hopes that Helen will want him to work outside today. However he will be disappointed as she wants him to begin clearing the garage. A bit of pottering in the garden as opposed to fetching and carrying all day would have been much more appealing.

"If possible I want to create enough space not just for the car but also to store some of the things that are in the summerhouse. I'm quite happy for you to discard things that don't look like they are worth keeping. Anything you're unsure of stack in the corner and I'll go through it with you."

"I see you got rid of that box that was there." Martin points at the empty space it has left behind.

"Yes, and you were right, it did fall apart." As she says this Helen remembers the keys. She slides her hand into the pocket of her jeans, they are still there. She pulls them out dangling them in front of Martin. "And if you find anything that you think these may belong to, give me a shout."

Martin takes the keys from her and spreads them across the palm of his hand.

"They are both slightly different," he says. "This one looks like a filing cabinet key and that one could be for a suitcase or briefcase."

"A filing cabinet," repeats Helen as she lifts them from his open palm.

"Possibly."

She takes him round to the summerhouse so he can see what he has to make room for. It's a bright, airy space furnished with willow furniture. All of the walls are adorned with pictures, except one that is dominated by a large shelving unit housing a collection of teapots. An old-fashioned rocking chair sits in a corner, alongside it is a metal magazine rack that is so overloaded with magazines it has become bent and twisted and no longer resembles its original shape at all. In the centre sits a coffee table with an incomplete jigsaw puzzle on it. He is surprised that she wants to do anything with the summerhouse. It looks perfectly fine to him, a little over-crowded, but fine. Helen, sensing his misgivings, shares her plans with him.

"I want to turn it into a studio."

"A studio?"

"An art studio."

"Oh I see. I had no idea you were an artist."

"I'm not," says Helen. Martin's confused expression makes her smile.

"But I know someone who is. This is for them."

Helen had spent a fitful night's sleep thinking only of Charley. Those thoughts were not ones of resentment or jealousy, but of sympathy and pity for her misfortune. She thinks of Charley and sees a young girl with life as a single mother ahead of her. She has no family support and no friends as far as Helen has been able to ascertain, and definitely no support from the father of her unborn child. And she is so talented; a talent that will be neglected instead of nurtured if no-one steps into help. The recognition of Charley's plight and the impulse to help is unusual for Helen who is not overtly empathetic. But Charley has stirred something in her that has given rise to an instinctive desire to care. These latent feelings engendered in her have lain dormant for so long; feelings almost maternal in nature.

Martin is exhausted by the end of the day; it has been a while since he has had to work so hard. He could easily lay down and sleep until morning but he has promised Audrey he will call in on his way home from Helen's. He doesn't mind too much, it will give him an opportunity to see if anything is happening at Joanne's. He may even ask to borrow Audrey's car and check out one of Ray's haunts.

"You look done in," says Audrey as she watches Martin slump onto the sofa.

"Your friend cracks the whip."

Audrey laughs at Martin's comment, but isn't surprised. She is sure Helen will get her money's worth out of him.

"I bought some beer today. Would you like one?"

Martin hesitates; he shouldn't really mix alcohol with his medication. But one wouldn't hurt.

"Please, that would be good."

Audrey gets a bottle of lager and a glass from the kitchen and places both on the coffee table.

"I'll let you pour," she says to him.

Martin leans forward to reach the drink and hears something scrunching underneath him. He puts his hand in his pocket and pulls out the letter he had put in there this morning.

"What's that?"

"Don't know yet," replies Martin as he roughly opens the envelope with his thumb.

Audrey watches him as he reads the letter and observes a smile growing across his face.

"Good news?"

"Yes, very. I've been offered a flat."

"A flat? Oh dear, has your wife vetoed any idea of a reconciliation then?"

"What? Oh, no. I don't know, it may take a little longer and I'm in temporary accommodation at the moment, which isn't ideal."

"Of course. Where is this flat then?"

"Park Close on the Turner Springs estate. I don't know where that is." Martin looks up as Audrey tuts loudly. "What is it?"

"It's probably better now."

"Better?"

"It was a bit rough, but that was a long time ago."

Rough; Martin can cope with rough and he needs to get out of the hostel.

"Maybe I'll take a walk over there this evening and have a look."

"Walk? You won't be able to walk there."

"Why not? I'm quite capable of looking after myself Audrey."

"No, it's not that. It's a long way."

"How far?"

"I don't know, ten miles perhaps."

Martins face cannot conceal his disappointment, he is crestfallen. Ten miles is too far. Too far from Joanne and Amy and too far to keep an eye on Ray.

Audrey is upset with herself for spoiling his mood and wants to try and make amends.

"I don't know exactly how far, that's a guess. If you like we could take a drive out and see where it is. It might not be that far after all."

A chink of light.

Not for long though. Audrey's estimate wasn't that far off after all and sadly she had under-estimated as it is actually a little further - 11.8 miles to be exact. That's in the car, obviously less as the crow flies. Either way it is too far. But if he turns it down he runs the risk of being put lower on the waiting list or maybe even removed from it altogether. This is his dilemma, another catch 22.

When they get back to Audrey's house she asks if he would like to come in for a cup of tea. Martin looks out of the side window of the car and rolls his eyes, she thinks a cup of tea solves everything.

"No thanks. I'm going to head home. Goodnight Audrey."

Audrey spent a fitful night's sleep thinking about Martin and his situation. In a short space of time she considers she has got to know him well. She likes him and trusts him and she has got used to having him around. And then there is his family, they mean so much to him and he needs to be nearer to them. Someone has to help him. The solution is obvious, although it did not reveal itself to Audrey until she was tucking into a breakfast of porridge and blueberries.

☯

Charley does not believe in fairytales, or happy-ever-afters. And she categorically knows that she does not have a fairy godmother. But, what if ... Recent events are making her question logic and reason. She is not accustomed to such kindness and generosity. A studio and a sponsor; long held wishes she had never imagined being granted. And with Helen's encouragement she has discovered that it is feasible for her to complete her course despite her circumstances, and when not at college she can come to the studio and work in order to build up a portfolio. A possible future not made entirely of sleepless nights and nappies is emerging.

☯

Martin does not believe in providence or good fortune. And his life has not been one blessed with serendipity. Chance and coincidence he also doubts. For him life is and has always been a series of challenges, never meant to be easy. So when someone offers him help he is often sceptical and looks for motive. But in Audrey he has found someone who is agenda-free. She is a rarity to him; a kind person. Her offer of a room is a godsend, an obvious step up from the hostel and the perfect situation for him to continue to keep an eye on his family.

☯

Helen doesn't believe in fate or destiny. Neither does she hold with the idea of preordination. But lately she has been drawn along a path, which she would never previously have taken, with a sense of inevitability. She is not complaining. This path brought her Audrey who has enriched her life with friendship and support and Audrey has brought her Charley who is filling a void - the barren, unoccupied spot that Helen buried long ago before the misery it sowed consumed her.

Nine

THE SOUND OF FOOTSTEPS crossing the landing rouses Audrey from her slumber. For a few seconds she holds her breath, unsure what to do, then a cough reminds her it is Martin, her lodger; relieved she exhales. It took her so long to get used to being alone, she hopes it will not take her as long to become accustomed to having someone live with her once again. She looks at the clock on her bedside table. The alarm is due to go off in twelve minutes time, she is not going to wait for it so turns it off and gets out of bed.

"Morning Audrey. Would you like tea? Kettle has just boiled," Martin greets Audrey as she enters the kitchen.

"Thank you."

"I hope we didn't disturb you last night?"

Audrey is a little disconcerted by his question. Did he have a guest in his room? Are they still there? Her mind runs away with possibilities as to what he is alluding to.

"Disturb me, how?"

"Joanne came over, quite late. She was a bit pissed."

"Excuse me?"

"I'm sorry Audrey. Erm, what I mean is she is none too pleased that I am living in such close proximity to her."

"Aah." Audrey tries to hide her relief. "I'm sure she will get used to it and it's nice for your daughter that you are close by."

"That's what I told her. Are you working today?"

"No, but I am going out. I'm meeting Helen for lunch."

Martin is glad to hear that. Before he goes to work he wants to look up a few more things on the internet and it's hard to do when Audrey is hovering around. As soon as she leaves he switches on the computer. He goes onto his bogus Facebook account, and smiles when he sees that one Ray Milner has accepted his friend request. He visits Ray's page and is interested to see that he is attending someone's birthday drinks this Friday. It is at a bar Martin knows as it's not too far from where he works. He feels confident it will be a 'men only' evening as it is not the sort of place that Joanne would go to, so he decides he may venture along too.

☙

Audrey is surprised to find Helen waiting for her at the restaurant, though she is not surprised to see that she already has a glass of wine.

"Sorry am I late? I hope I haven't kept you waiting."

"No I was early, I had to take Charley to an antenatal appointment this morning."

Audrey raises her eyebrows before suggesting that perhaps she is becoming more involved than she should be.

"Audrey, she has no-one else."

"She must have a family somewhere."

"Maybe. But they are not helping her - she hasn't got long to go and she is beginning to feel apprehensive."

"I'm sure she must be scared and it's good of you to help her, just don't become too attached because if her family do come back on the scene ..."

"I don't think they will and if they do Charley will not want anything to do with them."

"You don't know that Helen. After all blood is thicker than water."

The first thing Helen does on returning home is pour a large glass of wine. She only had one with her lunch as she was driving. She drinks it quickly then pours another. She loves Audrey but at times she can be incredibly infuriating. And today was one of those days. As much as she appreciates Audrey's concern and is sometimes buoyed by it today was too much. Her concerns when voiced bordered on the sanctimonious. She knows Charley has a family somewhere but she does not need to be reminded of it; after all they are not here and she is.

She finishes her drink and rinses her glass before upending it on the draining board. As she does this she spots the pair of keys from Robert's tin. She picks them up, glancing out of the kitchen window towards the shed as she does.

"I wonder," she whispers to herself.

She goes outside, opens the shed and pulls at the old raggedy picnic blanket to uncover the filing cabinet. It's bent and buckled façade, dented by her frustrated hammer blows, remind her what was revealed to her last time she was here. She tries one of the keys in the lock. It fits, as she knew it would. She searches through the shed to see if there is anything else in there that requires a key to open it but there is nothing. Helen looks back towards the house wondering where the item is that the other key belongs to.

❧

Martin is pleased the pub is busy. He hopes he can mingle and observe Ray without being seen himself. He finds a table which gives him a good view of the door, the bar and the route to the toilets. Ray arrives about twenty minutes later and joins a party that are standing towards the centre of the bar. They are already very noisy and rowdy. Alongside them are a group of girls who look barely old enough to be there. As the evening progresses the distance between the two groups lessens and it is not long before there is no clear definition at all as the two groups merge and become one. Initially the interaction between them seems friendly, a little flirty but nothing untoward. An hour or so later the language that began as light-hearted banter is becoming lewd and lascivious. It's hard for Martin to tell who is saying what but he has adjudged Ray guilty by association. There is movement as some of the men jostle for position, preening and posturing now as the interaction ramps up a little. Ray is saying something to one of the girls who throws her head back as she laughs. He says something else, she nods and he steps past her placing his hand on her behind as he does. Martin is sure he detected a squeeze which riles him up a little. He watches Ray disappear through the doors to the toilets. Martin downs his drink and follows him.

Ray looks up briefly as the door opens, catching the briefest glimpse of him in the mirror before he is out cold. Martin exits the pub as quickly but calmly as possible; he does not want to draw attention to himself. Once outside he runs, not even sure if he is running in the right direction. He runs and runs until his heart and lungs scream at his brain to make him stop. When he does stop his legs wobble and he falls to the ground, he is sweating and shaking and then he vomits. He lifts himself onto his knees, wiping dribble and puke from his face with the back of his hand. His hands hurt. When his breathing returns to an almost normal rate, he stands up, looking around to get his bearings. Thankfully he has been running towards home so he continues his journey, but at a slower pace.

Audrey is still up when he gets back; she has fallen asleep in front of the television again. Something she does often. Martin removes his shoes and walks gently along the hallway, but forgets to avoid the first stair which creaks as he steps onto it. He holds his breath and listens; he hasn't woken her. He breathes out, then takes another step but as he lifts his foot the stair reacts angrily emitting a loud crack as the pressure is removed.

"Martin, is that you?" Audrey comes out of the lounge and into the hallway switching on the hall light as she does. "Goodness, you look dreadful. Is everything okay?" She edges closer to him. "And what have you done to yourself?" She takes hold of his hands, inspecting his knuckles. "Let's get you cleaned up."

"I'm fine, Audrey. I just need my bed."

"We'll get you cleaned up first and then you can go to bed, where I'm sure you have been all night."

He gives a half-hearted smile, nods and reluctantly follows her into the kitchen.

Martin is woken by the not-so-tuneful sound of Audrey singing. She must be dusting or doing some sort of cleaning, he thinks. Housework is always accompanied by singing or humming. Neither a particularly pleasing sound; her singing is brittle and a little shrill, the humming monotonous. Although this morning he really would rather she were quiet, he has no intention of saying so. After all, if his memory serves him right then he is pretty certain she offered him an alibi last night. But do I need one, he ponders. He rolls onto his back and puts his arms up in the air bringing his hands down so he can take a better look at them.

They both have grazes across the knuckles and the right hand is a little swollen. The events of the previous evening are not all lost, but they are a little hazy. He remembers going out, going to the bar, watching Ray and … then Audrey telling him he was here all night. His hands say something else. He sits up, a little too fast, his equilibrium is not what it should be. He takes his time getting out of bed, turning by degrees, realising today may be a long day.

When he finally makes it downstairs he is greeted by a large mug of black coffee, a glass of orange juice and the smell of bacon frying.

"This is what I always made my boys if they had one over the eight," says Audrey as she places rashers of greasy bacon between white bread doorstops.

"Red or brown?"

Martin looks at her blankly.

"Sauce. Red or brown?"

"Red, thank you."

Audrey places the sandwich in front of him. Martin bites into it, nodding as he begins chewing. It is the best bacon sandwich he has ever tasted and the perfect antidote to his hangover. When his mouth is less full, he tells her this.

"I'm glad you like it. Now, about last night."

"I um …" Martin tries to speak but he is impeded by his breakfast.

"Shush," says Audrey sternly. "About last night. I don't wish to know what happened or where you were or who's unfortunate nose may have been on the end of your fist. As far as I am concerned you were here all evening, but if it happens again, I will be asking you to leave. Okay?"

Martin looks at her sheepishly before offering a heartfelt apology.

"I do know you are troubled at the moment and if you wish to talk then I will listen, but I do not condone violence at all."

"I don't really remember much about last night, I …"

"Then let us not say too much more about–"

Someone banging loudly on the front door ends Audrey's sentence prematurely. She and Martin exchange a look.

"Stay there."

Audrey goes to the front door, closing the kitchen door on her way. Martin can hear a raised voice but can't make out who it belongs to or what they are saying. Quite a few minutes pass before he hears the front door close and Audrey comes back into the kitchen.

"Well. We now know whose face your arm connected with last night. Do you know someone called Ray?"

Martin shamefacedly lowers his head.

"Yes, I would look like that too."

"I wasn't sure, I mean, I can't actually remember."

"Do you *actually* remember anything? Like the fact that you are *actually* divorced."

Audrey's accentuation of the word actually makes Martin a little nervous. He bites his bottom lip like a naughty schoolboy waiting for his mother's wrath.

"I think you had better start telling me the truth about yourself, Martin."

He does. He tells her:

About Afghanistan.

About Joanne and Jack and Amy.

About the blackouts.

He tells her everything.

Ten

"BRAXTON HICKS?" Helen asks the midwife.

"Yes. Let's call them practice contractions, your body getting ready but really nothing to worry about."

"But they are really painful," says Charley.

"They can be, but you still have almost three weeks to your due date and first babies are often late. Go home, but take it easy."

"Okay."

"Let Mum here take care of you," says the midwife with a nod towards Helen.

"She's not m–"

"I certainly will," interrupts Helen. "Thank you."

Once outside Helen explains to Charley why she let the midwife think she was her mum.

"I just thought it was easier, save you having to explain, save any embarrassment."

"Thank you. It was kind but I don't want you to feel obliged to do that. You've helped me so much already with the studio and college and all the things you have bought for me and the baby, and bringing me here today."

"Charley, it's fine. I really don't mind."

And she didn't mind, not one bit.

Audrey has to work this afternoon, but she is a little unsure about leaving Martin at home alone.

"I will be fine, a sore hand and a hangover are not life-threatening."

"Alright then, take it easy and I will see you later."

Martin hears the front door close and the distinctive rattle of the window that always accompanies it as Audrey has a tendency to slam the door. She says it is to ensure it closes properly. Just minutes later, or maybe even seconds, there is a frantic knock on the front door. Martin laughs to himself. What has she forgotten? Her keys most likely if she is knocking.

"Audrey, you would forget your–" he stops dead. It's not Audrey. It is Joanne.

"Hello," he says hesitantly.

Joanne does not wait to be asked in, she roughly pushes past him and stands hands on hips waiting for him to face her. Martin closes the door and turns to look at her.

"You have to leave," she says.

"And why would I do that?"

"Because if you don't Ray will tell the police it was you who attacked him. I don't care what that old biddy says, I know you were not here all night. I know it was you."

"Jo, I don't have anywhere else to go."

"Not my problem."

"I …"

"Two weeks, I will give you two weeks."

She pushes past him again as roughly as she did when she came in, opens the door then slams it shut as she exits. Martin is still standing in the hallway long after she has gone. Silence surrounds him, but he has his hands on his ears as if to muffle a sound. A sound loud and deadly that only he can hear, only he can remember …

… *panic, frantic panic. Bangs and explosions all around. Shouts and screams, screams loaded with pain. A salvo of gunfire overhead. A barrage of bullets discharged from a semi-automatic, it's distinctive clatter as the belt passes through the feed block. The bombardment is relentless. Whirring helicopter blades throw up choking dust. The dust and the smoke blending to create a harsh abrasive mix when inhaled. The coughs and cries are endless …*

… he is cold, he is shaking and his head hurts. He looks around initially unsure of his surroundings; his eyes are assaulted by a clash of colours that have no business being together. He soon determines that the swirling patterns belong to the carpet on which he is laying and the wallpaper that surrounds him. As he slowly reacquaints himself with his surroundings his headache eases a little. Turning over he makes his way to the stairs on all fours. He sits on one of the lower stairs looking back to where he was prostrate. He has a dry mouth which suddenly becomes desperate for lubrication. To quench his abrupt thirst he goes to the kitchen, glad to leave the hallway and its hideous decor. He guzzles three glasses of water in quick succession. Thirst slaked he goes for a shower.

In the shower Martin has recollections of his conversation with Joanne. He can't leave. He won't leave. He could try talking to her but he knows he has little to no chance of making her change her mind. So he thinks he will have to change someone else's mind, but is unsure how to approach him. He knows going over there is probably a non-starter, it's unlikely he will open the door to him and she may be there anyway. Martin decides to use his Facebook alias to deliver a message.

What a stroke of luck it was that he had bothered to take some photos last night. The majority are quite innocuous, but a few could easily be misconstrued and one, well, they say a picture paints a thousand words, though in this case none of the words would be particularly complimentary. Ray's hand is clearly placed on the backside of a girl who looks young enough to be his daughter. He could just as easily show this picture to Joanne, but he figures now is not the right time to do that. To convince her of Ray's unsuitability he needs a bit more than one grainy photo, but it is enough to make Ray see that talking to the police or making Martin move is not a good idea. Martin uploads the photo and sends it to Ray via messenger. The reply is instantaneous.

What do you want??

Martin replies.

I want you to leave Martin alone. No more accusations and no requests for him to move.
It's not me, it's Jo.
Persuade her to change her mind otherwise I will send her the photo- then it might be you she asks to move.
Then you will delete the picture?
I will delete the picture.
Ok, leave it with me.

Martin chuckles to himself. He has no intention of deleting the photo; in fact he is printing it along with a copy of his internet exchange with Ray. It will all help when he finally presents his case to Joanne.

Eleven

LIFE HAS CHANGED so much for Charley and in a relatively short span of time too. But the biggest change is on the horizon. She is almost full term and the apprehension has now grown into full blown fear. Fear of giving birth, fear of being a mother, fear of the future. Her fears make Helen's offer incredibly attractive, but even that makes her fearful. Helen has been so kind to her; attending appointments with her, giving her a place to work, encouraging her to pursue her dream despite her circumstances. Living with Helen would be very nice. Charley hates the hostel and there is not a lot of room. The mother and baby home is nicer, still small though, and she would still have to share with strangers. Helen has a very large house, so space is not an issue. It would be a short walk to the studio rather than a twenty minute bus ride. The college is closer too and she would have help with the baby should she need it. And she is sure she will need it. The pros far outweigh the cons, yet there is still this nagging doubt that it is not the right thing to do, but it is a doubt which she cannot give reason to.

Charley continues mulling over her dilemma as she waits for the bus, which is late. It is late so often that its late arrival time has now become its due time, unofficially of course. She is so preoccupied with her thoughts that she doesn't see the bus until it has stopped in front of her. She gets on and takes a seat at the front. There was a time she would only sit at the rear of the bus or on the top deck if there was one, but now, with her extra load, she is happy to take the first available seat. She gazes out of the window as the bus travels along its route. The houses are the biggest marker of how different one end of town is from the other. The neighbourhood she is going to is more affluent, but it's not only that which marks it as different. It is cleaner and that's not just the roads and paths. The air is cleaner and fresher. In the poorer, deprived areas – where the hostel is – the air is tainted, grubby and smelly. Hardship carries a scent of its own, a scent that Charley is happy to leave behind. As the bus approaches her stop Charley presses the bell and stands up, unaware that someone on the back of the bus is watching her with more than idle curiosity.

The woman watches her cross the road in front of the bus and then turn a corner. Once Charley is out of sight the woman jumps up pressing the bell several times as she makes her way along the bus.

"Stop, stop. I missed my stop."

"Well I can't stop here," explains the driver. "You'll have to get off at the next one."

"Give me a break. I'm gonna be late for work."

"You can get out at the lights, only if they are red mind."

They are red. The woman jumps off the bus and heads back to where she last saw Charley. She crosses the road and turns the same corner. She can see Charley up ahead, waddling along. The woman slows a little, she doesn't want to be seen. Charley turns the next corner so the woman breaks into a run to ensure she doesn't lose sight of her. When she reaches the corner she watches as Charley walks up the driveway of a house. The woman is mystified as to why Charley is here, unless this is where the father of her baby lives; after all, she knows Charley is not round this way for the same reason she is. Not in her condition anyway. A text disrupts her thoughts. She takes her phone from her pocket, noting the time as she does. It will be him as she is late now.

Are you coming?
5 mins. Bus was late.

Lizzie puts the phone back into her pocket and returns the way she came.

Helen opens the door before Charley reaches it; she has been looking out for her. With her due date approaching Helen gets a little anxious when Charley is late. She did offer to go and collect her but Charley insisted that she would make her own way over today.

"Morning," says Helen. "How are you feeling today?"

"Hi. I'm fine."

"Would you like a drink before you go outside?"

"No. I think I'll get cracking thanks."

Helen is disappointed. She had hoped they could discuss further her suggestion that Charley move in here with her. An hour or so later she takes a mug of tea and some biscuits out to the studio.

"I thought you might be ready for some refreshments."

"I do have a kettle out here," says Charley without looking up from the easel.

"I know, it's an excuse really for me to see what the painting looks like so far."

"There is not much to see yet," says Charley with a knowing smile and a shake of her head. She is sure Helen's interest in the painting is a ruse to come out here and find out if she has made a decision yet. After all, it was only last week that she said she did not want to see the picture before it was completed. Charley plays along regardless, taking a step back from the canvas so Helen can have a closer look.

"Have you given any more thought to my offer?" asks Helen before biting into a lemon and ginger biscuit.

"I have."

"And?" Helen speaks without looking up from the painting. She is unsure what the answer will be and if necessary it will be easier to hide her disappointment if she has her back towards Charley.

"I would love to, if you are absolutely certain it is okay." Any reservations that Charley had dissipated as soon as she stepped into the house. She would be foolish to turn down such an offer, it would be a far better environment for her baby and for her too. Helen makes her feel safe and secure and worthy, ingredients that thus far have been absent from her life.

Helen wants to let out a whoop. She refrains from doing so and instead puts one arm around Charley's shoulders and suggests a shopping trip to celebrate.

☯

Lizzie was surprised to see Charley this morning and surprised at how large she was. She has no idea when her due date is, but looking at her this morning it is obvious it isn't that far away. She looked well and Lizzie is glad; despite what happened between them she is still her daughter. But she is interested in more than Charley's welfare. What Lizzie would really like to know is why she was where she was this morning. She has convinced herself it is most likely something to do with the baby's father and if he does live in that big house either he is very wealthy or his parents are. Either way she thinks it is worth finding out; who knows it may pave the way to a reconciliation, which could well be in her best interests.

❂

The shopping trip isn't quite going as Helen had planned. She has pointed out quite a few things to Charley that she will need for the baby and that she thinks are nice, but Charley seems unimpressed. They stop for lunch and Helen decides to tackle Charley about her lacklustre attitude.

"Is everything okay?" Helen asks.

"Yes."

"You don't seem very keen on doing any shopping."

"I've got a couple of things."

"A couple of sleep suits and a packet of bibs are hardly enough and you don't have long left."

"I'm sure I don't need much."

"I'm sure you do. Crib, blankets, bottles, bath, clothes, pushchair, car seat …"

"Car seat? I don't have a car. I can't even drive for Christ's sake," Charley says, her voice rising above the clamour of the restaurant.

Helen takes a hurried look around aware that some of the other diners are looking at them. She looks back at Charley, ready to chastise her for her outburst when she realises that the girl is crying.

"Oh, Charley. What is it?"

"You need to stop being so nice to me."

"I er … Why?"

"I have to do this on my own."

"No, you don't."

"Alright. What I mean is, I have to do this my way. I am so

grateful to you and I can never repay your kindness, but I need to pay my way as best I can and all the things you keep pointing out and talking about, well, I can't actually afford them."

Helen listens intently to what Charley is saying to her, she understands completely. It is a question of pride, a virtue that Helen has witnessed before; Robert was a very proud man who would neither ask for nor accept help from anyone. Charley has her pride and does not want to accept charity, she wants to be in charge of her situation as best she can be. She appreciates so much what Helen has done for her, but she needs to remain in control and in order to do that she cannot be totally reliant on Helen.

"Of course," says Helen. "I understand and I'm sorry."

"No need to apologise," says Charley taking hold of Helen's hand. Helen puts her other hand on top of Charley's and smiles at her.

"Okay. Where would you like to go now?"

"Can we go to the charity shop, the one where Audrey works? I've seen some things there that would be perfect."

"Sec ..." Helen stops herself from decrying the notion of buying second-hand. "Of course, but can I buy a car seat first, for my car. I'm sure there will be times when I will be bringing you and the little one out."

"Okay."

Audrey is pleasantly surprised when Charley and Helen come into the shop, but her surprise soon turns to shock when Helen informs her that Charley is going to be moving in with her.

"Do you think it's wise to let her live with you?" Audrey asks discreetly as Charley looks over the nursery equipment on offer.

"Audrey, we've been through this before."

"Not this exactly. It's one thing helping her out with lifts to the clinic and buying her paintings but having her move in is ..."

"… is no different to what you have done for Martin," counters Helen.

Audrey has nothing to offer, she is beat.

"You're right. We are both a pair of old fools who can't stand by when someone needs a hand."

"Less of the old, thank you," says Helen with a look intended to remind Audrey that Helen is in fact several years younger than her. Their exchange is interrupted by Charley who comes over laden with things she wants to buy.

On the drive back to Helen's house she asks Charley when she would like to move in, suggesting that it would be best to do it sooner rather than later. They pick a day the following week, the same day that Charley has an antenatal appointment. Helen is pleased that a day is set and also that she has a few days to get the rooms ready. She intends to ask Martin to decorate the large guest room and its en-suite for Charley and then the other guest room will become the nursery. The thought of having a baby in the house fills Helen with joy, it is the one thing the house has always lacked. And a baby is the one thing she has always lacked.

Twelve

LIZZIE'S DETECTIVE WORK has uncovered more than she bargained for. She can't believe it is his house, or was. Although she threatened to go there many times, she never did and never bothered finding out where it was either. She was going to go after he died, see that bloody wife of his to get some money, but when she went back to the solicitor he told her it would be a waste of her time. The visit to the solicitor hadn't been a complete waste of time though, at least she had earned some money that day and gained a new client.

She has been watching the house and is pretty certain Charley is living there now. Lizzie supposes that Charley must have gone in search of her dad; after all she was always banging on about it to her. But how does she end up living here? That's what Lizzie wants to know. Maybe he left her the house; after all she must have been entitled to something. And if that's the case I reckon I'm due some of that too, thinks Lizzie.

"Stay with me."

"Are you sure?" asks Helen.

"Of course she is sure," says the midwife. "It's quite common for mums to come in these days, or sisters or friends."

Helen waits for Charley to tell the midwife that Helen is not her mum, when she doesn't a smile lights up Helen's face and heart.

It is not a quick birth but finally …

"It's a boy, you have a beautiful baby boy."

Charley is exhausted but overcome with love for her baby son. Helen is equally overcome and both women shed some tears as they hold one another and the newborn boy.

❧

Martin can hear someone knocking on the door, but he isn't going to answer it. It won't be anyone for him as this is Helen's house and as she is not here whoever it is can just come back another day. He needs to get this room finished as Charley and the baby should be coming out of the hospital tomorrow. He dips his paintbrush into the tin and is just about to run the brush along the cornice when the knocking starts again; whoever it is, they are persistent. He lays his brush across the top of the paint can, steps off the ladder and goes downstairs to see who it is.

Lizzie is taken aback when Martin answers the door.

"Who are you?" she asks, wondering to herself if this is the guy, the dad.

"I think that's my line."

"What?"

"I should ask who you are. Oh never mind," says Martin, who can see that Lizzie isn't on his wavelength at all. "Can I help you?"

"I want to see Charley."

"She isn't here. Who shall I say called?"

"You know Charley?"

"I do," Martin replies impatiently. He is keen to get on with the decorating.

"Do you live here?"

"No, I don't. I'm working here and I need to get on. Would you like me to give Charley a message?"

Lizzie is satisfied he isn't the one; she is glad, she could fancy this one herself.

"Can I come in and wait for her?" she asks seductively.

"No, but as I said I can pass on a message for you."

"Don't bother." Lizzie turns to leave, then changes her mind. "Actually tell her that her mum dropped by."

"Her mum?"

"Yes, her mum. I know I don't look old enough."

Martin closes the door without saying anything more to the woman who claims to be Charley's mum. Helen has told him Charley's story and he will not give any more time to a woman who threw out her kid when she needed her the most.

He is in the utility room washing the paintbrushes when Helen returns.

"How's it looking?" she asks.

"Go see for yourself. It's all finished."

Helen goes upstairs closely followed by Martin. She is really pleased with the room and glad that it has been finished in time.

"Will the smell of paint be gone by tomorrow?" she asks him.

"Yes, I'm sure it will. Just leave the windows open up here for as long as possible. Let in some fresh air and it'll be fine."

"You really have done a great job, Martin. Come and have a cuppa."

As Helen is making a pot of tea Martin tells her about the visitor. Although the news throws her for a second, when she thinks about it she is not really surprised. After all Charley's mother must have known that the baby was due around this time.

"Did you tell her about the baby?"

"No. I didn't say anything of any consequence to her at all, didn't much like the look of her to be honest."

"I would prefer it if you didn't tell Charley that she was here. I will tell her, but when the time is right."

"No worries. I don't think you should be telling her anytime soon. I remember when my wife had our two, emotions all over the place in the early days."

"Yes, exactly. How are things with you and your family?"

"I see Amy, my son is away at the moment. Jo and I are … it's complicated."

"Relationships often are. Health wise you doing okay? No more blackouts?"

"I er …"

"Sorry. I'm being nosey. Audrey mentioned it, but I shouldn't have asked."

"It's fine. Audrey has been very good to me, but she can be a bit indiscreet."

"She wasn't gossiping. She was just voicing her concern. She is very fond of you and she worries about you."

"And you too."

"Yes I know," says Helen. "I think she misses her boys and we are their substitutes."

"She was Skyping one of them the other night, the one in New Zealand. They were talking about her going over there. Not that I was listening, it's just she was talking rather loudly."

"She shouts when she is on her mobile phone too," Helen says laughing. "I think the one in New Zealand is Philip. She talks about going all the time but it never works out. Between you and me, I don't think her sons are that good to her. I know they are not close by, but they could phone more often. It is always Audrey who has to phone them and apparently the one who lives in Scotland,

I forget his name now, he was down this way recently but couldn't find time to see his mother."

Lizzie watches as Martin drives away from the house. She still thinks he is rather handsome despite the offhand manner in which he spoke to her. She saw a lady go into the house and she is certain she knows who she is, but it is Charley she wants to see. Not due to any maternal concern, although of course she hopes she is alright. No, she is keen to find out what is going on and why Charley is living here - and if, as she suspects, it is because there is money in this house that belongs to Charley. She can't wait too much longer though, Mo wants her car back in an hour. Lizzie wishes she hadn't sold her own car now, but at the time her cash flow was zero and she had a big bill to pay. Another ten minutes pass and there is still no sign of Charley. Lizzie is starting to worry that she may have to come back another day, unless … Boredom and impatience and a desire to know why her daughter is living here embolden her and suddenly Lizzie is out of the car and walking purposefully across the road. Her knock on the front door is loud and commanding, she means business. She doesn't need to knock twice as the door is opened quickly. Lizzie attempts to introduce herself before Helen speaks but she is thwarted.

"I know who you are. You had better come in," says Helen. She closes the door behind Lizzie. "What do you want?"

"I've come to see my daughter."

"She isn't here."

"I'm happy to wait."

"I don't think so. I will tell her you called round and if she wants to see you, which is extremely unlikely, I'm sure she knows where

to find you. In the meantime I can pass on any message to her."
When Lizzie doesn't answer Helen takes a step towards the door
and puts her hand on the latch ready to open it.

"Don't bother opening that. Like I said I can wait. It'll give you
and I a chance to become better acquainted," says Lizzie, who
begins walking across the hall to the kitchen. "After all, we have a
lot in common."

Helen is dumbstruck. She watches as Lizzie goes into the
kitchen, uninvited. She follows her and is astonished to see her
sitting on a stool. Helen watches as Lizzie places her bag on the
counter top and takes a nail file from it.

"Do you mind?" says Helen. "I have things to do. As I said I will
let Charley know you were looking for her."

"Tea, two sugars, thanks," says Lizzie ignoring Helen's obvious
request that she leave.

"I would like you to leave, now. I'm not discussing Charley with
you at all. As I have made clear it is up …"

"Then let's talk about something else, or someone else. Like, say,
Bobby …"

❧

"Good grief Helen. What did you say to her when she said that?"

"Nothing, well not immediately, I couldn't. I could hardly
breathe let alone talk. I was confused, was she Charley's mother or
Robert's whore? I never expected her to be both."

"And what does Charley say?"

"What?"

"Charley, what does she make of it all?"

"Nothing."

"Nothing? You mean you haven't told her?"

"She doesn't need to know."

"Now you are being ridiculous. Of course she has to know."

"I paid her off."

"Who?"

"The whore." Helen is no longer going to dignify her with a name.

"You still need to tell Charley."

"No, I don't. Do you know, the whole time that bloody woman was in my house she never once asked how Charley was. She did not even ask about the baby. All she was interested in was how much the house is worth."

"Charley still has a right to know."

"Why? Oh I see, you think she is entitled to something."

"No I …"

"I will give her whatever she needs. I have done more for her in a few months than her mother has ever done."

"I know you have, but it's not just a question of money or entitlement. It's about Charley, her parentage, her identity."

"I am not telling her," says Helen firmly. "And neither are you," she adds when she sees a disapproving look on Audrey's face. "Are we clear on that Audrey?"

"It's not my place to say anything, but I think that …"

"Exactly, it's not your place."

Thirteen

MARTIN HAS BEEN keeping a close eye on Ray and it seems he is behaving himself, at least for the moment. He goes to work and comes home straight after. The only other times that he ventures from the house he is accompanied by Joanne. Martin is disappointed. He had hoped that by now he would have gathered enough dirt on him to show Joanne what a waste of time and space he is. He realises Ray is probably being cautious; after all he is now aware that Martin has been following him. Martin wishes that he had been able to control his temper that night but when the red mist descends he is helpless. And not just helpless, oblivious too. When his rage is unmasked and laid bare he is completely impotent. His rage rains down like a tropical storm and the recipient will be soaked by the torrent. The medication helps, when not mixed with alcohol. The counselling Martin is not so sure of; he is not much of a talker. But he will persevere. He wants to be in control of himself, even though it is hard. He is competing against a force that has taken a part of him away, isolated it and made it very, very angry. Then when this part reveals itself, he is lost. Restraint, recognition and recollection all abandon him. Then the red mist is replaced by a darkness that creates a black hole in time. He does not like having these unaccounted for periods of time, so if there's a possibility the therapy might help he will stick at it. He knows that he will never win back his family if he does not win back himself first.

Joanne does not want to see Martin, or speak to him or hear him. She thought she had got rid of him, but Ray has convinced her that it wouldn't be fair on Amy to force her dad to move. So she has agreed to give him another chance, but it really goes against her better judgement. Over the years she has given Martin so many second chances, and for what? She still ended up on the receiving end of his wrath too many times. She knows it has been hard for him, some of the things he has witnessed have been appalling, and then there was Pete. He could not deal with that - blamed himself but took it out on her and the kids. Joanne is still unconvinced that he has got over that, maybe he never will, but she knows it was right to leave him, not just for her sake but for the kids too. So many regrets cloud her time with Martin, but she tries to remember the good times. There were some, but his behaviour makes it harder for her to recall them. Of course the kids are a reminder of happier times. They do have two wonderful children thinks Joanne as she plays around with the envelope in her hand. She should tell Martin she has heard from Jack.

Martin looks in the mirror to check that his name badge is straight; it isn't, although the majority of people wouldn't notice. His training however makes him acutely aware of slight imperfections that others do not see, so he unpins the badge and puts it on again. This time it is perfectly straight, sitting neatly across the left side of his uniform. He could do without work today, especially a late shift, although the silver lining is he won't have to listen to Audrey's moans this evening. It sounds to him like she has had a falling out with Helen, although she hasn't revealed any details. The only other topic of conversation is her possible trip to New Zealand, which Martin is sure will never happen. Her sons are a waste of space in his eyes. He would give anything to be able to see his mum again. He closes the door behind him and walks down the path. He is surprised to see Joanne coming towards him.

"Hello," he says. "Everything alright?"

"Fine," replies Joanne curtly. "I thought you should know I've heard from Jack."

Joanne hands him the letter.

"So he's finished his basic then," says Martin as he hands the letter back to her.

"Yes."

"Then he's got four more years of the army, at least four, the fool."

"It's what he wants to do."

"He doesn't know what he wants to do. A few months ago he was happy nicking cheap beer and getting drunk."

"I think that had a lot to do with some girl and you com–"

"Yes I know," interrupts Martin. "I know I helped screw him up, you don't need to remind me. But giving himself to the army …"

"Look, Martin, I would rather he was here doing something else too, but he isn't and it is his life. Anyway, I wondered if," Joanne pauses mid-sentence and takes a deep breath before continuing, "you would like to come with us to his passing out parade?"

"He doesn't want me there."

"Of course he does."

"Joanne, I read the letter. He invited you. You and Amy."

"I'm sure he would like you to be there."

"If he wants me there, he can ask me himself."

"Martin," pleads Joanne.

"I have to go to work."

Helen puts the phone down, she is glad that Audrey has called and she is looking forward to seeing her tomorrow. She hopes that Audrey has had time to reflect and understands that the situation with Charley is not her concern, then they can put all this nonsense behind them and carry on as before. Helen has missed her friend. Her musings are halted by the static crackles of the baby monitor, a gentle whimpering soon gives way a full-blown cry. Noah is awake.

Martin's shift drags, he longs for something to happen, just to interrupt the monotony and to stop him thinking. He is glad he has a day off tomorrow, although he is spending it working at Helen's. She wants a patio now, and he's happy to do that, he enjoys physical work. He likes being outdoors and getting dirty and sweaty, it feels like real work to him. And Helen is a nice lady, interesting too and Charley is good fun. And then there is the little fella. He is great, although when he sees him it does take Martin back to when Jack was a baby; happier and simpler times.

Charley can't believe how lucky she is. She has a beautiful, healthy son and he alone is enough to fill her life with boundless joy, but she is painting too. Her creative side is being fed and it is responding with some fabulous work. Helen has suggested staging an exhibition the following spring or summer. The only cloud in Charley's sky are her parents - or lack of them. She doesn't know her father and has resigned herself to never knowing him. Her mum is another matter entirely. Charley is determined Noah will not experience the same ignorance regarding his dad. But in order for that to be so, his dad needs to be told about Noah.

Fourteen

AUDREY PUTS A SMALL BUD VASE on the dining table and pops in the flowers that she selected from the garden. The blooms are a little past their best but they still add a little flourish to the table. She takes a couple of crystal wine glasses from the cabinet and adds them to the place settings. She figures it wouldn't do to deny Helen a glass of wine as that may irritate her before the evening has even started. Audrey steps back and gives her table an approving look before going to check on the fish pie. As she opens the oven a knock at the door startles her. She hopes it isn't Helen yet, she was rather banking on her tardiness to give her time to get changed.

It isn't Helen, it's the boyfriend of Martin's ex. Audrey wishes it was Helen; the last thing she wants at the moment is for Martin's drama to play out in front of her. She closes the door leaving Ray on the doorstep as she has no intention of inviting him in. After shouting loudly up the stairs several times Martin finally hears her and sticks his head over the banister.

"Everything alright, Aud?"

Audrey winces, she has told him many times not to shorten her name. "You have a visitor."

Martin bounces down the stairs two at a time, and as he passes Audrey she tells him who it is. He stops dead, pulls his stomach in and draws himself up, his manner changes too. The jovial Martin who came home today, happy and contented after his day at Helen's, has suddenly been replaced by a hostile and malevolent Martin whose balefulness is unsettling. Audrey watches uneasily as he goes outside. Instead of getting herself ready she goes into the living room and peers through the net curtain to see what occurs between the two men. The body language on display clearly shows that they are not having a pleasant chat. She can't make out what they are saying and curses having triple-glazed windows. She flinches as Martin takes a step closer to Ray who responds by stepping back and raising his arms, palms facing Martin, an attempt to pacify or conceding defeat, she isn't sure. Relief sweeps over her when Ray turns and walks away. She moves from the window and tries to get back to the kitchen before Martin comes back inside.

"All good?" she asks.

"Fine."

"Would you like some of this?" Audrey points to the fish pie. "I always make far too much."

"No thanks. I'm going out."

Audrey is glad to hear this, she was hoping he would go out anyway so she could talk freely to Helen about things, even more so now if he is in a bad mood. A glance at the clock on the kitchen wall tells her she needs to hurry up and get changed. As she buttons up her blouse she hears the front door close. She goes over to the window and catches the rear view of Martin as he marches up the road. She hopes wherever he is going he keeps himself out of trouble.

Helen is almost ready, she looks at her watch, running late again. It doesn't matter how much time she gives herself she is always running late. Still, she is sure Audrey won't be expecting her to be on time anyway. She sprays her hair, adds a dash of rouge and a flash of lipstick and she is done. Before she leaves she pops in to see Noah; he is sleeping soundly. Helen stands and watches the gentle rise of his chest and listens to the contented purring of his delicate breaths. She senses someone watching her and turns to see Charley leaning on the door frame smiling at her. She smiles back then quietly backs out of the room.

"What time do you have to be at Audrey's?" asks Charley.

"Now," says Helen looking at her watch to emphasise the point.

"You'd better get going then."

"Are you sure you will be okay?"

"I think I can manage," laughs Charley.

"See you later then," says Helen, kissing her on the cheek.

Finally, thinks Charley who thought Helen was never going to leave. She has plans this evening, nothing exciting, just important. She intends to write to Noah's dad and she would prefer to do it when nobody is around.

When Helen gets to Audrey's she is pleased to note that there are wine glasses on the table. She interprets this as a conciliatory gesture on Audrey's part and hopes that in other matters too she plans to keep her opinions to herself. The two women enjoy a delicious supper of fish pie and green vegetables washed down with a glass of Sauvignon Blanc. When they have finished eating Audrey clears the table and the two women move into the lounge. She tops up their glasses with the remainder of the wine, apologising that there isn't enough for a full glass each, her excuse being that she used some of the wine for the sauce in the fish pie. Helen regrets not bringing a bottle with her, settling for flowers and chocolates instead. They both sit down and inevitably the conversation is about Charley and Noah.

"He is adorable," gushes Helen.

"You sound like a doting grandmother," says Audrey.

"Do I? At times I actually feel like one."

"Only you are not."

Helen is slightly ruffled by Audrey's barb, but rather than retaliate she opts to change the subject. She tells Audrey about the garden and her plans for a patio.

"Yes, Martin was telling me about that."

"He was a great find Audrey. He works incredibly hard and he is good company too."

"Hmnn … sometimes."

"Oh. Something wrong?"

"Not wrong exactly. I get a little worried about his mood swings sometimes. And it doesn't help having his ex-wife living so close."

"He was in a very good mood today," says Helen. "But then I think Noah brings out the best in us all." Without meaning to, Helen has brought the conversation back to Charley and Noah once again.

"Has Noah met his grandmother yet?"

"Charley does not want him to."

"Oh. That's fair enough I suppose, it is up to her. But I'm glad you told Charley about her mum's visit."

"This wine is very good," says Helen determined to change the subject once more.

"You haven't told her." Audrey is not fooled by Helen's talk of the wine.

"And dinner was lovely, a hearty and homely meal. I haven't had fish pie for a long time." Helen presses on with inane chatter and small talk.

"Helen. Please tell me you have told Charley."

"Audrey, leave it. We have had a pleasant evening. Let us not sour it with a pointless discussion about something that is not your concern."

Audrey is seething; she does not like Helen's dismissive tone and she absolutely believes that Helen is wrong to keep this from Charley. Yes, her mother has behaved disgracefully but Charley should still be made aware that she has come looking for her even if it is with dubious motives. She can't let this go but before she can challenge Helen their evening is interrupted by Martin returning home. Audrey instantly knows he has been drinking. The slamming of the front door is partnered with expletives and when she goes out to the hallway his uncoordinated stumbling confirms his inebriation.

"Martin," she screeches at him. "Look at the state of you."

Martin is in no state to respond so just waves a dismissive hand in Audrey's direction before attempting to climb the stairs. His faltering footsteps alarm her and she steps forward to help him. Again he attempts to dismiss her with his arm, but his flailing limb catches her a glancing blow to her face. Her shock is matched by his horror and he offers drunken apologies to her. Helen hears the commotion and appears in the hallway in time to witness the unseemly event. She takes charge of the situation by helping Audrey and ordering Martin up to bed. Audrey allows herself to be led back into the lounge.

"Is that a common occurrence?" Helen asks.

"Not common, but more frequent than I care for."

"Tomorrow morning you need to tell him that behaving like this is unacceptable."

"He won't remember in the morning."

"Make him remember."

"It isn't entirely his fault. It has a lot to do with his medication, I think," says Audrey. "He shouldn't drink while taking it."

"You still need to tell him, he could've hurt you. Unintentionally I know, but even so."

"I hate to upset him."

"I know."

"And it's hard confronting people when you know they are troubled."

"The right thing to do is often the hardest thing, but it does not make it any less right."

"Do you practice what you preach?" Helen does not answer, she is well aware what Audrey is alluding to. "Helen?" snaps Audrey.

"Stop it. We are talking about Martin."

"And before he came home we were talking about Charley."

"I think it's time I left.

"Yes, it is, but promise me you will tell her."

"I will do no such thing."

"Then I will."

"You will not."

"You tell her or I will."

"You would rob me of my family?"

"They are not your family."

"They are now and you will not take them from me. Do you hear me?" Helen pushes Audrey as she speaks for she is stunned by Audrey's assertion, stunned and furious.

"Stop it, stop it and go. I have had just about enough for one night."

"I will go when you swear you will drop this and stay out of my affairs."

"I can't do that."

"Aargh!" Helen's scream is full of pain and anger, and as the wretched sound emanates from her throat her hands reach for the empty wine bottle that has been abandoned on the coffee table.

She grasps the neck and smashes the bottle down onto Audrey's head. Audrey stares at Helen for a second or two as a thin trickle of red drizzles down her forehead, before her legs fold beneath her and she pitches sideways. A direct fall to the floor is impeded by the coffee table and her head strikes the corner of it with a sickening thud as she goes down.

Helen does not look at the crumpled body at her feet, she doesn't need to. She has seen death before. What she has to do now is make a plan. First, she goes into the hallway and stands at the bottom of the stairs and listens. The house is silent and still. Martin's inebriation has anaesthetised him and he has slept through the deadly disturbance. She is glad, she would hate to have to deal with him too. Although he may prove to be a problem. Helen knows not many people will miss Audrey, her sons pay her no mind at all and her work colleagues would readily accept the news that Audrey has finally taken that trip to New Zealand; but Martin, he will be harder to convince. He will not believe that Audrey would have left without telling him. It would be easy to dispense with him in his current state. A pillow across the face perhaps, but how would she dispose of him? He is much larger than Audrey and Helen is beginning to have doubts that she can even manage her on her own. Helen leans on the wall, a hand on her head as the enormity of what has happened begins to sink in. She had not come here tonight with murderous intent, for her the evening had been about getting a derailed friendship back on track. A well of emotion threatens tears, and Helen pushes the heels of her hands into her eyes to prevent their release. This is not the time to succumb to her feelings, practicalities have to come first. She needs to get rid of Audrey's body.

Charley isn't surprised to hear from Helen, she had expected her to call and check that everything was okay. She is however, a little surprised when Helen says she will be spending the night at Audrey's. But then, she isn't surprised when she hears that too many glasses of wine have been consumed and Helen is unable to drive home.

Helen is able to move the body by pulling the rug beneath it across the wood floor but that is all she can manage. There is no way she will be able to lift it into her car. She needs help. But who could help her, who would? She will have to pay someone. But who? And she only has a few hours in which to find them and get it done. Audrey's remains have to be gone before Martin gets up. She could pay Martin to do it, she thinks.

"Don't be stupid," she says out loud, to no one but herself.

She knows there is no way Martin will have any part of this. Unless ... of course.

Fifteen

THE ALL TOO FAMILIAR feeling of being hungover greets Martin once again. The dry mouth and nausea are coupled with a headache that is making its presence keenly felt. Daylight offends and the sound of morning affronts and as Martin raises himself up in his bed an ominous sense of foreboding surrounds him. He tries to recall the previous evening; flashes come to him. A disagreement, Ray, Audrey, Helen. He remembers talking to Ray outside - or arguing, he is not sure which. But they probably argued. What did he do? Did he hit him again? Did Audrey see? Nothing is clear to him, except, he is sure he upset Audrey. Did she witness his dispute with Ray? And Helen, she was here too, he thinks. He has to stop this, drink is his downfall. It leaves too many voids. It is hijacking his body and taking it to a place where control and reason are absent. He has to stop this, before someone really gets hurt.

Footsteps overhead wake Helen from a fitful slumber. She stretches her aching limbs; she hasn't slept in a chair since the last few days with Robert. She looks around; although unaccustomed to her surroundings they are not completely alien to her. Her eyes scan the room, stopping at the odd shape laying alongside the coffee table. Helen gasps as her memory refreshes. The odd shape is Audrey who Helen covered with a throw from the sofa. The flush of the upstairs lavatory jolts Helen back to the present. She has to play this right, handle him carefully, for both their sakes. She stands and straightens her crumpled clothes as best she can, then goes out into the hallway. The mirror on the wall reveals how disarranged she looks. Her hair looks like a wild mane and attempts to tame it into something a little tidier are futile. The creak of the stairs draws her eyes from her reflection to Martin's descending frame. He stops half way down.

"Helen?" he says quizzically.

"Morning, Martin."

"I erm, sorry I'm surprised to see you here. Heavy night?" Helen does not respond, well not verbally. Her eyes say plenty and Martin again feels the unease that he woke with. "What is it Helen? What's wrong?"

"You don't remember?" she asks. Martin does no more than offer a timorous shake of the head. "You should sit down."

"Where is Audrey?" he asks.

"There was an argument, last night. You and …"

"Ray." Martin slides down onto the stairs. "What did I do? Is she really mad with me?"

"Who?"

"Audrey."

"It was Audrey you argued with."

"Not Ray?"

"Martin can you recall anything from last night?"

"I think I remember seeing Ray and going out and …"

"When you came back, what do you know of when you came back?"

"I'm not sure. Look, where is she?"

"You were very drunk last night and Audrey wasn't happy about that."

"I guessed that was coming. I'll apologise."

"She challenged you and the two of you argued. She was very angry and you were very drunk and you …"

"I what?" When Helen doesn't answer Martin asks again. "I what Helen? What did I do?"

Helen begins to cry. "You didn't mean to, I know."

"No, no, no." Martin stands and runs at Helen taking her by the shoulders. "Where is she?"

"In there." Helen points at the closed lounge door.

Martin approaches the door, putting his palm on it and slowly pushing it open. Helen stays outside, letting him go into the room alone. He reels a little as his eyes take in the blanket covered body, then kneels down beside it and pulls back the cover. He emits a loud gasp as he takes in the sight before him. Her skin has started to discolour and her eyes are open and so is her mouth. A brown stain sits across her forehead and part of her face. A face that looks quite grotesque. Not the sweet, homely, reassuring face that Martin has become accustomed to and loves. He allows the corner of the blanket to slip from his fingers and he begins to sob. A hand on his shoulder draws him back to his feet. He turns and leans heavily on Helen who allows him to continue his sobbing in her arms.

"I can't believe I did this."

"You didn't mean to."

"I wouldn't hurt her, I couldn't."

"It was a terrible accident Martin. It was not intentional."

"When are they coming?" he asks, freeing himself from Helens arms.

"Who?"

"The police."

"The police aren't coming."

"Who then?"

"No-one."

"What?" He is bewildered.

"No-one is coming. I haven't called or told anyone."

"But she is dead, Helen. She is dead."

"Yes and we can't change that, but your life does not have to be ruined because of an accident."

"I don't understand."

"I know you and I know you did not mean for this to happen. I also know Audrey would not want you to be punished as a result of an unfortunate accident."

"We can't do nothing. We can't just leave her here."

"No you're right. We can't. We need to move her and put her somewhere where she will never be found."

"Helen, you are talking about disposing of a body. That is illegal."

"So is murder. What do you prefer?"

"What about her family and friends? What about the shop?"

"Her family will not miss her, they rarely get in touch. We are her friends. As for the shop, we will tell them she has gone to visit her son."

"I don't know."

"You don't have much choice, unless you are happy for your children to visit you in prison."

"Alright. But how do we do it? I'm not cutting her up. If we are doing this, she stays intact and she is put somewhere nice."

"I know the perfect place."

Sixteen

CHARLEY HAS JUST FINISHED feeding Noah when she hears Helen's car pull onto the drive. She goes into the hallway to greet her and can't help laughing when she sees her, she looks more than a little rough. Helen explains that she has not had the best night's sleep as Audrey's spare room consisted of an old single bed with an extremely lumpy mattress. Charley raises her eyebrows as if to suggest there could be another explanation for her dishevelled appearance. Helen concedes that wine may also have played a part. She goes on to tell Charley that Martin is coming over later to do some more work on the patio and that he will be using some heavy duty digging equipment.

"I thought we could go out. It'll be too loud to concentrate on anything and the noise may upset Noah."

Charley is sure Noah will be fine, he can sleep through anything, but she needs to go out anyway. She has a few bits to pick up and she has a letter to post.

"So how was your evening?" asked Charley once they were in the car.

"It was nice."

"Just nice?"

"You say that as if nice is a bad thing."

"Sorry, I meant did anything interesting happen?"

Helen thinks for a moment before speaking.

"Audrey did have some news to share."

"Oh yeah?"

"Yes, she is going to visit her son in New Zealand."

"When?"

"This week."

"Blimey. That's a bit sudden."

"Not really. She has been talking about it for a while now."

"That shop won't be able to manage without her," laughs Charley.

"She would like to think that."

"Ain't that the truth."

Helen emailed Sheila before she left Audrey's this morning, as Audrey of course. Sheila replied straightaway.

Morning Audrey.

Thanks for letting me know. A little more notice would have been appreciated, but as you are only a volunteer I can't really reprimand you for it. As you are going for an unspecified period of time it may be necessary for us to take on another volunteer to replace you. However, when and if you return I'm sure we will be able to make room for you and avail ourselves of your service once again.

Have a lovely time,

Sheila

"There is something I need to discuss with you," says Helen.

"Okay," says Charley. "Have I done something I shouldn't have?"

"No, of course not. I just wondered how you would feel about having someone stay with us for a while."

"Well it's up to you. It's your house."

"It's your home now and I would like you to be happy about it."

"I suppose it depends who it is."

"Martin. I was going to let Martin come and stay. He doesn't feel that its right for him to stay at Audrey's while she is away."

"That would be fine. I like Martin."

❧

Martin has to move Audrey's body and soon. The longer he leaves it the harder it will be, literally! He doesn't want to look at her let alone touch her. A drink may steady his nerves, but alcohol is what got him into this mess in the first place. Thank God for Helen. If not for her he knows he would be in a cell somewhere with nothing to look forward to besides a long period of imprisonment. Any hope of reconciliation with Jo, any hope of reclaiming his family, any hope of a future would all be gone. However, the task before him is not made any easier by this knowledge.

He has put the car in the garage, which thankfully can be accessed from the kitchen. He decides not to carry her to the kitchen, instead he rolls her onto the rug and drags her along the floor. He has opened the door and the boot of the car, but he will need to lift her from the kitchen floor to the car. He wraps the blanket around her as best he can and lifts her up. She is far heavier than he expected, a 'dead weight', of course. As gently and respectfully as possible Martin places the body in the boot of the car, before going back inside to tidy up. The clean-up doesn't take him too long. Audrey's house has wood flooring throughout the ground floor. The rug is the only thing he is unable to clean; an unsightly stain has spread across it. He decides to get rid of it, so places it in the boot with Audrey.

When he gets to Helen's he is relieved to see that she and Charley and Noah have already gone out. He uses the key fob that Helen gave him to operate the garage door, watching in the rear view mirror as it slowly rises. It seems to take an age. When it has fully opened he slowly backs the car into the garage and presses the button on the key fob once more to close the door. As he watches it close he is thankful now that Helen had him clear out the garage recently. When it is fully closed he gets out of the car and goes to the back door of the garage which goes straight out into Helen's garden.

Martin studies the area that he has been working on, what will eventually be the patio. He has already dug down about 10 inches but he will need to go much further now and he will need to work quickly. He starts up the cement mixer and begins shovelling in the sand and cement and water, preparing the mix he will need later. He keeps the cement mixer switched on while he digs; the rotating drum will prevent the mix from drying out before he is ready to use it. Before long he has excavated an area large enough and deep enough to accommodate Audrey's remains. Martin wheels the wheelbarrow into the garage and places it by the rear of the car. He lifts the body from the boot and lays it unceremoniously across the barrow; an arm escapes from the blanket and dangles at the side. Carefully he lifts the arm and places it across her chest, then takes the rug that he brought from Audrey's house from the boot and completely covers her body with it. Thankfully Helen's garden is not overlooked so he does not have to concern himself with nosey neighbours. He wheels the barrow outside. When he reaches the hole he realises that the only way he will get Audrey into her grave is to tip her out of the wheelbarrow. He shakes his head; it is such an undignified end for a lady who showed him nothing but kindness. He raises the handles of the barrow and lets her fall. A dull, heavy thud is followed by a crack that sickens him. He tilts the drum of the cement mixer over the hole and watches as the grey gunk slides out covering Audrey entirely. As the remainder of the mixture drips from the machine, Martin's eyes mirror the scene as his tears fall.

Seventeen

LIZZIE PAYS FOR HER PURCHASES then walks away from the counter. She is still trying to put away her purse when she hears the voice. She turns and looks into the faces of the people nearby; the speaker is not one of them, but Lizzie is sure she heard her. She walks toward the escalator, but on the way her eyes are drawn to pair of striking looking boots. She stops to admire them, surprised she missed them first time round. She picks one of the boots up, the leather is incredibly soft. She has to at least try these on, she knows she will regret it if she doesn't. Lizzie scans the shop floor looking for a sales assistant. She doesn't see one, but she does see her. So, she had not imagined hearing her voice. She watches Charley, who is looking at a coat, a black coat. Lizzie isn't surprised, Charley will wear anything as long as it's black. She continues watching her, losing sight of her briefly as she walks slowly between rails that are piled high with sale items. When Charley re-emerges from the corridor of clothes, Lizzie breathes in sharply. She had forgotten there was a baby. She takes a couple of steps forward, daring herself to approach her daughter but an advancing voice halts her progress.

Helen puts her shopping bags in the basket beneath Noah's pushchair. Lizzie wishes she were closer, for the two women seem to be having a conversation that is amusing them both. Charley laughs out loud, then she and Helen move off, with Helen now pushing the pushchair. It is this that irritates Lizzie, despite actually forgetting that there was a baby until a few seconds ago. Is it jealousy or curiosity she is feeling? Whichever, she has a few seconds to decide whether to approach Charley and if she does, what then? There is unlikely to be an emotional reconciliation in the middle of a department store. And what of Helen? She has made it very clear that Lizzie is not to contact Charley ever. That is why she paid her, to stay away. But that was then, and she got the money so what is there to stop her? She hasn't signed anything this time so it's not like she would have to pay the money back. Which she couldn't do anyway as most of it has gone. And there it is, the answer. She won't approach Charley, not yet. She will wait to see if there is more money to be extracted from this situation first. And she really needs to try the boots on.

❧

After several days Lizzie's vigil pays off. She has been able to establish Charley's routine, which is anything but routine really. The only outings she undertakes with any regularity are when she goes to college. She attends college twice a week, on Tuesdays and Fridays. Although on a Friday she spends differing periods of time there, and because of this Lizzie decides that Tuesday will be the best day for her to pursue her plan.

❧

Helen is holding Noah and waving from the lounge window. Charley blows a kiss to them before walking to the bus stop. Tuesday mornings are always hard for Charley, initially at least.

She hates leaving Noah, although she knows he is in good hands. By mid-morning she will be fine. She will be absorbed in her latest project at college and for a few hours she may even forget that she is a young mum. She pulls her new coat tightly around her, glad that Helen had insisted on buying it for her as the weather has finally changed. A squally wind whips along the road dragging her hair across her face. She lowers her head and walks quicker, looking forward to the warmth of the usually overheated bus.

Once Charley is no longer visible Helen carries Noah into the kitchen to get his bottle. She takes it from the bottle warmer and goes back into the lounge where she sits and begins feeding him. She loves Tuesdays, the entire day is just her and Noah. Occasionally Martin may be around but he pays them no mind. No, Tuesday is her favourite day, devoted totally to 'the little fella' as Martin calls him. Helen hopes the wind dies down so they can go for a walk later.

Lizzie positions herself near the college, far enough away so as not to be spotted, but close enough to be able to see who goes in. She wants to be certain that Charley is at college today. It's a blustery day and Lizzie is finding it hard to stand still as she is buffeted by the wind. She is just beginning to wonder if Charley is coming today when she sees her. She watches her go up the steps and enter the building. Satisfied that this is where Charley will be for the rest of the day Lizzie leaves her observation post.

Following his feed, Noah falls asleep in Helen's arms. She sits with him in silence for several minutes, marvelling at him. She would happily sit like this all day but knows it is best to lay him down. Carefully she rises up from the chair and takes him upstairs, placing him in his cot and gently pulling his blanket over him.

She switches on the baby monitor before going back downstairs. Helen flicks the switch on the kettle before starting to clear away the breakfast things. She is washing up the few things that won't go in the dishwasher when she hears a knock on the front door. The interruption irritates her. Helen roughly pulls her gloves off, the rubber snapping as they leave her hands and she tosses them onto the counter top.

"Morning," says Lizzie.

"What the hell do you want?" asks Helen.

"That's not a nice welcome, I must say."

"That is because you are not welcome." Helen tries to close the door but Lizzie is one step ahead of her and roughly pushes it open before stepping inside.

"You and me have unfinished business."

"No we don't. I paid you and you agreed to stay away, for good."

"Well, I've changed my mind."

"Then you can give me back the money."

"No can do."

"We had a deal."

"So sue me," laughs Lizzie.

"What is it you want?"

"I want to see my girl and her baby. That's what I want."

Helen is unconvinced, but decides to call her bluff.

"Fine, I'll tell Charley you were here and get her to call you. Then you can arrange it with her, assuming she wants to see you of course."

This is not the response Lizzie expected, she was sure Helen would simply say 'how much'.

"No. I think I will wait right here for her to come back from college."

"What makes you think she is at college?"

"I err … guess that's where she is."

"She could be upstairs for all you know."

"I don't hear her."

"You know exactly where she is, and how is that I wonder?"

"Lucky guess," says Lizzie.

"I don't think so. You have been watching her, haven't you?"

Lizzie offers no protestation, she can't. She has been caught out. Helen studies her, trying to gauge what is in her head. She knows she hasn't come to see Charley. She has not asked about Noah and she said we had unfinished business. Helen gets it. Lizzie has come to see her, she wants more money.

"How much?" asks Helen.

"Same as before. I ain't greedy. Although, I think I'd like it every few months, regular like."

"Really? But you're not greedy. We have to have a proper agreement this time, a legal one."

"No way. I don't want to see that tosser again."

Helen smiles, well aware Lizzie is talking about Anthony.

"Well that's how it has to be. You can sign a contract and I will transfer the money into your bank account."

"No. No contract and no bank. You can take me to the cash point like before. We can go now for today's money and I'll come back in a few months for the next payment and so on."

Helen's patience is wearing thin and she is about to tell Lizzie this but the sound of Noah waking prevents her. The two women stare at each other as Noah's cry fills the hallway. Lizzie is the first to divert her gaze, her eyes following the sound up the stairs. Helen swiftly moves across the hallway so she is standing between Lizzie and the staircase.

"You're not going to let me see my grandchild?" asks Lizzie.

"You need to leave," replies Helen.

"I don't think so, not without my money."

"I am not giving you money without a contract."

"It's either money or the baby," threatens Lizzie.

"Get out, before I call the police," threatens Helen.

"The police. Now that's a good idea. I reckon I have a greater claim on that baby than you do. I'm its grandmother after all."

"It! He is not an 'it'."

"He, so I have a grandson." Lizzie takes her phone from her pocket and waves it at Helen. "I am going to call the police and tell them you have kidnapped my grandson."

Helen lunges at Lizzie snatching the phone from her. Lizzie tries to get it back and the two women end up on the floor. Lizzie is sitting on Helen trying to prise her phone from Helen's clenched hand. Their struggle is punctuated by Noah's cries, which gives Lizzie another idea. She punches Helen, stunning her for a second, then gets off her and runs up the stairs. Helen, realising Lizzie's intentions, launches herself up the stairs too. She grasps Lizzie's ankle and pulls sharply. Lizzie falls forward, her face taking a direct hit. Helen drags her down until once again they are both at the bottom of the stairs. Helen manages to stand and walks towards the front door. Lizzie manages to get herself on all fours before sitting back on her haunches. This hasn't gone well. She looks up at Helen ready to concede defeat, but everything goes black.

Robert's grandmother's old iron. Cast iron, very heavy, served no real purpose other than as a doorstop on very hot days. Until now that is. Now it's perfect for removing Lizzie from Helen's life for good. It's so heavy Helen can only manage one swing, but that's all it needs. Lizzie's lifeless body lies at the foot of the stairs. Her smashed face etched with her final expression; a look of horror as she grasps Helen's objective. This one is a mess, but worth it thinks

Helen. Her satisfaction is short-lived though, once she realises that Noah is still crying.

Helen settles Noah before beginning the grisly task of moving Lizzie. She manages to get the body as far as the utility room, but it is abundantly clear that she is not going to be able to get her outside. And then what would she do with her anyway? Bury her? Dismember her? Helen does not have the strength to dig a hole or the stomach to cut her up. Help is required and the only person who can deliver such help is Martin. He should be easy to persuade, after all he still thinks he is indebted to her. Although this time will be different as there is no way she can convince him that this one is his fault. Helen sighs heavily; this will bring their relationship back on an equal footing which she doesn't really want. She likes having the upper hand, an element of control. Taking charge and asserting authority are her strengths, but her options are limited - in fact she has no options. Martin is the only one who can help her and the price for his help will be the relinquishing of her power over him.

While she waits for him to return from work Helen begins the unenviable task of cleaning the hallway. When the worst of it is done Helen mops over the floors, following the slimy, blood smears that were created when she dragged the body through the house. She also washes down a wall that has been dappled by blood spatter. She is sure everywhere is clean, but scrutinizes it anyway. Good job she does for on the console table alongside today's post is the iron. Helen picks it up and notices the corner has something stuck to it. Closer inspection tells her it is a small piece of Lizzie. She takes it into the utility room and holds it under the tap, the running water changing to a pinky hue as it washes the hair, skin and blood down the drain. Once it is clean Helen places it back in its regular spot near the front door.

Reluctantly Martin begins digging. Despite the recent rain the ground is still quite hard and why wouldn't it be, the seasons are changing. He knows Helen will have a few jobs for him to do, she always does, but grave digging is not what he expected to be doing today. He was shocked when Helen had relayed the day's events to him. He knows the bond between Helen, and Charley and the little fella is strong so he kind of understands; but what has shaken him is that Helen is capable of such violence, that she is not so different from him.

Eighteen

CHARLEY TURNS THE ENVELOPE OVER and over in her hands; she knows it is from him. She recognises the handwriting and the Woking postmark confirms it. She is pleased that he has bothered to write to her, but she is anxious about what the letter may say, which is why she didn't open it straight away. And she does not want anyone around when she reads it. She has never discussed Noah's father with Helen or anyone else, and Helen has never asked about him either, but has often stressed that Noah has all he needs with her and Charley. She may well be right, thinks Charley. Noah may not need his father, but he has a right to grow up knowing who he is. Not knowing your parentage sucks and it was this reason that made Charley write to Jack.

Tentatively she opens the envelope and pulls out the letter. There are several sheets of paper, more than she expected as she doesn't have him down as much of a writer. It begins angrily: he had heard about the baby, but assumed it had nothing to do with him. His actual words are:

'How could you keep something this fucking important from me? And why wait until now when I'm in the middle of my pissing training to tell me? WTF?'

After a couple of pages the ranting subsides and a gentler tone emerges. He is sorry her mum has thrown her out: 'I know all *about the hassle that families bring with them.'*

He empathises with her but he is a little disconcerted by her new living arrangements.

'You could be living with a fucking psycho for all you know.'

He explains that he isn't due anymore leave until Christmas, but suggests they get together then. The letter ends on a better note than it started with:

'I don't know how I feel about all this or you to be honest, but I won't let you deal with it by yourself.'

Charley puts the letter in the drawer of her bedside cabinet. He says he will get in touch with her when he comes home, so now she has to wait.

❦

Martin has been looking forward to this lunch with Amy for a while. His daughter is growing into a beautiful young lady and he is proud to be seen with her, but now he just wants her to go. The news she has just shared with him is devastating, for him anyway. For Amy it is joyful and exciting, and her own excitement makes her oblivious to the distress she is causing her father.

"I have never been a bridesmaid," gushes Amy. "I don't even think I've been to a wedding before."

"You have," says Martin. "But you were a baby."

"I can't remember that, so it doesn't count. I hope Mum doesn't pick some hideous colour for my dress."

"Well, make sure you tell her that," says Martin, desperately trying to hide his despair.

"I have, don't worry about that. Now let me tell you the other news."

"There's more?"

"Yes Dad. I told you I had two things to tell you."

"Okay, go ahead sweetheart. Tell me." Martin knows whatever else Amy has to say will not be nearly as depressing as the news that Ray and Joanne are going to get married.

He is wrong.

Helen pulls on her old fleece jacket and goes outside for a cigarette. She has started smoking again recently, not a lot, two, sometimes three a day. It is a guilty pleasure which she goes outside to indulge as she knows it isn't good for Noah. And she does not want to listen to the inevitable criticism and bemoaning of smokers that Charley and Martin feel the need to share with her. She wipes the garden bench with an old towel and sits down, surveying her surroundings. The garden is looking good, regardless of the bleakness that the winter season encourages. The changes she has made, with Martin's help, are definite improvements. The extension to the patio is her favourite addition. It isn't quite finished, but when it is, it will run across the entire width of the house, bringing the outside in or the inside out, depending how you look at it.

The door opens behind her and Charley comes out. Helen tries to extinguish her cigarette.

"Don't bother. I know what you're doing," says Charley as she sits down next to Helen. Helen smiles and has a last drag before stubbing it out properly. "I wondered if you would mind if I pop out later."

"Of course not. Going somewhere nice?"

"For a pizza and then a few drinks in town, as it's end of term."

"Do you need a lift?"

"I can probably get a lift."

"Does he have a name?"

"*She* is called Emma. It really is a few of us from college, nothing more."

"Okay. Did you get your letter?"

Charley hesitates before answering. She is unsure whether to reveal that the letter is from Noah's father. She is well aware how attached to Noah Helen has become; maybe too attached. Yet the support and unwavering kindness has prevented Charley from becoming overwhelmed by her situation. Helen's steadfast devotion is what you usually expect from your mother, not a stranger. And although given unconditionally, with no demands for explanations about her life before they met, Charley feels now is the time for honesty and transparency.

"Yes I did. It was from Noah's dad."

"Aah."

"I'm going to let him see Noah."

"I'm not sure that's wise," cautions Helen. "He hasn't been interested thus far."

"That is because he didn't know of his existence until I wrote to him."

"I take it he isn't local then?"

"He is. But he's erm, well he is away at the moment, he will be back around Christmas time."

"I see. Well let's just wait and see what happens then," says Helen through pursed lips.

❧

Helen is not happy. Once Noah is settled she goes downstairs and pours herself a large glass of red. She keeps going over her conversation with Charley about Noah's father. Charley didn't offer much, but what she did say has led Helen to believe that he is an unsavoury type. The few details revealed have led Helen to assume that he is most likely in prison, due for release around Christmas. She pours a second glass and ponders more about this unknown entity who she already dislikes intensely. He might be violent or dishonest, or both. He could be a pervert or drug addict, or both. She pours a third. He may be many things but what he won't be is part of this family, she'll make sure of that.

Martin is freezing by the time he returns home. He has been walking the streets all afternoon, trying to process what Amy has told him. Helen hears him come in and calls out for him to join her in the kitchen. He would rather just go to bed, but he does as he is told. When they see each other they both know the other is troubled and simultaneously ask what is wrong.

"You first," says Martin.

Helen tells him about Charley's letter and relays her concern that Noah's father is a convict.

"You might be right, but he is still the boy's father," stresses Martin.

"An ejaculation doesn't make you a father," spits Helen.

Martin can see she is upset so decides against contradicting her further. A brief silence stalls the conversation before Helen asks Martin what is bothering him. He tries to speak without displaying emotion, but it is hard and his voice falters as he tells her Joanne is marrying Ray and she is having his baby. Helen puts down her glass and puts her arms around him, allowing one hand to gently rub his back. He leans into her and wraps his arms around her too. They stay like that for a moment, comforting one another before both letting go. Martin is surprised to see tears on Helen's cheek and he wipes them away with his thumb. Helen takes his hand and lightly kisses it before placing his thumb in her mouth and sucking it. His surprise is soon replaced by desire, especially when her other hand moves lower.

When they are both spent Helen declares that she needs a cigarette and goes outside.

Martin is confounded by what has just happened. Helen is several years older than him and he has never had longing or lustful thoughts about her. But what just happened was amazing, probably because it has been a while. Of late the only sex he has experienced is with himself, accompanied by Joanne's photograph or a top shelf magazine. He cleans himself up and goes outside to join her.

"Do you have one to spare?" asks Martin pointing at the cigarette packet.

"Help yourself."

"Thanks."

"What for?"

"This," replies Martin, waving the cigarette. He looks at her and realises she is smirking at him. "Yes, thanks for that too," he says nodding his head back towards the kitchen worktop.

"My pleasure."

"Yes it was," he says laughing. "Mine too," he adds.

"This patio looks good."

"Are you trying to change the subject?" he asks.

"No, not at all. I genuinely think it looks good."

"It will do when it's finished."

Helen stands up and walks along the patio, stopping at the unfinished end, which at present is a hole and a mound of earth. She bends down and runs her hand over the earth, scooping up a handful as she does.

"I'm not happy about Noah seeing his father," she says.

"I know Helen, but just wait and see what happens. It may all work out fine."

"And if it doesn't," she pauses for a second before continuing, allowing the dirt in her hand to slowly slide through her fingers and into the hole, "I'm sure we can find room for one more …"

Nineteen

OPPORTUNISTIC SEX. Exciting and gratifying, yes. But it lacks something, for Helen anyway. She and Martin have now had several liaisons. Always spontaneous and urgent, fulfilling a need in that moment. Like scratching an itch really. But now the physicality of the act needs balance; it needs tenderness. The two of them have shared so much, but their shared experiences are steeped in violence and anger. The anger has been living alongside them, fuelling their encounters and controlling their emotions. But no more. It is no longer enough for her to have animalistic sex up against the kitchen worktop. She wants the intimacy and gentleness that has vacated her life to return. And she knows it is time. No longer does she feel empty or bereft by Robert's absence and she certainly feels no guilt now that she has given herself to Martin. The grieving has stopped, both for Robert and her marriage. A red-letter day ...

Martin is worried that Helen is looking to make more of recent events. He has heard her refer to Charley, Noah and himself as family. He has a family. A family that he still dreams of being reunited with. Although he is grateful to Helen for her help he no longer feels beholden to her; after all they are the same. Neither has leverage to use against the other and both have a lot to lose. But she is beginning to frighten him a little; 'room for one more', that's what she said. She was talking about Noah's father this time, but if Martin doesn't play by her rules, could he be next? This thought has crossed his mind on more than one occasion. And what about her husband? What really happened to him? Martin thinks it is time to find out more about his partner in crime.

❧

The approaching yuletide season is making Charley feel melancholic. It was always her favourite time of the year; the colours, sounds and smells that accompanied advent would thrill her. Her thoughts travel back to her schooldays. The last couple of weeks of the school term would be spent singing carols and making paper chains and Christmas cards. The school itself would be more colourful and shiny as it sparkled with decorations and lights, and the excess glitter that lay on floors and desks would twinkle like fairy dust. Her Christmases were not about over-filled stockings or over-stuffed bellies. For her there was no anticipatory delight on Christmas Eve as she waited for Father Christmas; she had been told early on that he was not real so she should not expect a sackful of toys. But still it was magical and at home things were different. Her mum had no 'work' over Christmas, so there were at least two days that did not see Charley banished to her bedroom. She would sit with her mum watching television while dipping into the tin of Quality Street that sat on the coffee table. Sometimes she would be on the floor quietly colouring in festive images in her new colouring book. Mum might even play snap or a board game with her, as long as it wasn't one of those games that went on for hours as Mum bored easily. A sad smile briefly crept onto her face as she recalled those days. She knew her nostalgic mood was brought about by motherhood. It was also reminding her that she did have a mother, who despite all that had passed between them did mean something to her. In her head Charley conceded that her mum's lifestyle was not brought about by choice, it was necessity. Who knows? If Charley had not been blessed with meeting Helen maybe she would have been forced to make some unpalatable choices. This more charitable view of her mother has led Charley to decide it's time to visit her. After all, it is the season of goodwill.

Twenty

DISCONSOLATELY, CHARLEY WALKS AWAY from the landlord's office. She can't believe her mum has gone. The landlord told her she just disappeared.

"Went round to collect the rent, which was overdue, and she wasn't there. Went back a couple of times but she was never in and neighbours said they hadn't seen or heard her. They would've heard her as she wasn't a quiet one. Eventually had to assume she had done a bunk. Just surprised me that she left everything."

"What did you do with her stuff?" Charley asked.

"Got rid. Well most of it. There's a couple of boxes of stuff, personal bits like. You can have them, be glad to be shot of them really."

"I'll have to come back for them. I won't be able to manage them on the bus."

"That's fine. I gotta get them from my lock-up anyway. Come back in a couple of days, but there's not a lot worth anything and just so you know her deposit is gone. Forfeited, as she broke her tenancy agreement by not giving me notice."

"Fair enough."

Charley is surprised at how disappointed she is not to have seen her mum. But as she left no forwarding address there is nothing Charley can do to ease the disappointment. She sees the bus approaching and sticks out her arm. The bus stops and its doors open; she moves to step onto the bus, then hesitates.

"Come on luv, ain't got all day," says the driver.

"Sorry," says Charley as she turns the pushchair around and heads back the way she came. Charley can't believe she didn't think of it before - she'll go and see Maureen. Maureen will know where Mum is, Charley says to herself.

"Blimey. What brings you round here?" Maureen asks.

"Hello Maureen. I'm looking for Mum," Charley answers.

"Aren't we all? You'd better come in."

Maureen holds open the door and watches as Charley awkwardly manoeuvres the pushchair into the hallway. The narrow passage is made narrower by a couple of bicycles and a large parcel.

"Probably easier if you leave your buggy here, doubt you'll get it up my stairs. It'll be perfectly safe," adds Maureen who spots the look of unease on Charley's face. "We're all honest people in this house."

Charley lifts a sleeping Noah from his warm cocoon. His initial protests subside by the time they have reached the top of the stairs and when she is seated in Maureen's lounge he is fast asleep once more. The room is dominated by the stench of stale tobacco, which is extremely unpleasant, so Charley listens carefully to what Maureen has to say as she does not want to stay here longer than necessary. She is sure the air in this unventilated room is not good for either her or Noah.

"Yeah, let us all down has your mum. She owes me a fair bit of money too. I wasn't worried though, not right away; after all, she has always been good for it before, always paid her dues. But it is a considerable amount for me you know." Maureen pauses to allow Charley to make some comment or at the very least ask how much money is involved. Charley says nothing; she neither wants to know nor does she care about Maureen's financial issues. She just wants answers regarding her mum's whereabouts, but it is obvious that Maureen is no wiser than she is on that count. Maureen continues speaking once she realises that Charley has nothing to offer; neither words nor money.

"Yep, she promised me. She actually said that she was coming into some money, quite a bit by the sounds of it. We even started planning a holiday. She was going to treat me on account of how I had always helped her out. I sent off for my passport which set me back £74.50, waste of money that was. So I'm well out of pocket and no holiday to look forward to."

"So you have no idea where she might have gone?" Charley needed Maureen to clarify this for her.

"Nope. At first I did think something may have happened to her, but … well if that had been the case they would've found her by now. She's done a bunk, plain and simple."

Charley thanks Maureen and leaves. She is puzzled though. She can't imagine her mum going off on her own. Perhaps she met someone. But surely she would have told Maureen, unless she didn't want to or couldn't pay her back.

Twenty-One

TODAY IS THE PERFECT DAY for Martin to continue his search. He has dropped Helen at the train station as she is going to meet her former assistant. She will let him know when to pick her up but warned him it could be quite late as they might take in a show. So he has all day to go through the house. Charley is out too although he is unsure what time she will be back. Still, that doesn't matter, he can easily convince Charley that whatever he is doing is at Helen's behest. Not that Charley pays a lot of attention to what is going on in the house, and she has been rather distracted of late. Martin reckons this is due to the possibility of meeting up with Noah's father.

His initial snooping has already told Martin that there was nothing unnatural about Robert's death, albeit untimely. Despite learning this his growing sense of unease has not lessened. Statements and documents that he read through were all straight forward and revealed nothing more than the fact that Helen is indeed an incredibly wealthy woman. He moves upstairs to continue his search. In her dressing room in the foot of a cupboard he finds a small safe and another document box. The safe is bolted to the floor, and requires a key and a code to open it. The document box, though locked, is not attached to the floor so Martin carefully lifts it from the cupboard. He fiddles with the lock for a few seconds before placing it on a chair. He systematically begins searching through drawers in the hope of locating the key that will open it. When he has exhausted every possibility in the dressing room he moves into Helen's bedroom, taking time to ensure he does not overlook any place where a key could be hidden. After a futile search of the bedroom Martin goes back into the dressing room and replaces the document box back where he found it. He assumes the key to both the safe and the box are probably with Helen. If the opportunity arises he may have to search through her handbag.

Martin heads down to the kitchen taking the stairs two at a time. He puts the kettle on to make a coffee and while he waits for it to boil he considers where else he should look. He has already been through all the downstairs rooms, except the kitchen. He doesn't think the kitchen has much to reveal, as they all have access to the kitchen and its contents at all times. It certainly doesn't seem like a logical place to conceal something, but while he is here he may as well have a look. The cupboards are home to nothing but crockery, glasses, and other assorted tableware. The food cupboard is just that – a food cupboard. The drawers prove to be a little more interesting, housing an array of strange and sometimes unidentifiable objects. The dresser drawers contain assorted chargers and wires, many of which are tangled together, a bag of coins, picture hooks, small screwdrivers and some keys. Martin takes the keys from the drawer and studies them. He has seen these keys before; Helen had asked him to look out for what they might open. He puts them back into the drawer; if Helen doesn't know what they are for, it is unlikely these keys are concealing anything of any importance. He makes his coffee and considers what to do next. The only place left to search is the attic. He is not convinced that he will find anything up there either as it isn't a place that Helen ventures into, but it is the only place in the house which he has yet to search.

❧

Charley is relieved to be back home. It has been a long walk. Noah's pushchair is so laden with carrier bags that it would have been impossible to lift it onto the bus. The bags are full of the things that her mum had left in the flat. She could have asked Helen or Martin to take her to collect them, but she didn't want to explain about her mum or answer any awkward questions - and there would have been questions. Helen is out all day and Martin won't notice or care what she is doing so Charley can go through her mum's things without interference or prying eyes.

❧

The attic is a treasure trove of miscellaneous items. A genuine Aladdin's cave. There are the usual seasonal items like luggage and the Christmas decorations. And boxes containing an assortment of junk as well as an array of objects that to Martin would not look out of place in an antique shop. Not a second-hand shop, a genuine bonafide antique shop. There are enough paintings to fill an art gallery. Martin looks through them and discovers they are all by the same person; they have been initialled R.J.H. Maybe Helen's husband did them, thinks Martin. So maybe they are not worth a huge amount, but some of the other stuff is sure to be worth something. Tucked into the corner of the attic are smaller boxes and bags. They are draped with thick cobwebs, strands and strands of them, evidence that they've been sitting in the same spot, untouched for many years. Using the already dusty sleeve of his jumper Martin swipes his arm across the silvery fibres that hang like greying tresses from the joists and rafters. He pulls the boxes from the corner and starts looking through them. They contain nothing of interest so he pushes them back. As he does, he spots an old briefcase lurking in the shadowy alcove. He pulls it toward himself. A layer of dust lays heavy on it. Martin shakes it and blows at it causing the dust particles to flutter and dance in front of him like a swarm of tiny flies. He coughs and sneezes as some of the ash-like molecules end up in his mouth and nose. The briefcase definitely contains something, its weight tells Martin this. But it is locked. Martin looks closer at it and wonders.

In his haste Martin almost runs into Charley at the top of the stairs.

"Sorry," he mutters. "I didn't realise you were back."

"It's okay. More sorting out for her Ladyship?" Charley asks, pointing at the loft ladder and open hatch.

"Yes, she's a hard taskmaster," laughs Martin. "Where's the little fella?"

"He's asleep."

"I'll try not to make too much noise up there then," says Martin pointing upwards with his thumb.

"Don't worry. He would sleep through an earthquake."

"My son was like that," laughs Martin.

In the kitchen he opens the dresser drawer and removes the keys that he had earlier. He smiles to himself and heads back up to the attic.

❧

Charley is surprised by some of the items in her mum's belongings. She never had her down as sentimental, but clearly she was. A large envelope contains some of the cards and notes that Charley had given her over the years. Many of them handmade when Charley was quite young. There are also some drawings. A small ashtray that Charley had made in pottery class is there too. Charley recalls giving it to her mum and her mum's response:

'That is too good for cigarette ash. I'll keep it on my dressing table and use it for my earrings.'

The rest of the stuff isn't particularly interesting although Charley is surprised her mum hasn't taken some of the things with her, like her make-up and toiletries. There is also a small painting that Charley doesn't recall ever seeing before; it's not one of hers. It is quite good, and in the bottom right hand corner are the initials R.J.H. She tosses it to one side and carries on looking through the rest of the things. There are some letters and papers which she flicks through. Amongst them is a small brown envelope with something hard inside, like a small book. Charley tips it up and is surprised when a passport falls into her lap. She opens it at the photo page and is astonished to see her mum's facing staring up at her.

❧

He knew the key was going to fit even before he got back to the attic; what he didn't know was what the briefcase would reveal. A slew of letters detailing tragedy and heartbreak, making for difficult reading. They lay bare the despair and sadness of a family. A sadness that may well have been the result of one person's heinous actions.

Twenty-Two

HELEN ENJOYED HER DAY OUT. It was lovely to catch up with Marilyn even though she did insist on bringing Helen up to date on the comings and goings of the office. Helen is not a part of that world and surprisingly does not miss it, but she likes Marilyn so feigned interest. However, despite having had a lovely time she is beginning to regret her jaunt as she is sure something has occurred in her absence. She senses tension in the house, a palpable tension that grows daily. When Martin picked her up from the station he seemed rather tense and was not very talkative. Helen initially put this down to the late hour but now she's not so sure, he is preoccupied by something. Helen has tried asking. She gently touched him and enquired if he was alright but he flinched violently as if alarmed by her touch. And Charley's mood is no better; she is distant and distracted. Helen is sure Charley's problem is Noah's father and decides to broach the subject today. Martin is working then apparently meeting up with an old army buddy, so he will be out all day.

"Morning," says Helen as Charley walks into the kitchen. "Coffee?"

"Nah, I'm good. I'm off out in a bit, just getting some bits for Noah."

"Going anywhere nice?"

"Not especially. I have some things to pick up, that's all."

"Give me 20 minutes and I'll come with you. We could have lunch out," says Helen.

"Don't worry yourself. We'll do lunch another day."

Helen is struck dumb at how easily Charley dismisses her offer. It is clear that whatever she is doing she does not want Helen to be a part of it. "Are you meeting him?"

"Who?"

"Noah's Father."

"No."

"So why so secretive?"

"I'm not being secretive. I told you I have things to do–"

"But I can't come with you," interrupted Helen.

"Look I'm going to see Mum. Well, some of her friends, Mum seems to have gone missing."

Once more Helen is struck dumb. "Do you think it's a good idea taking Noah to see your Mum's friends?" sniffed Helen. "I'm sure they don't inhabit a very child-friendly environment."

"What do you know of Mum's friends?"

"What?" said Helen nervously, realising her mistake.

"You know nothing of my mum or her friends or anything," shouts Charley.

"My opinion is only based on what you have told me."

Charley is sure she has told Helen nothing about her mum, other than she was a single parent who was unhappy when Charley became pregnant. "Your opinion is based purely on the fact that mum was a single parent. You are a snob, Helen. I know Mum was … I know she wasn't …" Charley struggles to find the words. "She is still my mum."

"Okay, but why don't you leave Noah here with me. And not

because I think you are meeting unsavoury types, but because you may find it easier and quicker without him."

Charley considers Helen's offer. It makes sense, as she will be less encumbered without Noah and it will also appease Helen if she leaves him with her. "Alright. I doubt I'll be long. I'm probably wasting my time, I reckon she is miles away."

"She is closer than you think," mutters Helen under her breath as Charley walks out of the kitchen.

❧

Martin is not meeting an old army buddy, as he had told Helen. He is not working either. Today he is on a train, Oxford bound, 'the City of Dreaming Spires'. He is meeting someone who he hopes will shed some light on the letters and papers that he discovered in the attic. As the train pulls into the station Martin takes a piece of paper from his jacket pocket, reads the hastily written directions and pops the paper back into his pocket. It takes little over ten minutes for Martin to reach the Ashmolean Museum, an impressive building with a stunning neoclassical façade. There are several people milling about including some standing in front of the building posing for photographs. They are obscuring Martin's view and so he struggles to spot the benches at the front of the museum. When he finally sees them he notices that one is occupied by a young couple looking at their phones and a man who keeps giving a surreptitious glance at his watch. A man who looks like he is waiting for someone. Martin is sure it is him.

"Mr. Blackmore?" enquires Martin of the gentleman on the bench.

"Yes."

Martin offers his hand. Following a brief handshake the

gentleman suggests they move somewhere warmer. "And call me Patrick, please, lest I'll think you are one of my students."

"You are a teacher?"

"Professor."

The two men go into the museum and head towards the cafeteria. It isn't busy but Patrick leads the two of them to a table in the corner. "Now Mr. erm …"

"Martin."

"Martin. What can I do for you? Your message was a little vague."

"I want to ask you about Helen."

"Did Robert send you?"

"No. I'm afraid to say Robert is dead."

"Oh dear. I'm sorry to hear that. Are you the police?"

"No I'm not. Why would you think …"

"Sorry. You said Robert was dead and I assumed …"

"Cancer. He died from natural causes."

Patrick issues what is quite obviously a sigh of relief before speaking. "So what is it I can help you with?"

"Like I said I would like to know about Helen."

"And why are you interested in my sister?"

Martin explains how he knows Helen (without revealing their macabre connection), that he has been doing some work for her since Robert died. "This and that: decorating, gardening, house clearance." He goes on to say that he discovered some papers in the attic.

"Which you just had to read," interjected Patrick.

"There were some letters from you to Robert. Rather disconcerting letters."

"What do you want, Martin? Is this about money? Because if it is you should be talking to Helen, not me. She is the one with the money."

"It is not about money. I just need to know more about her …"

"Because?"

"Because she is … sometimes she is a bit intimidating and …"

"So you are here because my sister frightens you." Patrick laughs. "Martin, she frightens everybody."

"I'm not frightened, I'm concerned. More for Charley and the little fella than myself."

"Little fella?"

Martin tells Patrick about Charley and baby Noah and watches as Patrick's irritated expression is replaced by one of horror.

☯

Lizzie's 'friends' are no wiser than Charley regarding her mum's disappearance. But none of them were surprised by it. They all told tales of her coming into some money, although none knew where this money was supposedly coming from. The assumption was that it could be one of her regulars.

"I reckon it was that solicitor bloke. He probably paid extra as he was a bit weird, you know."

Charley didn't know and didn't want to know but she did wonder who the solicitor might be. "Do you know his name?"

"No, but I know where his office is. Saw Lizzie go in there a few times. It's in town, on Duke Street opposite the bank."

The bus stops on Duke Street directly outside the bank. Charley gets off the bus and as it pulls away the building opposite is revealed to her. 'Villiers and Villiers Solicitors'. She crosses the street and goes inside. A wide entrance hall leads into a large room with thick plush carpets and oversized leather chairs. There are two doors at the rear of the room and in front of them is a desk occupied by a petite woman of advancing years. Charley approaches her and asks to see Mr. Villiers.

"Do you have an appointment dear?"

"No I don't, but I'm happy to wait."

"He and his secretary have just popped out for some lunch. You are welcome to wait but I can't guarantee he will see you without an appointment, he is a very busy man you know."

"That's fine." Charley sits in one of the large chairs, sinking into it as she does. She is relieved and surprised that the receptionist didn't ask her which Mr. Villiers she wanted. While she waits Charley scans the office, taking in all the detail. Her eye is drawn to a painting that hangs on one of the walls. It is quite distinctive. The paint has been applied in thick layers and there are visible brush strokes across the layers. Charley thinks this style of painting is called Impasto, a technique that adds light and expression. She stands up to take a closer look at it and immediately notices the initials in the corner, R.J.H.

"It's a wonderful picture, isn't it?" says the lady behind the desk.

"Yes, it is," agrees Charley.

"He was a lovely man, the artist. Just an amateur though."

"You knew him."

"Oh yes. He was one of Mr. Villiers' oldest friends. Sadly no longer with us. Dear Robert."

Martin takes his seat on the train. He tips his head back and closes his eyes, but he cannot sleep. Patrick's words are keeping him awake.

'Helen and I were very close as children, even though I am three years older than her. I was never allowed to go far from the house due

to my epilepsy. I don't have convulsive seizures, more like blackouts, but on one occasion my friends abandoned me when I had one of my attacks. After that my mother would not let me venture very far so friends stopped calling for me. Once she was old enough Helen became my playmate, we spent hours together and she soon learnt to tell when I was unwell. I was a very clumsy child too, something that could be attributed to my illness and on occasion I was responsible for breakages. Helen would repair or conceal these incidences for me or if she was unable to do either she herself would take the blame. As I got older my blackouts were less frequent but more severe, and sometimes I would suffer mood swings and memory loss alongside them. During one such episode our pet rabbit died. Helen took charge and buried the rabbit and then told our parents that she must have left the hutch open and the rabbit had escaped or been taken by a fox. I was so very grateful to her for this. So you see, she took good care of me. Sometime later, I think I was maybe 13 or 14, there was an addition to our family, a baby sister. She was adored by us all, especially Helen, although her attention towards the baby was very much discouraged by our parents. She was rarely allowed to hold the baby or feed the baby or play with the baby, but they were quite happy that I should do these things. I think it was at this time that I first noticed the animosity between Helen and our mother. Then Sarah died, she was eight months old. Cot death they said, even though most cot deaths occur under six months. However, I soon learnt otherwise. Helen told me I had killed Sarah during one of my blackouts, I had lain on her and suffocated her. Helen said she had placed her back in her cot and asked me to go to the park with her; she did this to give me an alibi. Our mother was never quite the same after Sarah's death, understandably. A kind of grief driven madness took hold of her and there followed several periods when she would go away, hospitalised. It was difficult for our father at this time so he decided that Helen and I should go to boarding school. Neither of us were particularly enthused by this but the decision was set. It was made worse by the fact that we would be going to different boarding schools. Then a couple of years later Mother had another baby, a girl again. The baby was a blessing for her as it brought her out of the shadow under which she had been living. It was about this time I left boarding school and started at the local college. Helen however had to remain at boarding school, a decision she was not happy about at all. When she came home for visits the atmosphere in the house changed. It was like she brought a swollen cloud with her and you never knew if the cloud would burst and we would all end up drenched. Mostly it would just be a shower, generally preceded by disagreements between her and Mother, but one time the cloud burst and there was a storm.

A fatal storm …

Mother had banished Helen from the nursery following one of their altercations. I heard her yelling at Helen, telling her the baby is mine not yours. Helen had shouted back at her, telling her she did not deserve children and she was a terrible mother. Later that day Helen and I were sitting in the garden chatting and drinking homemade lemonade when a scream so loud and piercing and full of pain tore through the air. I jumped from my seat and ran towards the house, then stopped as I was surprised that Helen had not moved. I asked her if she had heard what I had, she nodded and only then followed me into the house. Mother was sectioned and taken back to the hospital. Father said the police would need to speak to us both as was usual following an unexplained death. Before the police came Helen reminded me that we had been together all morning. We hadn't and when I said this to her she started talking about Sarah and what had happened to her and … the alibi she had given me. I knew then what I had to do.

They put Mother in a secure hospital, infanticide they called it. Latterly she was moved to a special unit and allowed home visits. She eventually died by her own hand on one of those visits. Our father lived a few years more. Towards the end, when he knew he did not have long left, we had a long conversation about the tragedies that had engulfed us and about Helen. He said she was a 'snake in the grass' and I should put some distance between us and never trust her. After he died and I was sorting through his things I discovered his journal. He wrote a great deal about Helen. He was sure that his youngest daughters died at her hand. After his funeral Helen and I discussed our childhood and growing up, we talked of our sisters and Mother and I was soon convinced that Father was right. I voiced my suspicions and she laughed, yet never denied it. All she said was that Mother did not deserve any more children. I wondered what had happened between her and Mother to cause such hatred. A hatred felt so vehemently it incited murder, or was Helen just evil all along? I thought about going to the police but to what end? My parents were both dead and I felt, well, that I did owe Helen some loyalty. However, I decided to take Father's advice and not see her again, sever all ties. Then fast forward several years, Helen is now married to Robert and Robert contacts me. He asks if I will visit Helen, I decline. He contacts me again saying that Helen is severely depressed and a visit may be beneficial to her. His letter goes on to explain that Helen's depression was precipitated by her inability to have a child. Even I.V.F. had proved futile. I wrote back expressing sympathy for their plight, although privately I was relieved and delighted that Mother Nature had realised Helen was not a suitable candidate for motherhood, but again I refused to visit. I heard no more from him for a while, then he wrote asking for information regarding our family. He said they were looking into adoption and some medical history was required. When I read they were considering adoption

I knew I had to tell Robert that it would not be safe to bring a child into their home.

I have not seen Helen for many years, but I do not think I would find her much changed. She fooled me into believing that I was responsible for so many things; breakages, the rabbit and ultimately Sarah's death. She is manipulative and devious and clever with it. So you are probably right to be frightened Martin.'

Martin wonders if he should call Charley, but what would he say? He has to tell her about Helen but over the phone may not be the best way to do it. Perhaps he should call the police, tell them what happened to Lizzie, but of course then he implicates himself - he did bury her. And then there is Audrey, though Martin is beginning to think that maybe Audrey is his rabbit.

Martin spends the entire train journey deliberating and agonising over what to do. He decides against going to the police, for now. At the station he jumps into a taxi. As the taxi approaches Helen's house Martin spots somebody lurking in the darkness. They are watching the house. He gets the driver to let him out a few doors up and then he silently creeps towards the unsuspecting figure. He grabs hold of the man and pushes him into a hedge, but the man fights back. He is younger and fitter and soon has Martin pinned to the ground. It is then they recognise each other.

"Jack?"

"Dad?"

Jack lets go of Martin and helps him to his feet.

"I thought you were at Pirbright."

"I'm on leave."

"Well, it's good to see you, Son, but you don't need to spy on me."

"What?"

"Hiding in corners, watching me. I would be happy to see you."

"Dad, I haven't been spying on you."

"Well what are you doing here?"

"No, what are you doing here?"

"I live here."

"Where?"

"There." Martin points towards the house. "The house you seem so interested in."

"Fuck."

The security light on the front of the house comes on and the two men are no longer in the shadows.

"Martin. Is that you?" asks Charley. "What are you ... Jack? Bloody hell. What are you doing here?"

"Hello, Char."

"You two know each other?" asks Martin.

"Yes, this is ..." Charley stops. "Do you two know each other?" She asks them both.

"My dad," says Jack.

"My son," says Martin.

"Shit," says Charley.

"Where's Noah?" asks Martin.

"He is with Helen. She's bathing him."

"Is she the psychopath?" asks Jack.

"I told you, she is not a psychopath."

Martin stares at Charley and Jack, taking in the exchange between them and then he sees it. "You are Noah's dad," he says to Jack.

"Maybe we should go inside," says Charley.

"I think you should," says Martin to Charley. "Make sure the little fella is okay."

"I told you he's fine. Helen is with him."

"Charley go inside, please."

Charley does as she is told, reluctantly. She assumes Martin wants to talk to Jack. She doesn't pick up on the anxiety in his voice. Martin watches her go back indoors.

"You should go home, Son. Call her tomorrow."

Martin knows what he has to do now. He has to protect his son and his grandson.

Twenty-Three

MARTIN IS SITTING in the kitchen waiting for Charley. She is usually the first one up and today is no different.

"Morning."

Charley is startled as she did not see him sitting in the corner. "Morning," she replies.

"Have you told Helen about Jack?"

"No."

"Good. Don't tell her. Not yet."

"Don't tell me what?" asks Helen.

"Nothing. A surprise," says Charley.

"Oh, I could do with a surprise. Don't have the best day ahead of me."

"Why?"

"I'm off to the dentist. Root canal treatment. Lucky me." Helen pours herself a coffee and goes back upstairs.

"Are you working today?" Charley asks Martin.

"Not today. I'm throwing a sickie."

"Oh." Charley is disappointed, she had hoped to go through her mum's things again and would rather be alone when she does that.

"Yes, and you and I need a chat when Helen goes."

Charley understands he wants to talk about Jack and Noah, but she wishes he could wait. Getting to the bottom of her mum's disappearance is her priority at the moment. She is not convinced that she has gone off with someone as many of her friends think; if that was the case why not take her passport? And what about the other things? Although there was nothing of value they must have meant something to Lizzie otherwise why did she hang on to them for so long?

Martin goes back to his room and comes out again once he hears Helen leave. He watches her drive up the road from the landing window. Once she has turned the corner Martin opens the loft hatch and goes up into the attic. He has decided to show Charley the letters that he found up there and tell her what he discovered in Oxford.

Charley has her mum's things spread across the bed; she sighs at the pitiful collection before going through it once again. They reveal nothing new, except the passport. Lizzie would not have paid out for a passport on a whim, so clearly she had some sort of trip planned. Charley picks up the passport and puts it into her handbag; she has made up her mind to officially report her mum as a missing person. She stands up and begins putting the other things back into the bags. She stops when she gets to the painting; picking it up she studies it more carefully than before. The initials cause her to breathe in sharply - R.J.H. - the same as the painting in the solicitor's office. She wonders why her mum would have a painting by the same artist; but then maybe the solicitor gave it to her, he was supposed to be one of her clients. Charley turns the painting over. The picture is too thick for the frame and it is starting to bend. The cardboard back is bowing outwards and only held together by strips of aging sticky tape. Charley peels away the once clear strips that have browned a little with age. They fall away easily and the cardboard pops from the back of the frame.

A folded piece of paper falls out from between the painting and the cardboard. Charley picks it up and unfolds it, and from the folds drops a photograph. It is a photo of a man, coming out of a building, possibly an office block. He is dark haired and wearing a suit. It is hard to determine how old he is as the photograph is not a particularly good one. It is rather grainy and he is not looking directly at the camera. Charley thinks he is probably unaware that he has been photographed. He certainly isn't posing for the picture. The piece of paper is blank. Charley drops it onto the bed along with the photograph which lands facedown revealing a scribble across the back of it. Charley picks it up again and is astonished to see two words written in her mother's hand:

'Charley's Dad'

A knock on the bedroom door brings her from a shock-induced trance.

"Come in."

"We need to talk, Charley."

"I know we do. But now isn't a good time."

"I don't think there will ever be a good time. Look, come downstairs when you're ready. I have some things you need to see."

He turns to leave and then spots the painting on the bed. "Where did you find that? I thought she had all of them hidden away."

"What?"

"The painting."

"It's my mum's."

"No, the painting."

"It's my mum's," repeats Charley.

"It can't be. How? She wouldn't have given one to your mum."

"Who?"

"Helen."

"Martin, you are not making any sense."

"Neither are you. That painting is one of Robert's, Helen's husband. There are loads of them in the attic. I just don't get why she would give one to your mum."

"She didn't," whispers Charley. "I think my dad gave it to her." Charley picks up the photograph with a shaking hand and gives it to Martin.

"This is your dad?"

"I think so. It was in the back of the painting."

"Is Noah asleep?"

"Yes."

"Okay, come with me."

Martin takes Charley up into the loft and shows her the other paintings. He also shows her some of the photographs that are up there.

"Helen had me put all these things up here. It was one of the first things I did for her."

Charley picks up one of the photo albums, tucks it under her arm and takes it back down with her. "Did you know?" she asks Martin.

"No. But I have learnt some other things that you need to know."

"So you don't just want to talk about me and Jack and Noah?"

"Not exactly."

Charley's sad and bewildered expression tells Martin he has to be completely honest with her. It is not enough to just tell her what Patrick has told him, he has to tell her everything.

Helen pulls onto the driveway. Before she gets out of the car she pulls down the sun visor and looks at her reflection in the small mirror on the visor. Her face doesn't look swollen, although it feels as if it is. She gets out of the car and goes to the boot to take out her purchases. She has tagged on some Christmas shopping to her trip to the dentist. Laden with bags she goes inside. The house is very quiet but she decides against calling out. She doesn't want to be responsible for waking Noah if he is having a nap, although she hopes he isn't. She has been looking forward to a cuddle all morning. Helen puts down her bags and goes through to the kitchen. From the kitchen she can see Martin and Charley in the garden. Curious, she thinks, then remembers. Charley had said there would be a surprise later.

She sticks her head out of the door.

"What are you doing out here?"

"We have something to show you," answers Charley

"Is it a surprise?" asks Helen excitedly.

"For sure."

"Give me a minute."

Helen quickly takes her shopping upstairs and puts it in her dressing room. Most of the purchases are for Noah but there are also some things for Charley and Martin. When she is done she goes back downstairs and out into the garden. Charley is sitting at the table which is covered with a table cloth. The cloth isn't lying flat on the table, there are several bumps beneath it. Presents, thinks Helen, excitedly. Martin is standing on the as yet unfinished patio, leaning heavily on the shovel. Charley gestures for Helen to sit down, which she does and then Charley very theatrically pulls the cloth from the objects on the table. Helen leans forward in her chair to take a closer look. It takes a couple of seconds for her to register what she is looking at: a photograph, a painting and some papers. It takes another couple of seconds for her to recognise that it is Robert in the photograph and the painting is one of his. The papers she is unsure of as without her glasses she can't see them clearly. She looks from Charley to Martin and back again.

"I don't understand."

"Neither did I," said Charley. "You can pick them up."

Helen picks up the painting. It is definitely one of Robert's, but she cannot recall seeing it before. She puts it down and then picks up the photograph. It is most definitely Robert but it is a very poor photo.

"I still do not understand."

"The photo is Robert, yes?" asks Charley.

"Yes."

"Turn it over. The photo, turn it over." Helen does as Charley says. "Now do you understand?"

"Not entirely."

"Robert, your husband and my father."

"According to who?"

"My mother."

"Really? Are you sure about that? I doubt she is even sure about that. Perhaps you should ask her." Helen's tone is a little menacing. Charley's eyes flash angrily, and in that moment Helen realises that Charley knows of her mother's fate. Helen stares hard at Martin who proffers no more than shrug of his shoulders. "You should consider your next move carefully, Charley. Why jeopardise all you have here? In the short time I have known you I have given you more than your mother gave you in seventeen years. You and Noah can–"

"Do not say his name," interrupts Charley. "I know what you do to babies. And Robert knew. He found out you were a monster. Maybe that's what drove him to Mum."

"Oh please. Your mother was a whore who did things that nice women refuse to do."

Charley lunges towards Helen and deals her a sharp blow to the side of her face.

"You are a vile baby killer. Your brother told Robert and he told Martin and we will ..."

"You will what? Come on, tell me. How does this end? What are you planning to ..." Helen's questions are halted by a wailing sound. The jagged noise of sirens. "Are they for me? I see."

"Do you?" asks Charley.

Helen looks at Charley, who looks at Martin, who starts digging.

"What are you doing Martin?" Helen asks. His reply chills her.

"Room for one more, remember ..."

Noah's Birthday

CHARLEY OPENS THE CURTAINS in the kitchen and is pleased to see that the sun is trying to put in an appearance. She recalls this time last year was a glorious day; not that she was able to get out and enjoy the sunshine. She was otherwise engaged. A smile lights up her face as she thinks of Noah, who is still sleeping, unaware that today is even his birthday. Charley looks at the box that is on the kitchen table. It is full of balloons and bunting and banners and napkins and candles and all the assorted paraphernalia required for a birthday party. Rather a lot for a one year old, who she is sure will be more interested in the box. But today is about so much more than Noah's birthday. For Charley, today marks a new beginning. Since first discovering she was pregnant her life has been chaotic. It has been tender and turbulent, dramatic and dangerous, heart-warming and hysterical, even mind-blowing and murderous. And now she wants normal; if there is such a thing.

"Morning, Charley. You're up early. Excitement too much for you?"

"Morning, Martin. Yes, something like that. Coffee?"

"No, I'm good. Had one earlier. I need to get going."

"Okay. I'm really looking forward to meeting Pete."

"You'll love him. Top bloke. Did I tell you he is Jack's godfather?"

"Yes, once or twice," laughs Charley.

Charley is trying to blow up balloons when Jack arrives. After several pathetic attempts she realises it is not the balloons that are faulty but her technique, or lack of. When Jack asks if there is anything that needs doing Charley throws the bag of balloons at him. She watches as he effortlessly inflates and ties them, then bats them around the kitchen much to the amusement of Noah.

"So, who is coming this afternoon?" he asks.

"Your mum and Amy, Ray, your dad of course and Pete."

"That sounds like a recipe for fun … My dad and Ray, in the same room. And my mum ready to drop any day."

"It'll be fine. Your dad is really chilled about it."

"Really? I'll believe it when I see it," says Jack sarcastically.

"Helping Pete and others like him has given him a focus and a different perspective on life. He is definitely in a good place. And I think he may have an admirer."

"Yes? Who?"

"A nurse who works at the rehabilitation centre. They are quite friendly. I said he should bring her today."

"Is he?"

"He said she's working, but he didn't just dismiss the idea so I'm sure there is a mutual attraction. He might be worried about how your mum will take it though."

"Mum will be fine. She wants him to be happy and she wants him to move on."

"Yes, I know."

"While we are talking of relationships, I was wondering where we are now." Jack slips his arm around her waist and pulls her towards him.

"Noah's watching."

As Jack turns to look at his son, Charley manoeuvres herself from his arm. She is unsure what she wants from Jack. She wants him in her life as Noah's father, but as for more than that she needs to see. They have shared a couple of intimate moments and physically, the attraction is still there. She is aware that Jack would like nothing more than to be with her and Noah, he has even suggested marriage. But life as a soldier's wife is not that appealing.

"Oh, I forgot, Anthony is coming too."

"Who is Anthony?"

"Anthony Villiers, the solicitor."

"Oh right. You know I can't believe she is just giving you her house."

"It was my father's house too."

"Yeah, I know, but even so. To give away a house, especially one this size."

"She has enough money."

"Yeah. Some people have it all. Where's she gone?"

"New Zealand. And that's enough questions. I need you to put the bunting up in the garden."

Jack does a mock salute, picks up the box of decorations and goes outside with them. Charley scoops Noah from his highchair and takes him upstairs to get ready.

The weather doesn't disappoint; the sun's rays add warmth and brightness that make the garden an idyllic paradise. All the guests are relaxed and enjoying themselves, although Ray does become a little tense every time Martin approaches him, even if it's just to offer him a beer. Noah has finished playing with the box and is now sitting in a paddling pool, which Jo and Ray bought him, with Amy. His infectious giggling is making them all laugh.

Anthony is the last to arrive, armed with gifts galore; many not age appropriate for a one year old. After offloading the gifts and having a drink, he tells Charley he needs to speak to her privately as he has some documents for her to sign.

"This one needs to be witnessed. Perhaps one of your guests can do it? Not a relative though."

Charley looks out of the study window at the party guests. She is related to none of them, yet they all feel like family, especially Martin. She taps on the window and beckons Martin inside. When the forms are all signed Anthony turns and shakes Charley's hand.

"Congratulations, Charley. You are now a very wealthy young woman."

"Thank you," says Charley nervously.

"Can I get you another drink, Anthony?" asks Martin.

"No, I need to get off. One more thing. I received another letter from Helen. She is in France now. Planning to travel through Europe. Having a blast by the sound of it. It's such a shame though."

"Shame?"

"Well, for me. Always had a soft spot for her you know. Fine looking woman, strong woman. I like that. An honourable woman too, making sure you receive what you are entitled to." Anthony pauses for a moment, lost in his thoughts, before continuing. "I could have made her happy, I think. But I understand she needed distance from this … erm … situation that Robert left behind."

"And she always wanted to travel. That's what she told me," adds Charley.

"Yes, she did. That was what she and Robert had planned before he fell ill."

Martin shows Anthony out and Charley files away her copies of the documents she has just signed, then they both go back outside to rejoin the party.

"These little cakes are delicious," says Joanne. "Where did you get them from?"

"They are madeleines, from France. A friend went there recently and brought them back for me."

☙

Charley lays Noah in his cot; he is already asleep. The party has exhausted him, and it has exhausted her too. It has been a perfect day though; the party and everything else went to plan. The future is set for her and Noah. Yet, she still feels unsettled. She hopes this feeling will pass soon. She had hoped it would be today, but now knows it will not pass until she reconciles herself with all that has happened.

Clearly revenge isn't always sweet, and if an eye for an eye is true, perhaps we will all end up blind.

The Kindness of Strangers is a great choice for a book club. Please find below a few suggested discussion questions for your book group:

Discussion/Book Club questions

1. Part 1 of the book is written in the first person. Did this allow you to gain an understanding of the characters and empathise with them?

2. Do you believe Helen's father's assertion that she was a 'snake in the grass' and always capable of murder? Or do you think the arrival of the baby supplanted her, causing the deterioration of her relationship with her mother and this led to murder?

3. Audrey believed in following the rules and always thought she was right. Her desire for truth at any cost ultimately led to her death. Do you think these are admirable qualities?

4. Helen had not 'planned' to kill Audrey or Lizzie. However, following their deaths she began thinking about getting rid of Noah's father - 'room for one more'. Do you think the killing of Audrey and Lizzie reawakened her murderous tendencies?

5. Martin was still coming to terms with his experience in Afghanistan and the perceived loss of his family. Do you think these things made him vulnerable and easily manipulated?

6. The female characters in this book appear stronger than their male counterparts. Do you think this is reflective of today's society or has the idea of women as the 'weaker' or 'fairer sex' always been out of date and unjust?

7. Why do you think Charley and Martin decided to kill Helen? Was it to avenge Audrey, Lizzie and the babies or to save Jack from the same fate? Or was it simply to gain Helen's home and money?

8. The final sentence in the book includes the phrase 'an eye for an eye'. This phrase can be found in the bible and it was written into Babylonian law; in fact there are still some regimes that adhere to this principle. What is your view on revenge? Can it ever be justified? Or do you believe an eye for an eye will leave the whole world blind?

The Kindness Of Strangers

Acknowledgements

There are many people to thank. Too many to name, for I am fortunate to be blessed with an amazing family and an army of friends who have encouraged my writing endeavours. You know who you are, and I thank you all.

I must thank my publisher, Urbane Publications for their continued belief in my work, in particular Publishing Director Matthew Smith whose support is invaluable. Thanks also to the bloggers and advance readers who take time to read and review urbane titles. You provide an essential service.

Love and thanks to Richard, Tom & Hayleigh who are quite simply my world.

Finally, thanks to my darling Nan from whom I inherited a love of books and the written word.

Julie was born in East London but now lives a rural life in North Essex. She is married with two children. Her working life has seen her have a variety of jobs, including running her own publishing company. She is the author of the children's book Poppy and the Garden Monster. Julie writes endlessly and when not writing she is reading. Other interests include theatre, music and running. Besides her family, the only thing she loves more than books is Bruce Springsteen. The Kindness of Strangers is Julie's second novel following her gripping debut, Beware the Cuckoo, in 2017.

You can follow Julie on Twitter @julesmnewman and visit her author website at https://julienewmanauthor.com/

HAVE YOU READ JULIE NEWMAN'S DEBUT NOVEL, *BEWARE THE CUCKOO?*

"Lies, deceit and dark secrets - this is a wonderfully addictive read"
Sheree Murphy, actress and television presenter

They were reunited at his funeral, school friends with a shared past. A past that is anything but straightforward. A past that harbours secrets and untruths.

Karen has a seemingly perfect life. An adoring husband, two wonderful children and a beautiful home. She has all she has ever wanted, living the dream. She also has a secret.

Sandra's once perfect life is rapidly unravelling. The man who meant everything to her had a dark side and her business is failing. To get her life back on track she needs to reclaim what is rightfully hers. She knows the secret.

As the past meets the present, truths are revealed - and both women understand the true cost of betrayal.